Praise for *Fox Tracks*

"Sister Jane makes for a memorable amateur sleuth, and the pack of animals sure added a new level of delight."
—Cozy Mystery Book Reviews

"An enjoyable whodunit . . . series fans will enjoy Sister's sleuthing."
—*The Mystery Gazett*

Praise for *Hounded to Death*

"The fun of Brown's series is the wealth of foxhunting lore, the spot-on portrayal of Virginians . . . and the evocative descriptions of the Blue Ridge Mountains. . . . And then there's Sister, the seventy-three-year-old heroine who becomes even more appealing with each successive book. Brown has a winner in this memorable character."   —*Virginia Times Dispatch*

"Will surely please fans of the series. The mystery is fast-paced and filled with scenes from the world of fox hunting. . . . Brown delivers the brush."   —*The Baltimore Sun*

"[A] paw-turner."   —*Dog Fancy*

"Anyone interested in rural sleuths, animals, Virginia, hunting, or horses will enjoy the engaging story, its countryside and its characters, all wrapped up in a high-quality modern cozy mystery."
—*Booklist*

Praise for *The Tell-tale Horse*

"Intriguing . . . Fans of the series will be fascinated with Jane's evolution under Brown's hand. With each book, Jane becomes more real—and more human—in the reader's imagination."
—*Richmond Times-Dispatch*

"A quality tale that is over all too soon."

—Charleston *Post and Courier*

Praise for *Hotspur*

"Dashing and vibrant . . . The reader will romp through the book like a hunter on a thoroughbred, never stopping for a meal or a night's sleep."   —*Publishers Weekly* (starred review)

"Brown combines her strengths—exploring southern families, manners, and rituals as well as the human-animal bond—to bring in a winner."   —*Booklist*

Praise for *Outfoxed*

"Compelling . . . engaging . . . [a] sly whodunit . . . [Brown] succeeds in conjuring a world in which prey are meant to survive the chase and foxes are knowing collaborators (with hunters and hounds) in the rarefied rituals that define the sport."   —*People*

"A rich, atmospheric murder mystery . . . rife with love, scandal, anger, transgression, redemption, greed, and nobility, all of which make good reading."   —*San Jose Mercury News*

The Sister Jane series

Outfoxed

Hotspur

Full Cry

The Hunt Ball

The Hounds and the Fury

The Tell-tale Horse

Hounded to Death

Fox Tracks

Books by Rita Mae Brown with Sneaky Pie Brown

Wish You Were Here

Rest in Pieces

Murder at Monticello

Pay Dirt

Murder, She Meowed

Murder on the Prowl

Cat on the Scent

Sneaky Pie's Cookbook for
Mystery Lovers

Pawing Through the Past

Claws and Effect

Catch as Cat Can

The Tail of the Tip-Off

Whisker of Evil

Cat's Eyewitness

Sour Puss

Puss 'n Cahoots

The Purrfect Murder

Santa Clawed

Cat of the Century

Hiss of Death

The Big Cat Nap

Sneaky Pie for President

The Litter of the Law

The Nevada series

A Nose for Justice

Murder Unleashed

Books by Rita Mae Brown

Animal Magnetism: My Life with
Creatures Great and Small

The Hand That Cradles the Rock

Songs to a Handsome Woman

The Plain Brown Rapper

Rubyfruit Jungle

In Her Day

Six of One

Southern Discomfort

Sudden Death

High Hearts

Started from Scratch: A Different
Kind of Writer's Manual

Bingo

Venus Envy

Dolley: A Novel of Dolley Madison
in Love and War

Riding Shotgun

Rita Will: Memoir of a Literary
Rabble-Rouser

Loose Lips

Alma Mater

The Sand Castle

FOX TRACKS

FOX TRACKS

A NOVEL

RITA MAE BROWN

ILLUSTRATED BY LEE GILDEA, JR.

BALLANTINE BOOKS
TRADE PAPERBACKS
NEW YORK

2013 Ballantine Books Trade Paperback Edition

Published in the United States by Ballantine Books, an imprint of
The Random House Publishing Group, a division of
Random House, Inc., New York.

BALLANTINE and the HOUSE colophon are registered trademarks
of Random House, Inc.

Originally published in hardcover in the United States by Ballantine Books,
an imprint of The Random House Publishing Group, a division of
Random House, Inc., in 2012.

ISBN 978-0-345-53299-2
eBook ISBN 978-0-345-53298-5

Printed in the United States of America on acid-free paper

www.ballantinebooks.com

2 4 6 8 9 7 5 3

Dedicated to the Three Foxhunting Muses:

Mrs. W. Patrick Butterfield (Kay)
Mrs. Gloria Galban Fennell
Mrs. David Lamb (Sally)

CAST OF CHARACTERS

THE HUMANS

Jane Arnold, Sister, is master of foxhounds of the Jefferson Hunt Club in central Virginia. She loves her hounds, her horses, and her housepets. Occasionally, she finds humans lovable, too. Strong, healthy, vibrant at seventy-two, she's proof of the benefits of the outdoor life.

Shaker Crown is the huntsman. He's acquired the discipline of holding his tongue and his temper—most times. He's wonderful with hounds. In his early forties, he's finding his way back to love with Lorraine Rasmussen.

Gray Lorillard, a now-retired high-powered accountant is in his late sixties, and is in love with Sister Jane.

Crawford Howard, a self-made man, moved to Virginia from Indiana. He's egotistical, ambitious, and thinks he knows more than he does about foxhunting. But he's also generous, intelligent, and fond of young people. His great disappointment is not being a father but he never speaks of this, especially to his wife, Marty.

Charlotte Norton is the young headmistress of Custis Hall, a prestigious prep school for young ladies.

Anne Harris, Tootie, is one of the brightest students Charlotte Norton has ever known. Taciturn, observant, yet capable of delivering a stinging barb, this senior shines with promise. She's beautiful, petite, African American, and a strong rider. This fall is her first at Princeton. She'd rather stay at the kennels and work with hounds.

Valentina Smith was the Curtis Hall class president last year. Blond, tall, lean, and drop-dead gorgeous, the kid is a natural politician. She and Tootie clash at times, but they are friends. She loves foxhunting, and her first year at Princeton.

Felicity Porter seems overshadowed by Tootie and Val but she is highly intelligent and has a sturdy self-regard. She's the kind of person who is quietly competent. She, too, is a good rider. Every bit as brilliant as Tootie and Val, her life took a dramatically different course with an unplanned pregnancy.

Betty Franklin is the long-serving honorary whipper-in at JHC. Her judgment, way with hounds, knowledge of territory, and ability to ride make her a standout. Many is the huntsman who would kill to have Betty Franklin whip into him or her. She's in her mid-forties, a mother, happily married to Bobby, and a dear, dear friend to Sister.

Walter Lungrun, M.D., joint-master of foxhounds, has held this position for three years. He's learning all he can. He adores Sister, and the feeling is mutual. Their only complaint is there's so much work to do they rarely have time for a good talk. Walter is in his late thirties. He is the result of an affair that Raymond Arnold, Sr., Jane's husband, had with Walter's mother. Mr. Lungrun never knew—or pretended he didn't—and Sister didn't know until a year ago.

Edward Bancroft, in his seventies, head of the Bancroft family, used to run a large corporation founded by his family in the mid-nineteenth century. His wife, Tedi, is one of Sister's oldest friends. Tedi rides splendid Thoroughbreds and is always impeccably turned out, as is her surviving daughter, Sybil Fawkes, who is in her second year as an honorary whipper-in. The Bancrofts are true givers in terms of money, time, and genuine caring.

Ben Sidell has been sheriff of the county for three years. Since he was hired from Ohio, he sometimes needs help in the labyrinthine ways of the South. He relies on Sister's knowledge and discretion.

Kasmir Barbhaiya is in his mid-forties, widowed, and a college classmate of High Vajay. He falls in love with Virginia while visiting High and Mandy. Eventually he will fall in love again guided by his deceased wife's spirit, but not in this book. He has made over a billion dollars in pharmaceuticals but would give it all up if he could bring his wife back. He keeps this to himself and is fantastically generous.

Tariq Al MacMillan, a Coptic Christian from Egypt, teaches at Custis Hall. He's in his mid-twenties, good-looking, and innovative in his Middle Eastern Studies class.

Art DuCharme is always described as not living up to his potential. As he's in his thirties, works in his father's garage as well as having a delivery service, no one is holding their breath.

Binky and Milly DuCharme are Art's parents. They have come to terms with their son's lack of ambition. Binky does not speak to his own brother, Alfred.

Alfred DuCharme is widowed and the father of the very successful Margaret. He oversees the land of Old Paradise, the family estate, but the grand old house is in desperate need of repair which takes a lot of cash.

Margaret DuCharme has more than made up for her cousin's failures. She is an MD in Sports Medicine, well liked by all and a go-between for the brothers. She is not much in evidence in this volume.

Donny Sweigart, a jack-of-all-trades, has a can-do attitude. He's in his mid-thirties, an outdoorsman and rugged. He has been dating Sybil Bancroft Hawkes for over a year. While he can never match the Bancroft fortune, he wants to make more money for his own satisfaction and so Sybil doesn't think he's a dud.

THE AMERICAN FOXHOUNDS

Sister and Shaker have carefully bred a balanced pack. The American foxhound blends English, French, and Irish blood, the first identifiable pack being brought here in 1650 by Robert de la Brooke of Maryland. Individual hounds had been shipped over earlier, but Brooke brought an entire pack. In 1785, General Lafayette sent his mentor and hero, George Washington, a pack of French hounds whose voices were said to sound like the bells of Moscow.

Whatever the strain, the American foxhound is highly intelligent and beautifully built, with strong sloping shoulders, powerful hips and thighs, and a nice tight foot. The whole aspect of the hound in motion is one of grace and power in the effortless covering of ground. The American hound is racier than the English hound and stands perhaps two feet at the shoulder, although size is not nearly as important as nose, drive, cry, and biddability. It is sensitive and extremely loving and has eyes that range from softest brown to gold to sky-blue. While one doesn't often see the sky-blue eye, there is a line that contains it. The hound lives to please its master and to chase foxes.

Cora is the strike hound, which means she often finds the scent first. She's the dominant female in the pack and is in her sixth season.

Asa is in his seventh season and is invaluable in teaching the younger hounds.

Diana is the anchor hound, and she's in her fourth season. All the other hounds trust her, and if they need direction she'll give it.

Dragon is her littermate. He possesses tremendous drive and a fabulous nose, but he's arrogant. He wants to be the strike hound. Cora hates him.

Dasher is also Diana and Dragon's littermate. He lacks his brother's brilliance, but he's steady and smart. A hound's name usually begins with the first letter of his mother's name, so the *D* hounds are out of Delia.

Giorgio is young and just about the perfect example of what a male American foxhound should be.

THE HORSES

Sister's horses are **Keepsake,** a Thoroughbred/quarter-horse cross (written TB/QH by horsemen), an intelligent gelding of eight years; **Lafayette,** a gray TB, eleven now, fabulously athletic and talented, who wants to go; **Rickyroo,** a seven-year-old TB gelding who shows great promise; **Aztec,** a six-year-old gelding TB, also very athletic, with great stamina and a good mind; and **Matador,** a gray TB, six years old, sixteen hands, a former steeplechaser.

Shaker's horses come from the steeplechase circuit, so all are TBs. **Showboat, HoJo, Gunpowder,** and **Kilowatt** can all jump the moon, as you might expect.

Betty's two horses are **Outlaw,** a tough QH who has seen it all and can do it all, and **Magellan,** a TB given to her by Sorrel Buruss, a bigger and rangier horse than Betty was accustomed to riding, but she's now used to him.

Kilowatt is a superb jumper, bought for the huntsman by Kasmir Barbhaiya.

Nonni, tried and true, takes care of the sheriff.

THE FOXES

The reds can reach a height of sixteen inches and a length of forty-one inches, and they can weigh up to fifteen pounds. Obviously, since these are wild animals who do not willingly come forth to be measured and weighed, there's more variation than the standard just cited. **Target;** his spouse, **Charlene;** and his **Aunt Netty** and **Uncle Yancy** are the reds. They can be haughty. A red fox has a white tip on its luxurious brush, except for Aunt Netty, who has a wisp of a white tip, for her brush is tatty.

The grays may reach fifteen inches in height and forty-four inches in length and may weigh up to fourteen pounds. The common wisdom is that grays are smaller than reds, but there are some big ones out there. Sometimes people call them slab-sided grays, because they can be reddish. They do not have a white tip on their tail but they may have a black one, as well as a black-tipped mane. Some grays are so dark as to be black.

The grays are **Comet, Inky,** and **Georgia.** Their dens are a bit more modest than those of the red foxes, who like to announce their abodes with a prominent pile of dirt and bones outside. Perhaps not all grays are modest nor all reds full of themselves, but as a rule of thumb it's so.

THE BIRDS

Athena is a great horned owl. This type of owl can stand two feet and a half in height with a wingspread of four feet and can weigh up to five pounds.

Bitsy is a screech owl. She is eight and a half inches high with a twenty-inch wingspread. She weighs a whopping six ounces and she's reddish brown. Her considerable lungs make up for her small stature.

St. Just, a crow, is a foot and a half in height, his wingspread is a surprising three feet, and he weighs one pound.

THE HOUSEPETS

Raleigh is a Doberman who likes to be with Sister.

Rooster is a harrier, willed to Sister by an old lover, Peter Wheeler.

Golliwog, or Golly, is a large calico cat and would hate being included with the dogs as a pet. She is the Queen of All She Surveys.

SOME USEFUL TERMS

Away. A fox has *gone away* when he has left the covert. Hounds are *away* when they have left the covert on the line of the fox.

Brush. The fox's tail.

Burning scent. Scent so strong or hot that hounds pursue the line without hesitation.

Bye day. A day not regularly on the fixture card.

Cap. The fee nonmembers pay to hunt for that day's sport.

Carry a good head. When hounds run well together to a good scent, a scent spread wide enough for the whole pack to smell it.

Carry a line. When hounds follow the scent. This is also called *working a line.*

Cast. Hounds spread out in search of scent. They may cast themselves or be cast by the huntsman.

Charlie. A term for a fox. A fox may also be called *Reynard.*

Check. When hounds lose the scent and stop. The field must wait quietly while the hounds search for the scent.

Colors. A distinguishing color, usually worn on the collar but sometimes on the facings of a coat, that identifies a hunt. Colors can be awarded only by the master and can be worn only in the field.

Coop. A jump resembling a chicken coop.

Couple straps. Two-strap hound collars connected by a swivel link. Some members of staff will carry these on the right rear of the saddle. Since the days of the pharaohs in ancient Egypt, hounds have been brought to the meets coupled. Hounds are always spoken of and counted in couples. Today, hounds walk or are driven to the meets. Rarely, if ever, are they coupled, but a whipper-in still carries couple straps should a hound need assistance.

Covert. A patch of woods or bushes where a fox might hide. Pronounced *cover.*

Cry. How one hound tells another what is happening. The sound will differ according to the various stages of the chase. It's also called *giving tongue* and should occur when a hound is working a line.

Cub hunting. The informal hunting of young foxes in the late summer and early fall, before formal hunting. The main purpose is to enter young hounds into the pack. Until recently only the most knowledgeable members were invited to cub hunt, since they would not interfere with young hounds.

Dog fox. The male fox.

Dog hound. The male hound.

Double. A series of short sharp notes blown on the horn to alert all that a fox is afoot. The *gone away* series of notes is a form of doubling the horn.

Draft. To acquire hounds from another hunt is to accept a draft.

Draw. The plan by which a fox is hunted or searched for in a certain area, such as a covert.

Draw over the fox. Hounds go through a covert where the fox is but cannot pick up his scent. The only creature who understands how this is possible is the fox.

Drive. The desire to push the fox, to get up with the line. It's a very desirable trait in hounds, so long as they remain obedient.

Dually. A one-ton pickup truck with double wheels in back.

Dwell. To hunt without getting forward. A hound who dwells is a bit of a putterer.

Enter. Hounds are entered into the pack when they first hunt, usually during cubbing season.

Field. The group of people riding to hounds, exclusive of the master and hunt staff.

Fieldmaster. The person appointed by the master to control the field. Often it is the master him- or herself.

Fixture. A card sent to all dues-paying members, stating when and where the hounds will meet. A fixture card properly received is an invitation to hunt. This means the card would be mailed or handed to a member by the master.

Flea-bitten. A gray horse with spots or ticking which can be black or chestnut.

Gone away. The call on the horn when the fox leaves the covert.

Gone to ground. A fox who has ducked into his den or some other refuge has *gone to ground*.

Good night. The traditional farewell to the master after the hunt, regardless of the time of day.

Gyp. The female hound.

Hilltopper. A rider who follows the hunt but does not jump. Hilltoppers are also called the *second field*. The jumpers are called the *first flight*.

Hoick. The huntsman's cheer to the hounds. It is derived from the Latin *hic haec hoc,* which means *here.*

Hold hard. To stop immediately.

Huntsman. The person in charge of the hounds, in the field and in the kennel.

Kennelman. A hunt staff member who feeds the hounds and cleans the kennels. In wealthy hunts there may be a number of kennelmen. In hunts with a modest budget, the huntsman or even the master cleans the kennels and feeds the hounds.

Lark. To jump fences unnecessarily when hounds aren't running. Masters frown on this, since it is often an invitation to an accident.

Lieu in. Norman term for *go in*.

Lift. To take the hounds from a lost scent in the hopes of finding a better scent farther on.

Line. The scent trail of the fox.

Livery. The uniform worn by the professional members of the hunt staff. Usually it is scarlet, but blue, yellow, brown, and gray are also used. The recent dominance of scarlet has to do with people buying coats off the rack as opposed to having tailors cut them. (When anything is mass-produced, the choices usually dwindle, and such is the case with livery.)

Mask. The fox's head.

Meet. The site where the day's hunting begins.

MFH. The master of foxhounds; the individual in charge of the hunt: hiring, firing, landowner relations, opening territory (in large hunts this is the job of the hunt secretary), developing the pack of hounds, and determining the first cast of each meet. As in any leadership position, the master is also the lightning rod for criticism. The master may hunt the hounds, although this is usually done by a professional huntsman, who is also responsible for the hounds in the field and at the kennels. A long relationship between a master and a huntsman allows the hunt to develop and grow.

Nose. The scenting ability of a hound.

Override. To press hounds too closely.

Overrun. When hounds shoot past the line of a scent. Often the scent has been diverted or foiled by a clever fox.

Ratcatcher. Informal dress worn during cubbing season and bye days.

Stern. A hound's tail.

Stiff-necked fox. One who runs in a straight line.

Strike hounds. Those hounds who through keenness, nose, and often higher intelligence find the scent first and press it.

Tail hounds. Those hounds running at the rear of the pack. This is not necessarily because they aren't keen; they may be older hounds.

Tally-ho. The cheer when the fox is viewed. Derived from the Norman *ty a hillaut*, thus coming into the English language in 1066.

Tongue. To vocally pursue a fox.

View halloo (halloa). The cry given by a staff member who sees a fox. Staff may also say *tally-ho* or, should the fox turn back, *tally-back*. One reason a different cry may be used by staff, especially in territory where the huntsman can't see the staff, is that the field in their enthusiasm may cheer something other than a fox.

Vixen. The female fox.

Walk. Puppies are *walked out* in the summer and fall of their first year. It's part of their education and a delight for both puppies and staff.

Whippers-in. Also called whips, these are the staff members who assist the huntsman, who make sure the hounds "do right."

FOX TRACKS

FOX TRACKS

CHAPTER 1

Brilliant strings of moving rubies rolled away in the snow. At least that's how it looked to Jane Arnold, "Sister," as she peered out the window of her hotel room at The Pierre. The tail-lights of all those cars crawling down Manhattan's Fifth Avenue sparkled in the dark like rubies. When she was young, she would have seen parallel lines of headlights like diamonds coming toward her as well. Those days were long gone.

"Do you remember when the streets were two-way?" she asked her boyfriend, Gray Lorillard, who was carefully removing items from his Gladstone bag.

"Uh-huh."

"Do you think creating one-way streets in 1966 really made New York traffic move faster?"

"I do not." He answered this with conviction, his handsome brow furrowed as he once more reviewed his close items.

"Close" meant small clothing: undershirts, underwear, folded good shirts, and his Dopp kit, as well as a beautiful calfskin jewelry case (although men never called it that).

"I don't think it helped either," she said, turning from the view, "but there were fewer cars then."

"Fewer people," he mumbled, searching for something in his bag. "Goddammit."

"Is this male PMS I'm observing?" she asked, half smirking at him.

He rolled his eyes. "Men don't have mood swings."

At this, the elegant seventy-two-year-old woman with the incredible silver hair let out a whoop.

Younger by perhaps seven years—the year of his birth had a habit of sliding backward—Gray, taller than Sister, who was six feet, brushed his steel-gray military moustache while looking in the mirror above the desk. "Well, I don't have them—it's well known that I'm even-keeled."

"Honey, you are smoking opium. You're a lot moodier than I am."

Looking at the beautiful woman who never made the slightest attempt to look younger than she was—perhaps one of the reasons she was so striking—Gray shrugged. "Janie, we're all moodier than you. I've never known such a cool customer."

"I don't know if that's a compliment or an insult." She crossed the plush carpet and put her arm around his waist. "What's the problem here?"

"I'm missing one of my studs."

"Oh no, the chased gold fox-head ones with the ruby eyes?"

"I know I put it in here. I did. You know how meticulous I am."

"I do." She bit her tongue because she wanted to say: *And sometimes I wish you were not.* "Maybe it slid behind the lining. Your bag has some years on it."

"Buy the best. Then you only weep once." He sat on the side of the bed, taking a deep breath. "I am not going to panic."

She sat beside him. "Neither am I. Those were your Christmas present three years ago. I bought them from Marion at Horse Country." The proprietor had sneaked Jane the elegant studs when they'd driven up to buy tack for the staff.

As Master of the Jefferson Hunt, Sister, and her joint-master of three years, Dr. Walter Lungrun, were responsible for "the furnishings"—as horse equipment was properly termed—as well as for the paid staff, which consisted of one huntsman and one whipper-in. Newly added to the payroll, Betty Franklin had served as an honorary, which means amateur, whipper-in for decades.

Betty and her husband faced tightened financial conditions thanks to the sinking economy and the fact that they owned a printing press. Few people patronized true presses anymore so after much discussion, Sister and Walter had worked out the necessary details to give Betty a salary of $25,000. The good woman wept at the offer, tried to refuse, but the two masters insisted. That $25,000 kept the wolf from the Franklins' door.

"Sugar, if you truly have lost it, I will buy you another," said Jane.

"I didn't," he insisted. "It has to be here."

"Go back over the last time you saw it."

"Did that." He rose, kissed her on the cheek, patted his chest pocket. "Dammit."

"Your language is going to Hell."

Her cursing as well made them both laugh.

"My mother would wash my mouth out with soap." He smiled at the memory of the formidable, late LuAnne Lorillard, a power in the African American community long before integration. Nobody messed with LuAnne without ample opportunity to repent later.

"Well, humor me," said Jane.

"All right. I was back home the last time I saw the studs. I went to my dresser after packing my clothing in this bag. I opened the top drawer, lifted out my personal case, carried it to the safe behind the painting that Daddy did, opened it, and took out my studs. I opened the little green leather case, counted them, closed it, and put it in my Gladstone bag."

"Why don't men say jewelry case?" Jane interrupted.

"How many years were you married? As I recall, it was twenty-eight. Did you ever ask Raymond?"

"No, but I didn't talk to Raymond as openly as I talk to you," she said.

"Really?" he asked, smiling, liking the compliment.

"Really. I loved him in my fashion, but it was a different time. Ray had a bombastic streak, which meant he had a difficult time dealing with anything that didn't emanate from him."

"I lived in D.C. for most of your marriage, but Ray did not strike me as the sensitive or introspective type. How could you stand it?"

"I had a son, remember?" This was said in an upbeat tone. Any memory Sister recalled of her son, who died in a tractor accident in 1974, still brought her happiness.

She loved Raymond, Jr., beyond reason, but then doesn't every parent feel that way? Jane long ago came to terms with his death at age fourteen, growing determined to live each day with joy. Her son would have wanted that for her, not a lifetime of grieving and anger.

"It's not that I forget," Gray quickly replied. "It's only that I don't associate you with sorrows. You're a force of nature."

"You know, that may be the most wonderful thing you ever said to me. Now back to your studs."

"That's the chain of events until now." His hand went to his left pec again.

"Do I need to buy you a man bra?"

"No." He laughed. "I'm out of cigarettes."

"You can't smoke in hotel rooms anymore, at least not in this town. Actually, Gray, you can't smoke in public parks, the list goes on. If the mayor sees you smoking, he will assume you are a lowlife, possibly a cheap criminal. It never occurs to these health nuts the damage they do to others."

"You mean the loss of jobs in our state, North Carolina, and Kentucky? Devastation."

"That, too, but I was thinking about the people who love laws that inhibit other people's choices. Is smoking a good thing to do? No. But those sanctimonious rule-makers live rather luxurious lives. They aren't working on an assembly line or in scorching sun outside. If your job is repetitive and boring or dangerous, sometimes that little hit of nicotine takes the edge off. The people that make the laws go get prescriptions for Prozac, and how does anyone know the long-term effects of all that crap?"

He blinked, as he hadn't heard her that impassioned in months, in fact, not since a person blundered and turned the fox back toward the hounds at a hunt in November. Fortunately, the fox escaped.

Sister and Gray, this January 27, had traveled from central Virginia to attend the Masters' Ball, an annual extravaganza under the aegis of the Masters of Foxhounds Association of America. For forty years, Sister had attended the annual ball, always at the end of January. She loved to dance, loved to catch up with old friends scattered across the United States and Canada.

Over the last ten years, oftentimes when she spoke to city dwellers or suburbanites about foxhunting, she would notice the concern or distaste in their faces, so she invariably hastened to add that in the New World, foxes were chased, not killed. Usually, that opened up a torrent of quite intelligent questions and Sister would once again be reminded of how far most people lived from nature.

The last thing Jane Arnold ever wanted to do was kill a fox. She wouldn't mind dispatching a few humans, though, one of whom would be at this very ball. She wondered, could you kill a man with a butter knife?

Gray couldn't find a cigarette. "I am hooked and that's that." He came and sat down again, forlornly gazing into his opened Gladstone bag as though it would croak an answer concerning his stud. "I have stopped many times. Then pressure gets to me and I light up. I hate being controlled by an outside substance."

"I can't say that I understand. I don't have an addictive personality. I wish you could stop if only to suit yourself. However, smoking doesn't make you crazy, you don't lose your teeth like those pathetic meth people, and it isn't illegal. And although you say you aren't moody, honey, there are times when I would happily shove a cigarette in your chiseled lips."

"You say."

"Look, you search for your stud. We have three hours until the Ball. I'll pop around the corner to Madison Avenue. As I recall, there's a beautiful little tobacco shop there that sells gorgeous small humidors, cigarette lighters, cases from as early as World War One and, of course, tobacco."

"It's snowing out there. I'll go."

"Gray, that stud is more important than a little snow on my nose. We hunt in weather worse than this."

"Yes, but you don't hunt in high heels."

"I'll start a fad. I've got my pull-on rain boots. My skirt is wool and my sweater is glorious cashmere. You look on your DROID to make sure the store is still operating and I'll ring up the girls. They can come along to keep me company."

The girls were two young women, freshmen at Princeton, who

had hunted with Sister while attending an exclusive girls' school, Custis Hall, in central Virginia. They and quite a few other young women hunted with her for the duration of their secondary school education. Some of the faculty hunted, too, always swearing it made environmental studies more exciting for students.

Within minutes, Sister had rounded up one of the girls, Anne Harris—who was called "Tootie." Using his phone, Gray verified the store was still in business.

"You can calculate minute by minute the national debt on that thing." Sister admired his toy, as she thought of it.

"If I do that, I won't enjoy the Ball."

As it turned out, none of them enjoyed the Ball for entirely different reasons than the national debt.

CHAPTER 2

A gust of wind sent snow swirling around Sister and Tootie as they walked on a side street toward Madison Avenue.

"I think there have only been about three times in forty years that I've come to this Ball and the weather hasn't been filthy. No wonder they stop hunting in New York State early. Genesee Valley stops when the river freezes, which has to be now."

Sister was telling Tootie about a hunt founded in 1876 by hard-riding upstate New Yorkers, among them the Wadsworth family, who still led them.

"I'd love to go up there and hunt," said Tootie. "I can take a train up to Rochester and then rent a car to drive down to the Genesee Valley." Turning her head from the wind, the snow on her creamy café au lait skin added to her considerable beauty.

"Next year. I'll come with you. Watching Marion Thorne hunt hounds is always a treat. Then again she has good whippers-in. You know, that's the hardest position to fill."

"That's what you always told us." Tootie listened closely to everything the older woman had ever told her, as the gorgeous young woman loved hounds, horses, foxes, and Sister, herself.

Another gust of wet snow smacked them right in the face.

"Well, who needs skin abrasion up here?" said Sister. "Just go outside. You'll get a few layers peeled right off."

Tootie wrinkled her nose. "Sounds awful."

"Ah!" Sister stepped faster as the shop came into sight.

"Ladies." The owner rose from behind the store's counter when the two swept into the shop. "Welcome."

"We're glad to be here." Sister laughed, brushing off her snow-covered coat.

Adolfo Galdos, balding, pudgy, and sixtyish, smiled broadly. "One must submit to the weather. That's what my dear papa always said. He never could fathom how people endured this."

"Cuban?" Sister inquired.

"How did you know?"

"I've never met a proprietor of a tobacco shop from Barcelona." She smiled, but she had recognized the lilt in his voice.

"There you have it." He beamed anew. "For us, tobacco is gold, is art. Someday, and I hope I live to see it, we will return and once again, the finest cigar tobacco in the world will be available to you."

Tootie quietly studied the shop. Cigarette cases with sapphire clasps, lighters of perfect weight and simple design, sparkled alongside impossibly long cigarette holders.

Adolfo noticed the object of Tootie's scrutiny. "A Dunhill. 1938. That lighter will work as good as the day it was made."

Now also studying the display case herself, Sister murmured, "Beautiful. Oh, look at that."

He reached into the case, retrieving a heavy silver cigarette case with handwritten names incised. "This was given to a British officer by his surviving men." He flipped it open where it was gold inside, the officer's name—Cpt. Mitchell Markham—was inscribed therein.

Sister's hand flew to her heart. "What a tribute. My father fought in World War One. He never spoke of it, but I expect it affected him all his life and may be one of the reasons he married so late."

"Do we not ask impossible things of people?" Adolfo's beautiful green eyes met hers. "We left Cuba in 1959. My own father, who owned a tobacco plantation, saw there was no hope and left. Those who grew sugar also fled. Others, thinking the revolutionaries would not come for them, lost everything. Everything."

"This is called progress." Sister grimaced. "No one learns. It didn't work for the French in 1791 and it will never work, period."

Adolfo spoke to Tootie, delighted by her youth and femininity. "I hope, Señorita, that you will never encounter such foolishness."

Shyly, Tootie responded, "I hope so, too."

"Ladies, allow me to show you the humidor. The aroma alone is intoxicating." He stepped out from behind the counter, twirled one hand like a drum major, walked to the rear of the store, and opened a glass door—the fragrance of various cigars, cigarettes, long-cut pipe tobacco, filled the room. "After you."

The two entered the well-organized room. It was larger than it appeared from outside, looking at the glass door.

Closing the door behind him, Adolfo pulled a wooden box off the shelf. "I regret I cannot sell true Cuban cigars, but this is made from seeds taken from Cuba and planted in the Dominican Republic. It's a very good cigar, sophisticated and mild." He handed one Montecristo to Tootie.

She held it, in the wrapper, under her nose. "It's almost like perfume."

"A bit stronger. This one." Adolfo handed her a Pleiades. "Now this is a large cigar, a large gauge, but such a cigar draws smoother, easier than the small ones you often see women smoking. Granted those may be more ladylike, but I think in any social gathering it is the women who set the tone. If *you* smoked a Churchill," he cited a monster gauge, "it would become the fashion."

"Well, I—"

"We'll take that," said Sister, "and while I'm here, a box of Tito's, if you have them. They're somewhat hard to find."

"Madam, I have them." Adolfo leaned down and slid a box off the bottom shelf. "Not one of the famous brands, but a cigar for a discerning individual. Yourself, perhaps?"

"No, my gentleman friend. When he truly wants to relax, he smokes a cigar. When he's nervous, he smokes a cigarette."

Adolfo laughed. "Yes, well." Then he lowered his voice. "So much has changed. Tobacco additives. Well, there was always that, but if you bought a pack of, say, Dunhill Regular, you knew they were made with the best leaf from the tobacco plant. Whether it's cigarette tobacco or cigar, the upper leaves are most prized. The lower you go in price, the lower you go on the plant until you get to those discount brands—those are just chop." He squinted his eyes for a moment, shaking his head. "How anyone can put one in their lips, I don't know. Smoking should be a ritual of pleasure."

"We have few true rituals of pleasure in this country. No siestas. No teatime. Other nations have a special part of the day to relax, recharge, give thanks. We do not."

"Well"—Adolfo paused for a moment—"I cannot criticize a nation that took us in as refugees where we flourished. It took some time but we have made our way, the Galdos family."

"Galdos?" Tootie's eyes opened wider. "Do you know the designer, Sophia Galdos?"

He broke into the biggest smile. "My middle child. My oldest is a vice president at Altria, my youngest is a lawyer."

"Then, painful as your exodus was, I am grateful you are here." Sister reached out and took his hand, squeezing slightly.

Tootie couldn't stop grinning. "I can't believe I've met Sophia Galdos' father."

"She gets her talent from me, of course," Adolfo joked.

Sister plucked two packs of Dunhill Menthols to put with the one Montecristo, one Pleiades, and the box of Tito's. "Ah, I think I must have that World War One cigarette case."

He bowed slightly, handed her the case as well as the small white card, good stock, with the price: $2,800.

Sister noted it. "This is good fortune. And each time I hold it, I'll remember my father and yours, too."

"I believe it will bring you good fortune." He wrote out the ticket for the items, carefully deducting fifteen percent from the cigarette case, which he then slid over to Sister for her approval.

"Mr. Galdos, you are very kind." Sister misted up.

She didn't know why she was getting emotional.

"To think of a beautiful woman with this case in her hands pleases me." Then he looked over at Tootie. "Two beautiful women."

Sister rooted around in her purse, pulled out the slender little cell phone, found her small wallet with only the credit cards, and handed over her American Express Platinum Card.

The transaction completed, the merchandise secure in a plastic bag, Adolfo came around the counter again and gallantly kissed both ladies' hands.

"Go with God," he said, and he meant it.

"And you, too," Sister replied and Tootie echoed her.

Out into the fray they charged. If anything, the storm had worsened.

"I bet Galdos Senior nearly died when he suffered through his first New York blizzard," Sister said, head down.

"I got spoiled at Custis Hall." Tootie was born and raised in

Chicago. "Princeton reminds me of why I love Virginia. Four seasons of equal length. No long winters. I have good professors but, Sister, I hate it. I want to be an equine vet. I don't need to go to Princeton, but Dad swears he will cut off the money if I don't finish."

"Princeton is one of the best universities in this country, honey. You can go to vet school after your undergraduate work. That gives you three more years, well, three and a half, to work on the parental units. I'm assuming your mother is in league with your father."

"I guess," Tootie responded with no enthusiasm.

After another big blast smacked them, Sister ducked into a doorway. The two women huddled there for a moment as Sister opened her bag, fishing for her cell phone.

"Oh no, I left my phone on the counter." She sighed. "You go on back to the hotel. No point in both of us being out in this."

"How can I ever dream of whipping-in if I can't take a little bad weather on foot? We can sprint."

They did, despite the slippery pavement.

Pushing the door open, they laughed to be out of the storm but they did not see Adolfo behind the counter.

"Maybe he's in the humidor room." Tootie shook the snow off her head, then passed the counter as she walked toward the large climate-controlled room. She turned slightly as Sister triumphantly spotted and retrieved her cell phone: right on the counter where she left it.

"Sister!" Tootie called, before running for the back of the counter.

The older woman followed Tootie, now kneeling down.

"Dear God!" Sister exclaimed, for Adolfo Galdos lay on his back, beautiful green eyes staring straight up to Heaven. He'd been shot neatly between the eyes. On his chest lay a pack of American Smokes cigarettes.

CHAPTER 3

A glorious swirl of red, white, and black filled the ornate ballroom of The Pierre. Tradition dictates that all hunt balls should be white tie, but over the years they had devolved into black tie for those men not awarded their colors.

From her table, Sister watched the men entitled to wear evening scarlet: formal tails with the colors of their hunt on the lapel. Hard to fault even a hefty fellow in such splendor. The women in attendance wore white or black gowns. A few refined ladies even wore long evening gloves.

Concentrating on how much she wished the other less stylish gentlemen had worn black tails with white tie, Sister tried to keep her mind off Adolfo's shocking murder. It wasn't working.

Gray, usually on the dance floor, returned with a glass of alcohol for her. "Not bad."

"You would know better than I." She took the glass.

He slightly flipped up his scarlet tails to take the seat next to Sister. "Runs in the family," he stated matter-of-factly.

Indeed it did. His brother, Sam, a Harvard graduate, once lived at the train depot in Charlottesville, being moved nightly along with the other alcoholics. They slept under whatever bridge, overpass, or deep doorway they could find, until again being chased off. Over the years, Gray and his sister, a total snob, would discuss Sam, but only Gray would actually drive down from Washington to talk to his brother. Three years ago, Sam agreed to dry out, which he did. This more or less had a happy ending except that Sam was now employed by Crawford Howard, Sister's enemy. After just five years of habitation in Charlottesville, Crawford was the only person to give Sam a chance. People who had known him all his life worried that sooner or later Sam would backslide.

Sister found herself wishing she and Tootie had found Crawford Howard shot instead of Adolfo. However, furious as the pompous, rich, underhanded Crawford could make Sister, she had to admit he didn't shy away from reformed alcoholics, and to help young people, he would do anything—even, like Sister, sitting on the board of Custis Hall.

"Well?" Gray said with eyebrows raised, waiting for her verdict on the sparkly drink.

"Oh." Sister took a sip. "Bubbly. Tickles my tongue."

"It's odd that alcoholism shows up in every generation in the Lorillards, black or white, but my sister and I are unaffected. My Uncle George could empty a liquor store and still remain upright."

"People say it's in the blood or the genes or whatever but I also think it's in the culture." She took another sip. "No one has ever been a drunk in my family, both sides, but you know, there's still time."

At this, they both laughed, for Sister was a one-drink-a-night girl and that was that.

Hailing from Lexington, Kentucky, where she was Master of the Woodford Hunt, Jane Winegardner walked across the ballroom straight toward Sister, evening gown swishing as she did so. She leaned over Sister, kissing her on the cheek.

As Sister's Christian name was Jane and she was the elder by quite a bit, Jane Winegardner was referred to within these circles, as "O.J."—the other Jane.

"You doing okay?" asked O.J.

"I am, really."

"What a shock." O.J. sat next to Sister in one of the empty chairs at their table. Tootie, her date, and Val and her date, were off dancing.

"You know, it really was," said Sister. "Adolfo was a delightful gentleman." She thought for a moment. "Well, you and I have endured shocks before."

"Life." Jane looked up to wave at Lynn Lloyd, MFH, from Red Rock in Nevada. "But when we had our adventure, we found out why it all happened."

Sister well remembered the dreadful mess they had stumbled upon when hunting together in Kentucky.

Gray joined the conversation. "He was from Cuba. He came here as a teenager in 1959. That's what he told my beautiful date. I can't help but wonder if some of his talk about the old Cuban fortunes before the Revolution has something to do with his murder."

"Well, could be," O.J. said, considering it. "You let me know if there's anything I can do. And come hunt with me! It's been a first-rate season."

"For us, as well." Sister smiled. "Good weather, an abundance of healthy foxes. The pack just thrills me as they're so good and our hunt staff is working so smoothly together."

"Working with hounds is easier than working with people." O.J. laughed, a mellow rolling chuckle.

"Isn't that the truth." Sister leaned toward her friend. "But our field is in good shape, no dramas. Well, once we got rid of Craw-ford, the dramas did abate."

"What's he doing here tonight?" O.J. asked, wrinkling her nose.

Gray leaned toward Sister to speak to O.J. over the loud music. "New master up in eastern Maryland. Crawford's been shining on Brian Bocock, taking hounds, giving him tidy sums of money for this and that, hunting up there with this kid about once a month. So, without knowing Crawford's unsavory history—I mean the man runs an outlaw pack, for Christ's sake—Brian invites him to his table at the ball."

"What next?" Jane threw up her hands. "You'd think someone would have told him."

"The folks from Green Springs did. I think Elkridge-Harford did, too," Sister said, naming two solid hunts in Maryland.

Green Springs, established in 1892, occasionally hunted over the course for the Maryland Hunt Cup, and its masters over the years had ridden in that competition. You'd best be able to fly on a Thoroughbred at Green Spring Valley. And Elkridge-Harford did not countenance sloppy turnout, dirty tack, that sort of thing. Both hunts had the highest of standards and took excellent care of their hounds.

"Young Brian has to be dumb as a sack of hammers to ignore the advice of not just two senior hunts, but hunts with politically astute masters," said O.J. "He's going to have a less than easy time as master."

"Yes and no," said Sister. "Times are hard. Everywhere. Many hunts are having to breed fewer hounds, cut back on staff. We're all doing what we can to keep operating and to make sure all the hounds and horses in our care receive the best of everything. You can cut corners, but not there. And my feed bills just go up and up."

Sister twirled her forefinger upward. "We had to hire a professional whipper-in; it was necessary for both parties, so our budget is imperiled."

"Mmm," the younger woman murmured to herself. "Money. So you're telling me Brian took Crawford's money *knowing* he was inviting a man who runs an outlaw pack over your territory? And I doubt Crawford fixes one bloody fence if he knocks it down." O.J. frowned.

"Rumor has it that Crawford had spent about twenty-five thousand dollars at the Navy Man's Hunt," said Sister, sharing gossip about the hunt founded by a graduate of the U.S. Naval Academy at Annapolis.

O.J. folded her hands. "That's being a master. You solve problems. You look ahead. You do your best, knowing there's always someone who thinks they could have done it better, and maybe they could, but they aren't sitting in the driver's seat."

Both Sister and Gray nodded. "Imagine what it's like being President of the United States?" said Sister.

"At least we can ride out and feel the wind in our face, hear the hounds at full cry, see a beautiful red fox shoot across emerald meadows or fields of snow," said O.J. "What does he get?"

"Power over others," Gray remarked. After a long career in Washington, he'd seen enough of it.

"That's a peculiar type of person, isn't it?" asked O.J. "Someone who thinks they know better than you do about your own life, and wants to force their ways on you." The lovely woman stood up.

"Crawford is one of those types," Sister replied.

"I don't envy you him, but I do envy you your territory. You have some of the most beautiful hunting grounds in America." O.J. leaned down and kissed her on the cheek again. "My dance partner is searching for me. He doesn't have GPS."

As O.J. left, the girls returned with their dates, both good-looking young men clearly on the football or lacrosse teams. Big boys.

Jefferson Hunt paid for two tables. Charlotte Norton, Headmistress of Custis Hall and her husband, a physician; Walter Lungrun, jt-MFH, and his date; the Bancrofts; and Tariq Al McMillan, a handsome Egyptian teacher at Custis Hall, sat at the second table. While it wasn't written in stone, it was advisable that each table be headed by a master.

Tariq, single, in his mid-twenties, had come to the Ball and to visit friends at the Egyptian consulate, for he remained an Egyptian citizen. Some of the young men he had gone to college with worked at the consulate as well as the embassy in D.C. All were bright, beautifully educated, and carried the hope of leadership later in their lives. Egypt, still unstable, kept them all watchful, careful of conversation. Even with old friends, Tariq was circumspect. Above all, he did not want to be called home, which could happen for any number of reasons.

From the Jefferson Hunt standpoint, he was handsome and single. Always a great idea to have extra males, and since Tariq taught at Custis Hall, so much the better for his inclusion pleased the Headmistress. Tariq was a walking advertisement for the progressiveness of Custis Hall.

Tootie, seated with her date, Baxter Chiles, felt a tap on her shoulder.

"Miss Harris, may I have this dance?" Tariq beamed at his former student.

Smiling, she rose, touching her date on the shoulder as she left.

Baxter found this an excellent time to get a drink from the bar. Parched, he paid for tonic water. Not yet being twenty-one, he was smart enough to know he could compromise his hosts if he did purchase a real drink. Baxter figured he had the rest of his life to drink.

"Derek, sit here next to me for a minute." Gray patted the seat. "Val, oops, turn around."

The tall blonde, who had not yet sat down, turned just as one of the masters of Farmington Hunt was about to tap her on the shoulder.

Pat Butterfield asked, "May I have this dance?"

Pat and his wife, both educators, knew Val and Tootie from Custis Hall, as Farmington is the adjacent hunt to the Jefferson.

"Keep in touch with me as your studies continue," Gray said, sizing up the young man. "You're a junior, right?" Derek Joyner hadn't been drinking, nor had the girls. That boded well for these young people, and, Derek, especially, as he wanted to go into accounting, his sights being set on campaign finance.

"Thank you, Mr. Lorillard. Val told me all about your career in Washington. People don't think accounting is exciting. I bet you could tell some stories that would disprove that."

Gray smiled, his even teeth bright under his silver moustache. "It was exciting for me, and so many of the people I went to college with became CFOs of corporations. Oddly enough, only one other classmate went into campaign finance. He ran the numbers for the Democratic Party for years. I never worked for either party but for individual candidates, and then wound up as partner of the firm. At that point, all the action was in taxes so I had the field to myself. Well, too much about me. Call me." Gray reached inside his scarlet, pulling out a card. "The finance laws change by the minute. You will need to know exactly what's on the books in your state and nationally. But you know that."

"Yes, sir." Derek looked away to see Val and Pat. "He's a good dancer, isn't he?"

"Pat Butterfield? Yes, he is. Good rider, too."

"I've never been on a horse. Val, well, you know." Derek took a breath. "She wants me to learn to ride and I'm a little afraid."

"Did you tell her?"

"No, sir."

"Tell her." Gray was stern. "Whether you and Val wind up in a long romance or not. Any woman who comes into your life, tell her the truth. Be who you really are, fears and all."

"Val's such a strong person. I don't want to look weak."

Gray reached over and grasped Derek's muscular shoulder. "Derek, trust me. You'll look strong, not weak. It's the sorry twits putting up a big front who always, always crash. She'll respect you for it. I've known Val for four years. Trust me."

"Yes, sir." And Derek did.

Just then Crawford with Marty, his wife, swept past the table. He paused as his wife, who liked Sister a lot, tugged at him to move on.

"Ah, Sister, found another corpse, did you?" Crawford growled.

"Pity it wasn't you, Crawford," Sister snapped back, which wasn't like her.

His mouth fell open and he took a step toward the table, Marty tugged him back.

Sister rose from her chair, six foot three in her high heels.

Gray stood beside her. "Honey, what's gotten into you?" he whispered.

Marty succeeded in pulling away her slightly overweight husband.

Sister looked at Gray, surprised at how anger had just taken control of her. "I have no idea."

"You've had a shock," he said. "Come on, let's go upstairs."

"I'm all right. You were such a big help coming down for Tootie and me—well, Val and the boys came, too. And it made everyone an hour late to the Ball. But you don't know how glad I was to see you right then."

"Thank God for cell phones."

"Apart from the discovery of Adolfo, you know what else surprised me? How good the New York Police Department is."

"Are you sure you don't want to leave?"

"No, honey, I don't. The girls will go back to Princeton tomorrow. I want to spend some time with them. I miss them."

"I know." He fiddled with a gold fox-head cuff link.

He'd found the stud. As Sister had surmised, it had slipped behind the backing of his jewelry box. There was a small tear in the fabric not easily seen. His jewelry box had a false bottom where the stud had landed.

Seated again, Sister turned to Gray. "I will live to see that bastard dead," she said, staring again at Crawford's retreating form.

CHAPTER 4

The band, a small orchestra actually, played wonderful old standards from the first half of the twentieth century. When they took a break, a rock band played for the younger hunting set.

Sister loved to dance and stayed on the dance floor a good long time before returning to the Jefferson Hunt table when the rock music started. Known behind her back and to her face as "The Steel Lady," she didn't feel like it at that moment, ten minutes past eleven PM.

"Tired?" asked Betty Franklin as the whipper-in joined her. The expensive annual ball was beyond the Franklins' purse at this time, but Sister, well off, paid Bobby and Betty's way. As far as she was concerned, they were hunt staff who had served her for over thirty years. They deserved it. Tootie and Val, on the other hand, had been born with silver spoons. Their fathers paid their tickets, declaring this was the last year they would do so. Derek, a scholarship student, worked after school but he came up with the cash.

Tootie's date, Baxter Chiles, also worked for his ticket. The fellows had bunked up together at a much cheaper hotel downtown.

Sister took note of everyone's accommodations, and while she never interfered in anyone's personal life unless they asked her to, she liked both these young men. The girls could do a whole lot worse, but they were young and who knows what will happen? Then again, thought Sister, she fell in love with Big Ray when she was just twenty-one. She was married at twenty-two. Fifty years ago, and yet it seemed like yesterday. Puzzling as this contradiction was to Sister, all her older friends felt the same way about powerful emotional events long distant. Nothing ever truly fades except one's looks.

Betty affected a Philadelphia working-class accent, not Main Line, "I like da song. I can dance to it. Good beat."

Sister leaned forward, resting her arms on the table, which would have brought a swift reprimand from her mother, "I just miss *American Bandstand.*"

Glowing, Betty recalled, "Daddy put up a radio in the garage and we'd dance almost every night when we'd come home from the barn. There we'd be, a bunch of barn rats, gyrating."

"All girls?"

"For the most part. Sometimes the boys would come over after football practice in the fall or track-and-field in the spring. You know what was fabulous? We were having the time of our lives and we knew it. I don't know if young people are as happy as we were." She looked at the dance floor mostly filled with the young.

"Bet they are." Sister smiled.

"But what I don't understand is why they don't learn ballroom dancing? It's so, so erotic. A man holds you in his arms, you might even put your head on his shoulder and you move in rhythm. I like this kind of dancing, I'm not totally out of it, but there's nothing like being held in a man's arms."

"Favorite song?"

Betty's lips pursed. "I have so many. You know what I really love." She began to sing, "Heaven, I'm in Heaven."

The two of them finished "dancing cheek to cheek," then clapped for the joy of it.

"It's hard to sing with other music in the background." Sister fiddled with her earring. "You know what I remember? Cotillion."

Betty groaned as though in terrible pain. "The worst. The absolute worst and we'd have those hideous practice dances once a month. How did we live through it?"

"Fortitude. And we acquired considerable manners in the process. What I remember is sometimes we girls would practice. Not at cotillion, but sort of like you in your father's garage. Loathed it."

"Why? I thought it was fun."

"Betty, you're all of five foot six if you're an inch. I'm six feet now and was even a tiny bit taller back then."

"Well, so what?"

"I'd always have to lead. I really didn't want to push another girl around the floor, plus they all had their noses smack in my cleavage."

Betty stared at her dear friend's rack. "Did anyone suffocate?"

Sister lightly slapped her. "Do you eat with that mouth?"

"I do, but if I were you, I certainly wouldn't wear that gown near any hungry babies."

Sister let out a whoop, and the two of them nearly fell off their chairs laughing. Is there a greater happiness than laughter with an old friend?

Once recovered, Sister swept her eyes across the dance floor. "I see what you mean. No one holds anyone. I never thought about it before. Well, I don't think about much apart from hunting, geology, and history."

"That's not true. I've seen you work that credit card at Bergdorf's."

"Mmm. I like the men's store better than the women's. The tie display with all those colors in perfect silk." She looked directly at her friend. "You're right. It's not very heterosexual, this kind of dancing," she mused. "But I'm sure they'll figure it out."

"That they will, but they miss the frisson, the buildup, the gliding around, all that tension in your mind, all that music in your body."

"It is an unromantic time," said Sister. She noted the girls dancing with their dates. "Betty, I don't envy them. I love those girls, as do you, but I would not want to be young now."

"Me neither," Betty said forcefully. "Hey, before I forget, we're supposed to hunt at Old Paradise Tuesday. Bobby said he'd heard Art has fired up the old still just beyond the westernmost boundary."

Art was the middle-aged son of Binky DuCharme, the father being half-owner of Old Paradise. Art never fulfilled his promise, that's what his parents said, but they loved him anyway. Others said he was nice enough, but a bum.

"We'd better pray our fox doesn't head his way."

"The one time hounds ran through there, all that stuff exploded. Sounded like a small war. I never knew distilling could be so, uh, loud."

"Sure was that time," Sister agreed.

"They're now selling country waters in small batches. I mean the authorities are allowing it, but the distiller has to go through the process so he gets the stamp put on it. I even think one of the brands from Nelson County is called Pure Moonshine."

"More money to be made illegally." Sister frowned for a moment. "Well, we know our foxes at Old Paradise, so if we hop the big red who heads straight west we'll have to work to lift the pack, which I hate to do. They are doing their job. They should be rewarded, not thwarted."

"It will be an interesting day."

"Always is." Sister thought for a moment, then said above the music: "Know your quarry." She blinked. "I'm tired. It's past my bedtime. I feel like I've been hit by a Mack truck."

"You had a scare," Betty said wisely. "It's finally getting to you."

"I think it is." She looked directly into Betty's eyes. "Tootie and I had been gone from the shop maybe five minutes." She snapped her fingers. "Dead."

"You never know. I used to think my mother was so tedious when she'd say, 'Make every minute count.' I know what she means now." Betty inched closer to her friend. "You and Tootie didn't have to come to the Ball. We'd have missed you, but everyone would understand."

"We needed a distraction." Sister glanced out at the dance floor. The song had changed. "She's a strong person and she didn't want to disappoint Baxter."

"The boys are staying somewhere down in the Forties, I think. I asked Derek how it was, and he said clean. At least it's not a flophouse."

"Good for them."

"Maybe so, but after the Ball the girls are in one room, the boys downtown. I don't like to think of one of them going downtown and one staying here. I mean I don't like the idea of either Val or Tootie at a cheap hotel."

Sister pondered this. "Well now, Betty, let us trust their resourcefulness. Tootie did mention that she and Val had double beds so perhaps they will work it out."

Betty laughed. "It's better that mothers don't know these things, especially *their* mothers."

"Val's mother would be better than Tootie's but still, you're right. Better mothers don't know."

"Can I get you a drink?"

Sister shook her head. "No. Let's make our dates do that. I'm about ready for a tonic water with lime."

"Neither one of us are drinkers. Oh well, many of our hunt club members make up for us." She paused. "You know that Crawford will make trouble the minute he can. My bet is he'll cast his pack at Old Paradise. If not Tuesday, he'll be sure to try and screw up one of our hunts in the next week."

"He's the kind of man that keeps score." Sister felt a rush of anger rise again. "I try not to hate anybody, but I do hate him. Then I remember the good things he's done for Custis Hall, for Felicity." She mentioned a classmate of Tootie's and Val's who became pregnant at the end of her senior year. Crawford gave her and her brand-new eighteen-year-old husband a place to live.

"He's a walking contradiction."

"Maybe we all are." Sister shrugged, returning to the day's event. "What I can't get out of my mind, Betty, is the slightest whiff of gunpowder when Tootie and I returned to the tobacco shop. I discounted it, you know, city pollution. You don't think of guns in the city, not like home, but I smelled it." She paused for a long time. "We were detained, as we should have been, so we got to watch some of the police procedure, and do you know Betty, there were thousands and thousands of dollars in the glass display case? Lighters, jeweled cigarette cases, long cigarette holders, some with jewels, plus the cash register was crammed full of money. Nothing was touched. Nothing that one could see. You kill a man for cigars? Or cigarettes? I simply can't fathom it. And poor Adolfo had a pack of cigarettes set right on his chest. American Smokes was the name."

"Might be some kind of revenge thing," said Betty. They fell silent, and Sister's thoughts wandered. "I bought a cigarette case from him. I'll show you when we get back home. How can I look at it without thinking of him? Betty, he was so warm. You know how

Latin men radiate warmth, and Cubans ooze charm along with it. The man was delightful."

"Even delightful people have enemies."

"Yes." Sister paused, then raised her voice a bit. "I have never heard of American Smokes," she said, furrowing her brow in thought.

CHAPTER 5

Ornate wrought-iron lamps, installed in 1877, on the long curving main drive at Custis Hall, contrasted with the clean Federal architecture of the earliest buildings on campus built in 1812. The building bordered quads named after the trees planted on them. One could readily see when the money poured into the school, as it was reflected in the architecture.

Those buildings constructed in the 1980s were mercifully hidden around the Blue Spruce quad, way in the back, a half mile from the original Federal building. One good thing about these particular three long, low-slung buildings was they looked better than the examples from the 1970s.

At the rear of the blue glass building, Art DuCharme with Donny Sweigart, both men in their thirties, maneuvered a heavy wooden crate off the back of a small moving van onto a forklift. A Custis Hall groundskeeper drove the forklift and the two men followed him into the building.

A service elevator, thankfully huge, had enough room for the forklift to deposit the large box.

When the elevator reached the fourth floor, Tariq Al McMillan met Art and Donny. He rolled a low metal dolly over and the two delivery men jiggled it onto the dolly. Art steadied the end of the box while Donny walked beside it.

Tariq rolled the large, heavy object into a large office with floor to ceiling windows. The entire campus unfolded before him, to the west.

"Do you need a crowbar?" Donny asked, staring at the crate.

"Here, let's put it right here." Tariq directed them to the windows. "I think my big claw hammer will do."

Knowing it wouldn't, Donny left without a word, returning with a crowbar and a power drill with a Phillips head. Reversing the direction, he could spin out screws.

After twenty careful minutes, an ultramodern desk emerged. A heavy glass top—so heavy the sides were green—was supported by two graceful steel legs and supports. Like bridge cables, they ran diagonally between each side's front and rear legs. The desk resembled a suspension bridge.

"Ah." Tariq clapped his hands once the desk sat in place, directly in front of the large window.

"Pretty amazing." Donny admired the cool piece of furniture.

Tariq dug into his pocket, giving each man a fifty-dollar tip.

Donny looked at Ulysses S. Grant. "Tariq, this is too much. You paid enough to get the desk here."

"It's not too much. I've been waiting six months for this desk. I'm grateful for your help. And I'm grateful in the hunt field, too. Teenage girls can be a lot to handle."

Donny laughed. "I'm practicing. Sybil is pushing forty and she's a lot to handle."

The three men laughed.

Art checked his watch. "We've got one more pickup. Tariq, thanks for the tip."

As they left, Tariq settled in his comfortable desk chair, leaned his elbows on the desktop, and admired the steeple on the campus chapel, noticing clouds piling up behind the mountains.

Donny and Art walked to the small moving van, a square-box Chevy Topkick from the late nineties. Art said, "Margaret went to school here. She got a scholarship."

"She's made the most of it. I bet being a sports doctor she makes good money."

"You know, I make more than she does and I don't pay as many taxes." He laughed.

"Yeah, but you have to worry about getting caught."

Both men laughed as Art drove west from Custis Hall to Walter Lungrun's place, Mill Ruins. They did not go in the main entrance, a long gravel driveway that led to the huge mill where a two-story waterwheel still turned.

Instead, Art turned down a rarely used rutted farm road. "It's Lungrun's operating day. He wouldn't notice the tracks anyway. No one uses this road. Well, hardly."

The truck hit a deep rut sending Donny, not wearing his seatbelt, upward. "Jesus."

"Yep. Sometimes in the spring or summer, maybe Lungrun drives back here. He's got that Wrangler."

"Well, let's hope no one comes back here. Anyway, it's supposed to snow. That should cover our tracks."

"Place used to be full of people. Shootrough was what they called it because it was full of high grasses. Everyone would come in the fall, expensive shotguns. Walking through here, the quail would fly up— I bet there were hundreds of them. A lot of farms had shooting places then, but this one was special, more natural and full of game."

"Can't much do it now. The laws against shooting hawks and falcons means the big birds have about wiped out the ground nesters. Not that I'm a big fan of shooting anything but deer. Still. Seems too barren."

They drove up to a large metal-sided building, color faded, roof good, windows still intact.

They stepped from the warm truck into the cold.

Art, with conviction, said, "No broken windows after all these years. You know nobody comes back here."

"Sometimes the hunt does," said Donny, "but no one goes in the building. Well, let's get the stuff out of here."

Art slipped his key into the big metal lock and opened a side door. The two men then carried twelve-by-twelve-inch cartons over the concrete floor from the building. The truck's back door was rolled up and they loaded the cartons onto the bed of the box.

Donny pulled himself inside the truck's rear compartment as Art continued bringing cartons. Donny walked to the back, then reached into his pocket and pulled out a beeper, like one would use to open a car or truck door. Pressing its button, he heard a click and a beep. A flat door, what looked like the back of the truck, opened, revealing a three-foot-wide space spanning the width of the truck.

Donny rapidly packed the cartons into this space. Art brought out the last ones, then climbed aboard dragging a small metal stepladder over to Donny. He handed him cartons as Donny stacked them all the way to the top of the hidden space.

"They're tight as a tick," Donny remarked from the top of the ladder.

"Yeah, but let's use the cords." Art stooped to retrieve long, flat, heavy woven plastic cords, which the two men fastened into recessed large eyelet screws inside the hidden door. They tightened three bands of the plastic, further securing the boxes.

Once finished, Donny pressed the beeper and the false back closed. He handed the beeper to Art.

Back in the truck, Art leaned over Donny and opened the glove compartment where he placed the beeper, which had a long black ribbon attached.

"Cut the motor on, Art. It's colder than a witch's tit."

"How would you know?" Art sassed him. "You haven't been to bed with any witches."

"How do you know?"

Art cut on the motor and the mid-sized truck engine rumbled to life. "You're right. Sometimes I wonder about you."

"Well, Art, every time I open that door inside the box, I think, damn, you did a good job," said Donny. "You can do just about anything with a car or truck. I never wonder about you."

"Hey, that's my line of work, but building a false bottom or back or compartment is pretty easy. The trick is hiding the seams, fooling or diverting the eye."

They bounced back down the awful road.

Once out on the decent two-lane highway, Donny asked, "When do you want to deliver this?"

"Let me call and double check, but I figure middle of the night Sunday."

"I'm good with that." Donny unzipped his heavy jacket as the truck heater worked its magic. "People are saying you're running the still again."

"Mmm. Don't worry about it."

"If there's enough talk, Ben Sidell might have someone stop you on the road."

"Donny, don't worry about it. No cop is going to find the hidden compartment and I know every byway so we can avoid the weigh stations. Haven't gotten caught yet."

"Right."

"And you're making money. Good money." Art reached for the round can on the seat of the truck for a dab of chew. "What are you going to do with all that money?"

Donny smiled broadly. "I got plans."

Art smiled back. "Me, too."

CHAPTER 6

Snows had been light that winter. The last day in January felt cold and damp. Leaves hadn't mashed down enough to turn into humus. Dried leaves even this old sent off a distinctive odor.

Atop her trusted thirteen-year-old gray Thoroughbred, Lafayette, Sister Jane watched as the hounds soldiered through the wind devil, a tiny tornado spinning upward for perhaps two minutes, then vanishing as quickly as it came. There was a cold, low-pressure front coming in, the ground was tight, the day held promise. A wide allée in hardwoods on the eastern edge of Old Paradise provided a little protection from the increasing wind. The heavens looked as though they might unzip at any moment.

Sister Jane led First Flight, those riders who flew the fastest taking the jumps. Bobby Franklin led Second Flight, and he was welcome to it in Sister's mind. She thought this group harder to lead than her own because the ability of the riders and their mounts varied. A good rider might be back there with a green horse, the best place to bring along the animal. Those members smart enough to have bought a made hunter, one who knew the sport, themselves not made at all, also filled the Second Flight ranks. An experienced horse took care of them so the rider could learn much faster. Hunting could be complex, especially for green riders on green horses, a mixture not conducive to confidence.

Organizing a hunt was like producing an elaborate Broadway show, only you didn't know if your star, the fox, would show up.

Today, he sure appeared, and right on time. When hounds cast at ten o'clock, a glossy, medium-bodied, red, dog fox shot out from the sagging barn at Old Paradise, a once great estate. The dog fox headed straight for the sun.

When he broke covert, Sister sighed with relief. Hunting forced human, hound, and horse to focus intently. The cares of the day vanished, providing the energy and hope to successfully address them in one's own good time.

Shaker Crown, Huntsman, urged the pack on. Sleek Diana took the lead, a most intelligent hound. Shaker barely had time to get the horn to his lips, for the pace was scorching. He blew "Gone Away" more for the humans than the hounds.

On her beloved quarter horse, Outlaw, Betty Franklin whipped-in on the right while Sybil Hawkes, another long-serving staff member, covered the left on her Thoroughbred, Bombardier.

The grounds at Old Paradise demanded cool judgment. The terrain varied from sweet rolling pastures to thick hardwoods, and then there were sudden drops into crevices. These invariably led to or fed little streams into one of two bold creeks. Every time it rained, the crossings deepened or filled up, the latter more dangerous than the former. Years ago, Sister and Keepsake, another one of her horses, sunk in almost up to the animal's flanks. You don't soon forget such an experience. Had the water been any deeper there would have been nothing to forget. She would have most likely drowned. Both she and Keepsake knew it.

The wind played tricks on you here because Old Paradise backed up smack to the foot of the Blue Ridge Mountains. While it might be 42°F and calm in Charlottesville, out here twenty miles west, the mercury could suddenly plummet like a crazed bobsled competitor.

The wind, fifteen miles an hour at this moment, was already creating havoc. It switched directions and spun up wind devils. It slowed, then gusted.

The scent from the dog fox blew away from him to the left so the hounds followed that line, even though the fox could clearly be seen thirty yards to the hounds' right. But hounds knew their business. Foxhounds hunt by nose, not sight. Blessed with tremendous drive, the Jefferson Hunt pack would not surrender that line until the last molecule of *eau de vulpus* disappeared.

Once the fox blasted into the eastern woods, the line of scent returned to the fox's heels since the wind couldn't sweep over the forest floor, though it sure could bend the tops of the trees.

The hounds lost the scent. They cast themselves again. Sister held up and waited. Although a Tuesday, the field was large: thirty people, about half of them in Second Flight.

An eerie silence was broken by the moans of the trees. Branches rubbing on their neighbors created long strange creaks.

A hound of wisdom, Cora trotted over to the younger Diana. *"It has to be here somewhere."*

"I know, but the bear scent is overpowering." Diana's brown eyes nearly watered from the pungent signature of the bear. The younger "T" hounds patiently worked about a forty-foot area. These two litters, a year apart, were a new cross for Sister, who bred American foxhounds, a task she loved—but then if an animal had four feet Sister loved it, no matter what.

Tattoo was from the second litter, a youngster with a broad chest. He put his nose down, lifted it and uttered a little yelp.

His sister, Tootsie, joined him. She studied the scent. Her response was a clear signal.

"We got him!"

The other hounds moved toward the two young ones but they harbored some doubt.

Cora ran over, Diana by her side. *"Tattoo isn't smart about bears yet. Better make sure."*

A bit faster, Diana reached Tattoo and Tootsie first. She put her nose to the ground, inhaled deeply, her long nose warming the scent as it traveled to her brain.

"Yes!" she bellowed.

Cora seconded Diana's cry. The whole pack flew behind them, singing as a choir.

Right behind his hounds, Shaker encouraged them with rounds of "Yip, yip."

Betty could be momentarily glimpsed in her brown tweed bye-day jacket, as Tuesday hunts did not require a formal kit, then she disappeared down a slope. Being a saucy, confident fellow, the fox cut right toward her. He evidenced no fear of Betty or Outlaw. What's one human and a horse?

"Tallyho!" Betty yelled.

The red fox lifted his head at her cry, picked up some speed, launching himself off the steep bank of the creek. Betty knew the best crossing was a good football-field's length down the creek. No time for that.

"Outlaw, let's do it."

Without hesitation, the sturdy horse gathered himself at the bank's edge to leap straight down about four feet. The cold water splashed up on Betty, some running into her boots. The footing—good, not rocky, as she'd looked for that—held up. They half walked, half swam in the deep spots to the creek's other side, where an otter slide made getting out a whole lot easier than getting in.

"You are the best horse in the world." An invigorated Betty patted him on the neck as both horse and rider tried to keep the fox in view.

"I know," Outlaw replied.

In the field behind her, Sister galloped down to the easy crossing. A four-foot jump down into water could dislodge some riders, even strong ones like her. Not every horse in the field was as bold or handy as Outlaw.

Once on the other side of the creek, Sister stopped for a moment. Even with all the splashing behind her, she heard the hounds and kicked on. The easternmost forest of Old Paradise must have been where the glacier tired of pushing all that good topsoil down from Canada. Old rock outcroppings, some twenty feet high, appeared like a giant's cast-aside dominoes. They didn't seem to have evolved from the land but seemed to have simply been dumped in the spot. A few had shapes that could be mistaken for goblins. At least some of the horses thought so.

Kasmir Barbhaiya, a wealthy Indian gentleman who had moved to Virginia, proved his leg on this day when his extraordinarily beautiful Thoroughbred, a big fellow at seventeen hands, literally jumped sideways—all four feet off the ground. His leg never moved, his grip remained steady.

"It's a monster!" the deep bay warned the horses behind him.

Naturally, a few believed him so they shied from the odd stone formations.

Three riders parted company from their mounts, who did not have the good grace to stand and wait for their riders to remount.

Two scared horses thundered by the other riders, causing human cries of "Loose horse!"

Sister heard them and thought to herself, *Loose rider.* Not that she herself hadn't now and again provided entertainment for others over her long life by, for example, popping off, sliding face-first in mud, or taking a fence while her horse did not. The list could go on and on.

Sister's mother told her when she was a little thing on a lead line that you don't become a rider until you fall off at least seven times. Mother had seen many a spectacular crash, quietly proud that her daughter took it in stride: no excuses, no tears. Mrs. Oberbeck did not believe in raising wimps. She used to shout at Jane, "Leg. Leg, Janie!"

The two horses who'd dumped their riders came up, blowing hard, by Lafayette.

"You'll not get by me, you field peons," the talented gray snorted.

With that, Lafayette put on the afterburners, tears filling Sister's eyes. He pulled away from the two runaway horses—neither Thoroughbreds—as though they had stalled in traffic.

Once he put enough distance between himself and the interlopers, Sister was able to get him back to a hand gallop, sixteen miles per hour.

The fox was giving them one hell of a run while the ground was becoming treacherous in spots. When they first started, the temperature was 30°F. It had since climbed to the low forties. Ice tinkled when they ran through a shallow puddle, and the ground was greasy in spots where one thought it would remain tight.

This is why, even in the summer, Sister worked on keeping her legs strong, riding fifteen minutes a day without stirrups, mostly at a trot. Even more than your seat, all you had in a situation like this was your leg. Leg. Leg. Leg.

Good she had it because the hounds streaming in front of her, in picture-perfect form, leapt over the narrow drainage ditch between Old Paradise and the westernmost border of Kasmir's ever-expanding holdings. On the eastern side of this two-foot-deep drainage ditch were the remains of dry laid stone. This retaining wall for the land slipped toward the east, measured three feet high in some spots, while sunken in others. Sister leapt the ditch, and there was just enough land on the other side so that Lafayette could stop, gather himself, and pop straight up and over the wall.

Those straight pop-ups were harder to jump than a four-footer with an easy approach, at least Sister thought so as every filling in her teeth rattled when she dropped to the other side. She'd known when she sailed over that there'd been daylight between her bottom and the saddle.

Mother was right: leg, she thought, then laughed for the sheer joy of doing what she loved best.

On and on they flew, the sound of hoofbeats thrilling. Shaker rode well up with his hounds. Betty, feeling that water in her boots, on the right and Sybil, a swift-moving speck on the left, charged over undulating pasture. Sybil protected the road side, which fortunately carried little traffic, being a dirt state road. Depending on the state budget, stone would be put on the road about every three years. It never lasted long.

Sister heard gaining hoofbeats behind her. Turning for an instant, she saw that her field had diminished in number. Thank God for Bobby Franklin. As he passed them, he'd call back to his tail rider, the last person in his flight, to pick up the pieces.

Hounds disappeared over a swale. An old tobacco barn hove into view as Sister galloped down that incline, then up the other side. The hounds surrounded the old curing shed, some eagerly wiggling through spaces, logs deliberately built that way a century and a half ago. Other hounds found the open door and ran in.

Off his wonderful Hojo, who stood like a Life Guard's horse, Shaker joined the hounds in the tobacco shed.

Betty stopped on the other side of the shed, but at a distance.

If the fox emerged, she would not turn the fellow back toward the hounds. A good whipper-in has to know these things, it has to become instinct. The last thing Betty wanted to do was kill a fox. Give him plenty of time to get away if he bolted.

Sybil also kept her distance on the left.

Sister stayed about twenty yards away, the remnants of the field behind her. From there she could still see the tier sticks in the shed where four to six plants would be speared to hang, ropes tethered to them to raise and lower the orderly lattice framework holding the valuable leaves. In the center of the dirt floor would be a dug-out firepit, charred, looking like a dirty navel. Even from a distance, one smelled the magical perfume: old hardwood fire mixed with the sweetness of tobacco. The aroma could still tingle the senses, even decades after this shed's abandonment, more evidence of the destruction of the small tobacco growers due to antismoking legislation back in 1964.

Shaker emerged from the shed, a broad smile on his face after having blown "Gone to Ground" on his horn. The hounds dutifully followed him out, all but little Thimble, the runt of the second "T" litter. This was just too darn exciting. The fox was in that big hole in the corner and she couldn't leave him.

"I have him. I have him," she sang out in her reedy voice, not a desirable booming one.

Outside, Sister laughed, and saw Betty and Sybil laughing, too. The three of them, along with Shaker, worked with the hounds year-round. Sister and Shaker lived with them, the graceful kennels with their brick archways forming a square, had been built on Sister's farm. This was the first time Thimble had been in on a run that put a fox to ground.

Shaker, with big smile, cajoled little Thimble, "Come on, girlie, girl."

"No. I did an important thing," Thimble sang some more.

Senior hound Cora returned to the shed. *"Thimble, I will bite your tail. Come on. Time to go."*

Thimble sat down right next to the den, hearing the fox squeak. *"Why don't you move your sorry ass?"*

Her ears pricked up. She peered into the den to see two bright eyes peering back at her.

"He's right," said Cora. *"We've done our job. Come on, Thimble."*

She trotted out, puzzled, finally asking Cora, *"Are foxes allowed to sass us?"*

Cora laughed that dog laugh where they expel air in a short puff. *"All the time. Wait until you meet Aunt Netty. My God, that vixen's tongue could rust cannon. Come on now, young one. You did well."*

Thimble accompanied Cora back to the pack, patiently waiting, glad for the rest.

"Well done," Shaker praised his pack.

A sensitive man, Shaker knew his hounds. Far better for Cora to correct the youngster than for him to make a big deal out of it. If he had had to go in and bring her out, he would have. But the hounds live together, establishing their own society. Like nearly all pack animals, there is a clear leader. It's a peculiarity of humans, who are pack animals, that they so often fail to develop effective leadership. Neither hounds nor horses, who are herd animals, had any such problems.

Shaker easily swung up into Hojo's saddle, his dexterity a source of envy for many watching him. He walked over to Sister, their two horses touching noses for a moment.

"Didn't they do splendidly?" Sister glowed.

Also high from the successful chase, Shaker nodded. "Tell you what, Boss, they just get better and better." Looking fondly at the hounds, he said, "These youngsters are special."

"Yes, they are." She pulled her grandfather's pocket watch out of the watch pocket. "We've been out here a little over two hours. Doesn't seem like it. We'll have about a half hour walk back. Let's lift them. The ground's getting dicey. Let's get them back in the kennels and rub a little bag balm on those who need it."

Lifting hounds meant taking them off a line or ending the day's sport. The hounds literally lift their noses.

"Righto." Turning, he called the pack to them. They headed west at a leisurely pace.

Sister and Lafayette passed Bobby. "Got everyone?" Sister asked.

"Do. They had a soft landing when they popped off." He smiled. "What a go!"

"Was." She smiled back.

They reached the stone fence with the drainage ditch. Sister rode alongside it to find the fence's lowest point and stepped over it. She gave Lafayette a second, then they jumped again over the ditch. The field had jumped a lot that day, run a lot, no point pushing it. As it was, a few horses didn't find good purchase on the other side of the ditch, their riders having to stand up and lean forward to help the animal. It's easy to misjudge a ditch, especially for many riders since so few hunts had ditch jumps in their territory. Jefferson Hunt had only one other one, which was a whistling bitch. People learned.

The horses knew what to do. It was the rider who sometimes miscalculated and looked down. Never a good idea.

Once both fields were on the other side of the ditch, they hung together and entered the heavy woods. The clouds dipped lower now, the sense of moisture was heavier, too, and that respite where the mercury climbed to the low forties ended. The silver liquid plunged in the thermometers.

Eager to pull off her boots and wet socks, Betty rode along praying they'd get the hounds into the trailer quickly. Her feet were killing her.

In the woods, the trees swayed more as the wind increased. Dasher, a littermate of Diana's, stopped in his tracks. Diana, seeing her brother stop, put her nose down.

"Bear!"

When no fox scent is around, many hunts consider bear, bobcat, even cougars fair game. Jefferson Hunt was one of those.

For a brief moment, Shaker studied his hounds, milling around, then they took off. And with a roar so did everyone else.

Scent led south, and bears tend not to circle back or play tricks. They run in a straight line. Foxes can, too, if the mood strikes them.

No one had heard the bear crashing about, but his scent was relatively fresh and the hounds screamed.

The staff's horses were fit, and more than up to another hard run. As the day was so cool, that also worked in their favor. Had it been a hot day, such as one finds at the end of a cubbing run, cubbing being early in the season, Sister might have led the field back. In the old days, everyone hunting knew horses. They knew when their horse was tucked up, had enough. These days, a field master couldn't count on that. Those in the First Flight could ride, to be sure, but a rider is not necessarily a horseman. Sister kept a close eye on her field and if she saw a horse's flank draw up, a chest heaving, or an animal laboring in any fashion, she sent its rider back, ordering them to walk. Sometimes she had to tell them to get off and walk their horse back. Too many didn't know to do that. Sister always gave her orders with kindness, never treating the person badly. She knew many of these riders had come to horses late in their lives. Depending on natural ability and guts, one can learn to ride in a year or two, at least good enough to go Second Flight. Yet it takes a lifetime to make a horseman. Old as she was, Sister was still learning.

Running low to the ground, hounds covered ground quickly. They reached a deep ravine, the sun's rays long and slanting in winter, darkness gathering in the defile. The minute Sister picked her way down the narrow path, a deepening cold hit her. Hounds started up the other side, then turned back to run in the crease of the ravine. A narrow, often rocky trail rested alongside the crease, which turned into a thin hard-running stream emerging from underground.

Horses could trot but not much more. The ravine's end opened into a wide, fast eastward-running creek, its waters swollen with runoff from the mountains. Here, the first snowflakes fell.

The hounds leapt into the creek. Sister and Lafayette followed, the going slow, as the current was swift and the water about three feet high at that entry point. On the other side, hounds continued south, still on Old Paradise property. Suddenly they stopped, surrounding an old locust tree.

A small black bear nestled up in its branches, looking down. Small though he was, if he chose to come down, one swat from his paw could break ribs or the neck of a hound.

Lafayette loathed the bear, but he behaved himself. Some of the other horses got nervous.

"*Chicken,*" the hound Dasher called up to the bear.

"*I'm a bear, not a chicken,*" the young fellow sensibly replied.

"All right, let's go." Shaker looked up. "For a fat little fellow, you can move."

The fat little fellow clicked his jaws, a snapping sound that could be heard all the way back to Second Flight.

Sister looked down the creek west, then east. "If we follow the creek, there's a decent crossing farther down. We'll come out on the old farm road that leads up to the barns. Mmm, maybe a twenty-minute ride. Best to walk."

Which they did. By the time they reached Old Paradise, the ground was dusted white like a sugar cookie. The snowflakes, small, could even be heard as they hit tree branches.

Everyone put up their horses. Betty, boots and socks off, old muck boots now on, had a big thermos of coffee. Sister had tea. Most everyone had something. The weather was worsening and, much as Jefferson Hunt relished an impromptu tailgate or even a planned one, this wasn't the day.

Tariq Al McMillan, who rode out with the Custis Hall girls whose classes allowed them to hunt on a weekday, came up to Sister. "Thank you, master, and good evening."

She always enjoyed hearing his lovely British accent. "Wonderful day," said Sister. "Will I see you next hunt?"

"On Saturday. Thursdays I teach." He tapped his crop on his hard hat, slightly bowed, then turned to leave.

"Did you ever hunt in the Shires, Tariq?" she called after him.

"I did. America is wilder." He smiled, enhancing his handsome features. "At first, hunting outside of England was so different. I wasn't altogether sure if I would like it. But now, of course, I can't live without it." He turned to join the students at the Custis Hall van, who were calling to him.

Once back at Roughneck Farm, Sister untacked Lafayette, wiped him down, put him in a stall with fresh warmish water, three flakes of alfalfa, and an orchard grass mix. She topped this off with a big kiss on the nose, which he endured.

Her other staff horses, Keepsake, Rickyroo, Aztec, and Matador, watched this from their own stalls.

"*You're such a suck up,*" teased Keepsake, a nine-year-old Thoroughbred-quarter horse mix.

Lafayette then filled in all of them on the day's hunt, which he knew would create waves of envy.

Up in the barn's rafters, Bitsy, the screech owl, usually outside, fussed over her nest. She peered down, ruffled her feathers, wiggled her butt into her nest. It was going to be a long, cold night.

Knowing that, Sister checked everyone's blankets, cleaned her tack in the heated tack room, then threw on her father's old fleece-lined flight jacket from the Army Air Corps in World War II to trudge across the way to the kennels. Snow fell steadily.

On Saturdays and some Thursdays, Betty helped her with those chores, leaving her horse in Sister's barn. But on Tuesdays, she and Bobby needed to hurry home and get back to business.

The kennels, added onto by Sister and her husband, Ray, back in 1964, beckoned Sister in the failing light. The white snow contrasted with the old paprika-colored brick. The back of the kennel quad was lined with huge trees inside a chain-link fence. The male and female dogs lived in separate large brick units, whereas the larger square center building housed the office, special runs for hounds being bred, as well as a more sequestered portion closed off inside with a metal door, a place for injured hounds to recuperate. Each of the hound quarters had a large outside run. But now no one was outside except Sister. When she pushed open the heavy wooden door, she spotted Shaker, bent over the desk, writing in his hunting journal.

"Everything locked down tight?" she asked.

"Yeah, before the details slip away, I just want to recount the hunt, who did what. Then I need to go home and throw some wood in the fireplace."

"Me, too." The wood-burning stove in her basement needed feeding twice a day.

Shaker lived in the tidy clapboard house perhaps fifty yards from the kennels. It was part of his huntsman's contract. Sister kept everything in good order. If he needed a new refrigerator, she bought the best. Her father told her sixty years back when she was twelve, "If you have good help, keep them."

Her daddy had sure kept his. His friends had chided him for paying his help too much, but Peter Oberbeck had men who worked for him all their lives. He missed them when they retired or died. Of course, they turned out full force when his time came, a tribute to a good man. This respect for good people had been passed on to Sister. She didn't judge people on how much money they had, or who they knew. She judged them on what they did. Were they competent, hardworking? Were they as good as their word? And like everyone who came into her life, whether staff or friend, her ultimate criteria was, "Do they have a good heart?"

Someone with a very good heart drove slowly by the kennels in a Land Cruiser.

Shaker grinned. "Your boyfriend is here."

"Need a hand with anything? He can wait."

"No, everyone's fine. Hojo's wearing his new blanket. He's out in his pasture and I'll put him up in the barn in a minute." He glanced out the window, flakes falling hard and fast. "Looks like this is going to stick around."

"We need it. It's been an oddly mild winter. Well, if you don't need anything else, I'll go up home."

When she walked through the back door, Raleigh, her Doberman and Rooster, the harrier, a beautiful tricolor hound that resembled a small foxhound, rushed to greet her.

Naturally, Golliwog, the cat, made Sister come to her.

In the kitchen, Gray gave Sister a big kiss.

"What a hunt," she exclaimed. "I wish you'd been with us." She unfastened her titanium stock pin and began untying the tie.

"Me, too, but I promised Garvey Stokes I'd meet with him. He's a smart fellow, really." He noticed the pin. "Next time I see Garvey I'll tell him you always use the special pin he made for you."

Gray paused. "I saw Felicity, too. She looks good and is a smart one, too."

"That she is."

Felicity Porter, Tootie and Val's classmate, worked for Garvey while she and Howie, her husband, lived in a dependency on Crawford's estate. She took college classes at night and soaked up everything she could about Garvey's metal business.

Gray walked over and sat at the table, opening the *New York Times*, which he'd brought home. "Look," he said a few moments later, pointing at an article found on one of the back pages.

Sister read the column, read it again, then looked at him. "What in the hell is going on?"

"That's exactly what happened on Madison Avenue," Gray said, clearly perplexed.

The owner of an exclusive tobacco shop in Boston had been murdered. Just like Adolfo Galdos, a pack of American Smokes had been left on his chest.

CHAPTER 7

"A way of life swept away," Sister mused as she read from her computer screen, an activity they only had time for in the evening. "Nationalizing an industry is never as good as letting those who know how to run it do their job. Here, look at this."

Fretting over a crossword puzzle, Gray sighed and put down the paper to sit next to her at the desk. He'd learned long ago when Sister took a notion to go with it. "What is it you're looking at?" he asked.

Filling the right side of the screen was a grainy sepia photo of acres upon acres of mature tobacco plants.

"Southside?" he guessed, naming that part of Virginia below the James River, closer to North Carolina.

"No. Pinar del Río in Cuba. This was Adolfo Galdos' father's plantation."

Gray read the copy. "Four generations of tobacco growers. The Galdoses must have been among the first Spaniards to settle Cuba."

She scrolled down, and more photos of the family appeared. She'd fiddled around doing Internet searches on tobacco shops, then searched for Sophia Galdos, knowing the designer would have a great deal written about her. Sister couldn't erase Sophia's charming father Adolfo from her mind. She found photos going back to the beginning of photography. The family members were such a good-looking bunch, and Sophia was a knockout. A former model, she had become a clothing designer, the transition a great rarity in the fashion world.

Gray and Sister read an interview with her, in which Sophia, now in her early forties, explained why she turned to design. Gray read aloud, "I wore so many bad clothes on the runway I knew I could do better."

Sister laughed. "I like this girl. What a fierce business, though. A designer has to be creative, smart about money, and tough. Not only do you face the press with each season's showing, you have to deal with all the behind-the-scenes backstabbing." She studied Sophia's most recent fashion line. "How about that?" she said, raising her eyebrows at a spare, elegant off-the-shoulder evening gown.

Returning to the old family photos, Sister recognized that Sophia's cutting-edge designs also had echoes of the spare, gorgeous clothes that her female relations had worn long before air-conditioning.

Gray hunched forward. "So the plantation was nationalized and the Galdoses figured out that eventually they'd be imprisoned. Hmm. But when Adolfo Senior came with little Adolfo and his sister, he didn't try to break into the tobacco business—or at least not growing it."

"Well, this is just a shot in the dark, but back in Cuba they grew Criollo tobacco for cigars," said Sister. "Up here it's almost all cigarette tobacco. Cigar wrapper tobacco is grown in Connecticut, a little bit in Massachusetts. Who knows, honey, maybe after losing everything, Adolfo's dad just couldn't bear to start again in the same business. It doesn't say here whether or not he was able to smuggle out seed, but if he did, he probably sold it to other Cubans emigrating to Nicaragua or the Dominican Republic. Why does anyone think revolution improves life?"

"It does, if you're the revolutionary." Gray half laughed. "Ever notice how they're all intellectuals or lawyers? They stir up the lower classes, foment bloodshed, come to power, and perhaps the poor have more than before, but they sure as hell don't have any power."

She scrolled through more photos, more history, then returned to Sophia's webpage featuring her latest clothing collection. "I feel so sorry for this woman. To lose your father like that."

"Every day someone loses someone they love to violence, war, a car accident," Gray said, voice rising. "But this is uncanny. Somehow this Boston murder is related to Adolfo's death, don't you think?"

"It's certainly strange," said Sister. "The man who owned the tobacco shop in Boston was also a second-generation Cuban." She drummed her fingers on the highly polished surface of the mahogany desk. "There has to be a connection."

"Maybe. But it's all far away. I don't think our two tobacco shops in Charlottesville are in danger."

"Don't be so sure, Gray. The man who owns the shop in Seminole Square is Cuban."

"So he is. I forgot about that." Gray considered that. "Don't jump to conclusions. I'm sure he's safe."

"I hope so," she said before changing the subject. "You were groaning over there with that puzzle. Why do you do crosswords if they make you so miserable?"

"There's nothing quite as satisfying as one completely filled out."

"Sometimes I wonder about you."

"Ditto."

They laughed and she leaned in toward him, kissing him on the cheek.

He rubbed his unshaven cheek. "Sorry. A little rough."

"That's one of the marvelous things about being a woman. No scraping of the face. However, there are a few other drawbacks."

"You have no drawbacks."

"Oh, the honey dripping from those lips." She smiled at him. "Okay. While you were suffering the tortures of the damned with one down and twenty-three across, I looked up American Smokes. Nothing came up. The company isn't listed anywhere. There are a few small tobacco companies—one using white burley tobacco, which they claim is mild and has a lower nicotine content—but no American Smokes."

"Doesn't make sense," said Gray. "No cartons in the stores either, I guess, or the media would surely shoot a close-up of the brand, you know, a photo or explanation in the paper."

"Doesn't make sense." She returned to more online reading on the subject of tobacco. "Air-cured or fire-cured can affect nicotine content. I looked that up, too. I sure remember the fire-curing. Hey, did I tell you the fox we put to ground ran into the old curing shed at Kasmir's property? Still gave off that wonderful fragrance. You know, that smoky sweet smell that makes you want to close your eyes and dream?" She caught her breath. "But back to the subject at hand: nothing about American Smokes."

"So you've been researching tobacco, types, curing, all that? May I ask why?"

"Two murders occurred in tobacco shops, both with Cuban owners, no money was taken. All of this compels me in a strange way. I know this is really crazy but I almost feel I owe it to Adolfo Galdos. He was a true gentleman."

"Doesn't sound strange. Events happen in life that galvanize our sense of honor. This is one."

"Don't hear that word much anymore: honor."

He nodded. "When I walked over to take you back to the hotel, after the police released you and Tootie, they didn't know if anything was missing from the humidor or the safe. Did they ever find out if anything had been taken?"

"The paper said nothing. Same in Boston. I'll bet the police, the Feds, good old Alcohol, Tobacco and Firearms crawled all over those stories."

"It will all come out in the wash."

"I just hope no other bodies come out with it." She looked out into the darkness. "Our first real winter storm."

"Want to make a bet on how long the power lasts?"

"No." She cut off her computer. "Let's think good thoughts."

"Right. I stopped by the home place thinking I might see my brother. Thought Sam might have heard something about Crawford bitching about your tangle at the Hunt Ball. Sam wasn't there, but the place was pin tidy."

Gray and his brother lived in the Lorillard home place, a lovely large clapboard house maybe four miles from Sister's place as the crow flies, the Bancroft's land coming between the two farms. Gray spent more and more time at Sister's. Neither one mentioned living together. Gray liked getting away, keeping an eye on his brother. He soaked up memories when home. Sister enjoyed her independence, but she was equally happy when Gray stayed with her. Perhaps someday they'd cohabit. Sister was not a needy woman. She liked her own company.

"Don't you have to go to the bathroom?" the calico cat asked the dogs.

"Why?" Rooster picked up his head.

"*Soon it'll be bedtime. If you go now, you won't have to go in the middle of the night.*" Golliwog feigned concern. "*It's snowing hard. The dog door might be covered over and you won't get out! If you end up going in the house, you know she'll have a running fit.*"

The Doberman rose with a little groan. "*You're right.*"

Eyes half-closed, Golliwog waited on the back of the sofa until she heard the dog door flap shut. Then she shot off the sofa.

Sister turned her head as the cat sped toward the kitchen, but she didn't think too much of it.

Golliwog pressed through the animal door from the kitchen into the mudroom, then positioned herself right by the next animal door, cut into the mudroom entrance. The heavy plastic flap had a magnetic strip so when animals went in and out the door would fasten shut, thereby keeping out the heat, cold, rain, and snow.

She waited. Given the bad weather, neither dog wished to be out in it, so it wasn't too long before Raleigh stuck his head through the door to enter. Golliwog gave the sleek black dog a nasty rap on his tender nose.

"*That hurt!*" Raleigh cried out.

"*Die, dog!*" Golliwog puffed to twice her size, ego to match.

"*I'll get in. I'll break her neck,*" Rooster growled. Golly, having heard the threat, moved to the side. When Rooster stuck his head through, he didn't see her at first, and out came the claws. Golly drew blood this time.

"*Ow, ow, ow!*" the harrier howled.

Hearing the commotion, Sister hurried out to the mudroom. Golly didn't budge.

Sister opened the mudroom door, a gust of wind blew snow on the floor and the two dogs, heads down, hurried inside. Drops of blood fell on the slate floor. Neither dog looked the cat in the eye as she was prancing sideways, hoping to incite even more terror.

"Hateful. Hateful. Hateful." Sister knew exactly what the cat had done.

"I am the Queen of All I Survey! Dogs do my bidding. Humans feed me right on time." With that loud declaration, she shot through the door into the kitchen, crossed the floor at a good clip, and ran up the narrow back stairway to the main bedroom. Then she dashed out into the long upstairs hallway to run victory laps.

Gray heard the paw-pounding even down in the den. Sister came in and listened as the dogs joined them.

"She's mental. She needs counseling." Rooster had watched enough TV talk shows to parrot such claptrap. *"Anger management, that is what's called for."*

The laughter rolled out of Sister in waves as she told Gray what the conniving cat had done.

"Cats and women." Gray laughed. "They'll do as they damned please and we'd better get used to it."

This made Sister laugh all the more. She reached for a Kleenex to dab her eyes. Up above, Golly was still running victory laps.

"She has to slow down sooner or later." Sister sat down. "You know I forgot to tell you the Custis Hall girls came out Tuesday. Tariq rode with them. Rode well, too. Their coach has the flu. He had to keep up with those girls, then get them all back to school. Being a coach is quite a job. Being a stand-in coach can't be easy either, but what fun working with young people.

"He's better off here than in Egypt. Sooner or later things will stabilize there. It seems like the world is turning upside down, doesn't it?"

"It does." She switched back to the hunt. "Actually we had quite a few people for a Tuesday."

"Bet a lot of them figured we'd be snowed in for Thursday's hunt."

"That's what the Weather Channel said, but this part of central

Virginia doesn't seem to pay much attention to forecasts. It's the mountains. They create their own weather system."

"Don't know how those forecasters do it, but I wish I could be wrong half the time and still keep a job." He chuckled. "I learn a lot from the channel, though. I really like it when they explain things like plateaus, vortexes, and stuff like that."

"Bull. You like the weathergirls."

He smiled devilishly. "Yes, I do. Sister, when a man stops looking, it's all over. And I hasten to add no one is as fascinating as you."

She nodded at the compliment before returning to the topic of Tuesday's hunt. "Oh, Donny Sweigart was out and on one of Sybil's older horses. He said the hauling business has really slowed down. Tough times. Given that it started to snow the last half hour of the hunt, no one had the time to catch up or chat. We all know how quickly the roads can go bad, especially out there at Old Paradise."

"McMillan." Gray smiled. "The Egyptian teacher. Just thinking about his last name. Ever notice the more sophisticated a society gets, the more people mix and marry?"

"The Scots and Irish blanket the world," she playfully reported. "So some Scot somewhere fell in love with an Egyptian. You know, Nicaragua has many people with Scottish surnames. There were so many troubles in Great Britain over the centuries that in certain historical periods, a person's best shot might just be to get the hell out."

"Well, it made our country great."

"Yes, it did." She was ever mindful of her nation's odd genetic makeup, one often covered up, too, as certain groups were once considered undesirable.

Sooner or later, as Gray said, it all comes out in the wash.

He lit up one of his Dunhill Menthols, which cleared his sinuses, and put his feet up on the leather hassock.

"How come you never started?"

"I don't know. It never appealed to me. I wish you wouldn't, but it's not my business to live anyone else's life for them. I feel the same way about smoking as I do about alcohol and drugs. If you can handle it, fine. If you can't, seek help. None of those substances does a body much good, but I really don't think demonizing them helps. And I think sin taxes are just vile. In my little foray on the computer, I was looking at the demographics of who smokes. For cigarettes, it's overwhelmingly those who are less well educated. So we punish them with taxes. How many poor people do you know who make the laws?"

"Such taxes are punitive," Gray said, crossing his legs. "I tell myself I'm going to stop smoking and then I don't. It really is a bad habit."

"There are worse."

"Oh?" He gave her an expectant look.

"Yes, like not taking care of your goddess."

"Come over here. I'll do my best."

As she walked over to him, she stopped for a moment, cocked an ear. "She's stopped."

Finally, Golly had ceased. She was most likely in the bathroom then, unspooling the toilet paper.

CHAPTER 8

Silver silence. The snow had fallen to a foot and a half. Sister waded through it to get to the equipment shed. She needed to plow a path to the kennels, to the barn, to Shaker's house, and back to her own. As nothing was shoveled, the going was tiring.

The snow, light and soft, barely crunched as she pushed through. Raleigh and Rooster followed, letting her be the bushhog.

Golly remained in the kitchen. Sprawled on the sink windowsill, she watched the three creatures flounder along. Not for her. She hated when ice formed between her toes and she never, ever enjoyed getting her dainty paws wet.

Halfway between the house and the barns was the equipment shed, hidden by graceful Leyland Cypress. Once inside, Sister reached up and grabbed the tractor's hand bar to swing herself up. About as old as she was, the 80-horsepower tractor was plenty versatile. Every now and then, she'd dream of a big 120HP John Deere with a batwing bushhog attachment, but who could afford tractors like that? Then again, she consoled herself with the fact that her old green monster was all steel, with no computer parts. It had no cabin either, a fact she regretted the minute she pulled it out of the shed.

The sky, gray and low, kept the glare off, but nothing could keep the wind off, which blew at a steady pace. A twenty-mile-per-hour wind in 18°F cut like a knife. She'd wrapped herself up, even putting on the earmuffs she disliked. The great old machine rumbled along, and she dropped the snowplow, slowly pushing the snow to the side of the paths. Funny, you can walk down a path for fifty years and yet, when it's covered with snow, you're not quite sure where the edge is.

The lights shone in the kennels and in the barns, too. Shaker, bless him, was feeding the hounds a warm gruel. He had a potion and a recipe for everything, devoutly believing that on cold days animals need to be warm from the inside out.

The state roads had to have been plowed because Betty Franklin's yellow Bronco, another old vehicle made of heavy steel, was parked by the tack room door.

On and on Sister chugged, feeling the same satisfaction she felt when she mowed the lawn or cut hay. There's something about seeing an immediate result for your effort. So much of her labor took years to come to fruition. Training the horses she'd bred took about five years before she felt they were secure in the hunt field. But then some horses that had been donated to the club or that she'd bought herself, like Matador, a former steeplechaser, took hardly any time at all to train, if you know how to buy them in the first place.

You had to study the animal's mind.

"You can't put in what God left out," her mother used to say.

Boy, was that the truth and not just for four-legged animals.

The plowing took two hours of careful, cold work. She'd slaved too many years over her herringbone-brick walkways, her English boxwoods and other gardening delights, to mess them up now. She'd put burlap over most of her bushes and all the boxwoods. They could withstand the cold, but snow deformed their lovely shapes. The branches didn't always bounce back. Sister had a thing for symmetry.

Finally, task completed, she drove the serviceable tractor into the shed, cut the motor.

"You have no more sense than a sack of hammers," she called down to the two dogs who'd followed the tractor the entire time she'd plowed.

"You never know when an enemy might jump out of a bush," Raleigh soberly replied.

"Yeah, something big and hairy," Rooster agreed.

Sister swung down a lot more stiffly than she had swung herself up. The cold gnawed into her joints. Even with the superheavy gloves, she couldn't feel her fingers. She knelt down to kiss the two canine heads.

"Come on."

They fell in behind her.

Pushing open the door to the tack room, she felt a welcome envelopment of warmth. Betty sat perched on a chair.

"Coffee?" she offered. "I made a big pot. You've got to be frozen."

Sister poured herself a cup. "Last winter was so mild and the start of this one was, too. Making up for it, now, but I sure hope this isn't our only snow. We need moisture."

"Yes, we do," Betty then agreed. "But did you hear those leaves crunching yesterday in some places in the thick woods? We usually don't hear a thing this time of year when we hunt. Not that sound anyway."

"Yeah. Every time I think I know what the weather will do next,

I don't." Sister sat down, the dogs plopping at her feet. "I could have done all this."

"Wednesdays are my day in the stable," said Betty. "You need your shopping day and the roads aren't bad. If you're going into Charlottesville, Garth Road is a holy horror, but everything else is okay."

"Not plowed?"

"No. People fly up and down those curves. Idiots."

"Betty, speaking of idiots, have you seen Crawford since the Ball?"

"No. Nor Marty either. Sam Lorillard told me he's been lining up his hay purchases early, giving people half the money before their first cutting."

"Smart. I think we'll get enough hay off our land and the Lorillard place."

"That's rich soil over there." She polished a horse's bit with a clean soft cloth. "Not one little pit. Tell you what, there's nothing like English steel. This bit has to be seventy years old if it's a day."

"Good luck finding an English bit these days. Nothing like their leather either." Sister admired quality.

"Forgot. Brought you your paper. Haven't looked at the headlines yet."

Sister picked up the paper from the coffee table, an old door affixed to four heavy wooden legs. She read silently, flipping through until she reached page three of the first section.

"What? Tariq Al McMillan is being accused by some parents at Custis Hall of belonging to the Muslim Brotherhood!"

"Anyone making accusations like that is pretty stupid." Betty smacked her knee. "If he were a member of that organization, he wouldn't be teaching at an exclusive girls' school."

"Listen to this. One of our congressmen is expressing concern for our security and will investigate."

"Don't people have anything better to do?" Betty raised her eyebrows.

Sister read more. "Congressman David Rickman fears Mr. McMillan might be spying for the Brotherhood or planning harm in D.C. 'Charlottesville is so close and filled with former officials, military people. He could insinuate himself with those people who have security clearance.'" She shook her head. "Remember when Rickman accused the president of being un-American because he owned a Mercedes in 1985? And he still gets reelected!"

Betty nodded. "Rickman has a lot to answer for."

Sister read aloud. "Mr. McMillan categorically denies the charge. Headmistress Charlotte Norton responded that such unfounded attacks on any staff member of Custis Hall will be met with legal redress." She snapped the paper closed and put it back on the table. "Well, all I can say is if Tariq Al McMillan is a member of the Muslim Brotherhood and they all can ride like he does, they're welcome in my hunt field."

"Big problem," Betty deadpanned.

"You mean the Feds will come down on me, too?"

"No. I don't think the Brotherhood would accept a woman as their leader."

"I could wear a black bushy beard," Sister replied with solemnity.

"Silver. You aren't as young as you used to be, Babydoll. And we'd have to strap down your girls, but that might do it."

They laughed.

"I'll call Tedi and Edward later." Sister was back to hunting. "They've read the paper, the Bancrofts know everyone in politics. They'll have more insight about this than I do."

Betty paused for a moment. "Age is starting to tell on Tedi and Edward. They stoop a little now or maybe I'm just noticing it. I always thought the Bancrofts were indestructible."

"None of us are, but we have to live as though we are. What's the point of going through life worrying about everything? Just go. Just do it." Sister's philosophy was simple, but it served her well.

"Yep." Betty hung the bridle pack up on the small wooden half-moon nailed to the wall, upon which Aztec's name was neatly painted.

"Come on up for lunch," said Sister. "We could all use hot soup. You go tell Shaker to come up and I'll go and get started. Give the three of us a chance to talk about the hound breedings I planned. I am not having much luck this year. Only one of my girls caught. Driving me crazy."

When she pushed open the door to the kitchen, Sister found every dishtowel on the floor. Her cookbooks had been expertly thrown off the shelves, too.

"I will kill that cat."

"No, let me," Raleigh begged.

By the time her huntsman and best friend came up, the chicken corn soup was bubbling, the spoon bread ready.

As they sat to eat, the phone in Sister's pocket rang.

She looked at the screen. "Gray. He rarely calls at this time. Will you two excuse me?"

She punched the "talk" square. "Hello. What's up?"

Betty and Shaker watched as her face changed, her cheeks reddened.

When the call ended, she growled, "That son of a bitch. Crawford has bought hay in advance just like you said, Betty, but according to Gray, he has also offered to put up new gates at Old Paradise, replace all the fences and to buy a new furnace for the abandoned big house."

"What the hell?" Shaker was dumbfounded.

"Crawford says he'll do all that, but only if Old Paradise will no longer allow us to hunt their place. He wants all the rights to hunt there."

"He can't do that." Shaker exploded. "He's an outlaw pack and the DuCharmes know it."

"Yes, they do know it, but there's nothing the Masters of Fox-hounds Association can do to landowners. Their only weapon is to deny anyone who hunts with an outlaw pack the ability to hunt with a recognized pack. Crawford couldn't give a shit. No one hunts with him anyway, unless they work for him. Damn. This is my fault. I should have kept my mouth shut at the Ball."

"Perhaps," Betty said, not lying to her. "But Crawford has been laying for us for some time. The only thing I can think of is that you and Walter"—she said—"pay the DuCharmes a visit."

Sister placed her hands on the table palms down, then folded them in her lap. "We will, and you know what we'll have to say? That we understand. No hard feelings. They haven't got a pot to piss in. Those two brothers have been fighting about that property for decades. The result is nothing gets done, especially to the main house. There is no way we can solve this problem. We haven't the funds to make those repairs, to replace their fences. Also, if we did it for them, we'd have to do it for every fixture we are allowed to hunt. We'd be bankrupt in a skinny minute."

The land on which a hunt is allowed for their sport is called a fixture.

"Plus it violates a central tenet of hunting," Betty coolly added.

Shaker nodded, his dark red, closely cropped hair reflecting the kitchen light. "Funny, isn't it? When the Masters of Foxhounds Association came into being in 1907, one of the rules they formulated was that no hunt pay for the use of territory. The land must be freely given to hunt over. Those men knew what they were about."

"Yes, they did, and they were all men of great wealth," Sister agreed. "They knew if a master could pay, then any poor hunt, even a farmer pack, would be out of business. It was a most farsighted idea."

"What does Crawford think he can do?" As upset as Shaker was, he could still eat, and he reached for more spoon bread. "He can't ride but so much. He can't hunt his own hounds and he can't hire a good huntsman because no one wants to be tainted by his brush. Who would hire them if and when they left Crawford?"

"Money," said Betty. "He'll throw so much money at someone that he'll get a decent huntsman. Maybe even a good one."

A long silence followed, then Sister said what the other two had been thinking. "We need to go through our landowners. Let's determine who is solid and who is having financial problems. We'd better get to them before Crawford does."

"Janie," Betty called her by her Christian name, "we still can't pay them."

"No, we can't, but we can appeal to their sense of fairness, and we might be able to offer labor. There's no reason we can't rouse our club members. We go to these fixtures to clear paths and build jumps. There is no stricture from our national organization that prevents us from offering services."

"Like what?" Shaker said, knowing he'd be on the chain gang.

"They will have to tell us," said Sister.

CHAPTER 9

After Shaker and Betty left, Sister checked the big old wall clock. It was two-thirty. Walter Lungrun, her joint-master, was a physician. No matter how bad the roads, he made it every workday to the hospital using his teeth-rattling Wrangler. The Jeep could go through most anything, plus it looked so cool that Sister broke down last summer and bought one herself, black with a gold pinstripe.

The major roads would be cleared and by now most of the secondary roads as well. But as the sun's rays, long and low, finally set, the roads would turn to ice.

She'd call Walter later, once he returned home from the hospital. Throwing on the old flight jacket, earmuffs, gloves, and her wonderful cashmere scarf—which really kept her neck warm—she opened the mudroom door, inhaled deeply, feeling the cold air fill her lungs.

While many household chores awaited her, she preferred outside ones. A disciplined woman, Sister would return later to the dreary repetitive round of cleaning house, washing floors, and organizing papers.

Raleigh and Rooster came out the dog door.

"If you're going to walk with me, then walk with me. No running off. Do you hear me?"

"Yeah," the dogs replied.

They walked past the kennels, the barn, turning left on the sunken farm road. Tiny rainbows glittered on the snow as they pushed along. Reaching the apple orchard, they stopped to marvel at the mature fruit trees wrapped in snow, sparkling little crystals on those branches.

Jammed in her pockets were fake hot dogs, a dog treat she bought at Pattie Boden's pet store. Moving quietly, she crept over to a fox den in the orchard inhabited by Inky, a glossy black vixen.

Putting her finger to her lips, a gesture the two dogs knew well, she knelt down, placing four of the treats just inside the main den entrance.

Inky had several escape routes but she, like most humans, preferred her front door. In the snow her footprints showed she was a gray fox. A red fox's prints would betray a bit of fur between the toes and they'd be bigger.

Since the big snow, Inky had ventured outside just once. The snow was deep enough to make it tough going for her: She'd sink. Once a good icy coating covered the snow she could move about more easily. Smart, she'd emerge later that night and use Sister's tracks to go to the kennel. She liked visiting the hounds, getting the gossip, telling them what she'd seen, since she could roam everywhere. But tonight the hounds would stay tucked up. Still, Inky would probably walk down to pick up any edible tidbits that had been discarded. The best place was the barn because the horses always dropped some of their sweet feed, plus Sister and Betty left out jelly beans and small dog bones. Inky lived good.

"Here you go, Inky." Sister stood up, headed north.

The woman and two dogs reached a coop in the fenceline bordering the vast easternmost field of her property. A coop is a jump that looks like an old chicken coop. Lush in spring and summer, she could cut enough hay off this land to feed all her horses, except in drought years. And fortunately, she had other good fields, too. Sister believed in stewardship of the earth and its creatures, plus she loved the work.

Throwing one leg over the coop, she slid the other one over. Slippery and wet on the westernmost side where the sun now shone, it was tight as a tick on the other side. The dogs leapt over effortlessly.

How glorious to have four legs. Making do with two, Sister trudged through the snow, encountering a drift here and there until she reached the stone ruins of a foundation. Slightly over two hundred years old, the ruins testified to the wisdom and tenacity of those first farmers. They first built a small cabin with a stone foundation. As they prospered, they moved to the site where Sister now lived.

One giant walnut tree grew out of the center of the foundation. The tumbled stones—surrounded by locust trees and one lone chestnut not touched by the blight—hinted at what might have been. The rise in the land to the west offered some protection from the steady northwest winds. Plus Sister owned Hangman's Ridge, which was a thousand feet above sea level. A half mile distant, it also blocked the wind in this lower meadow.

Under the walnut tree, a large round hole signaled the home of Comet. He could have used some domestic help. Unlike Inky, Comet threw his debris outside his den. A mound of bones, snow-covered, rested on the left side. A denuded bird wing, fresh, lay on the right. Clearly, Comet was a good hunter.

Sister left him a few tidbits, then retraced her steps, again clambering over the coop. She stopped and looked up toward Hangman's Ridge.

"You know, boys, I'd like to see it in fresh snow, but I don't feel like that climb."

"Let's go home. I don't want to go up there," the Doberman said.

"Me neither. Full of ghosts. Full of misery." Like the other animals, Rooster could feel and sometimes see what humans denied.

"Interesting," she informed her dogs. "It's protected here, the snow stayed on the branches. When we reach the places exposed to winds, they're cleaned off. It's always good to remember these things when I'm hunting."

"Right." Raleigh agreed.

"Those two foxes know where the wind currents are. If they run headfirst into them, the odor goes straight to the hounds. If they hook a turn, they move their scent. You know, I will never know what the fox knows, I will never know what you two know with those incredible noses."

Having come to Sister as an adult, Rooster complained. *"People think we're dumb dogs."*

"Not her, but think about it," said Raleigh, *"she knows things we don't. She can look at a piece of paper and know things."* Raleigh loved his person.

A large shadow overhead made all three freeze. Athena, the huge Great Horned Owl, two and a half feet tall, flew right between them and the sun. Her feathers were built for silence. She had startled all of them.

Another owl, Bitsy, had to flap her wings much more than Athena, but she still flew silently. Bitsy was only eight and a half inches tall, the large bird's sidekick. Swooping past, both owls regarded the ground animals.

Sister waved. She might have looked stupid, but she didn't feel stupid.

"Golly is such a liar." Raleigh stared at the talons on Athena's feet. *"She swore she scared the big owl off."*

"My favorite is when she charges into the pastures just when the horses are running around," said Rooster. *"She puffs up, tail and everything, then she turns and says she made them all run. You can't believe one word that comes out of that cat's mouth."* He said this with forceful conviction.

"Maybe we could convince the owls to turn around and chase her." Raleigh skipped a step at the thought. *"Except the horses love that rotten cat. They'll talk her up when she visits the stalls. They even come over when she sits on a fence post. I like horses, but they can't be but so smart if they're taken in by her."*

Finally, they reached the house. Sister hung her gear on a Shaker board with pegs. The dogs walked over a thick sisal rug, which cleaned their paws.

"All right," said Sister. "I have to make this call."

Before she could pick up the landline phone in the kitchen, however, it rang. The caller ID signified it was Tootie's cell phone.

"Tootie."

"Oh, Sister, I'm so glad to hear your voice."

"You doing okay? I guess you must have heard about the murder in Boston."

"Yeah, weird, exactly like what we found." Tootie paused and Sister heard Val in the background.

The two were roommates, a feat in itself, since Tootie planned ahead and Val left everything until the last minute, including every paper she had ever written at Custis Hall. Princeton proved no different.

"Snow up there?" asked Sister.

"Still is. I love to hunt in the snow. You taught me that." Tootie paused. "Can I come down and hunt with you this weekend?"

"Of course, you can. I'm assuming you'll drive. Can the car make it?"

"It can."

"Is Val coming?"

"She's spending the weekend with Derek."

"Ah."

A long silence followed this, broken only when Tootie tearfully begged, "I want to hunt with you and I don't want to come back here."

Val heard this, came over, and spoke into the phone. "She's being a big wuss."

"Shut up, Val." Tootie moved away from her roomie. "I don't belong here," she told Sister.

Hearing the tears, Sister simply replied, "Sweetie, come on down. We can talk about all this when you get here. It's a long drive. Be careful."

"I will," Tootie promised.

After hanging up, Sister sat at the kitchen table for a time. Golly jumped up in her lap. Absentmindedly, she stroked the calico fur, so soft. "Let's hope I get the whole story this weekend." Sighing, she dialed Walter, who should be home by now.

"Hey." He, too, had caller ID.

Sometimes Walter's voice startled her for he sounded so much like her late husband Ray, whom a series of circumstances had revealed to be Walter's natural father. However, Walter's mother and her husband had always pretended otherwise. Sooner or later these things do see the light of day. Sister had found out a few years ago. Walter, who loved her, feared the truth would result in distance between them. On the contrary; it made her closer to him.

Sexual peccadilloes rarely affected Sister, but screwing around with her hunt territory sure did.

The bottled-up frustration of dealing with Crawford's underhandedness for the last two years poured out as Sister told Walter about the Old Paradise problem, her fears about other farmers whose land they hunted, the whole nine yards.

"Well, we'd better get over to the DuCharmes'," said Walter. "Shall I call them, or would you like to do it?"

"Oh, I will. I've known both brothers since the earth was cooling. We'll have to see them both on the same day, too, or one will inflame the other because he was chosen first."

"Exactly. You know my schedule. I'm ready when you are." He thought for a moment. "We probably won't hunt tomorrow, right? It's at the old Lorillard place and those back roads will be treacherous in this weather. They're calling for more snow tonight."

"I'll cancel. I do so love to hunt in the snow, but I don't like hauling horses in it. We should be roadworthy by Saturday, though."

"Right."

"Walter, forgive me for spewing fury. Old Paradise has been a fixture of this hunt club for over one hundred years. Since 1887."

"I know. You're right that all of us should sit down and identify what landowners might be shaky."

"We will. Next week if all goes well."

"February is starting off like its usual dismal self." He laughed. "It's the longest month of the year."

"Actually, I like it. But this landowner thieving, I sure don't. You know, I had what Raymond used to call a volcanic moment and then I had to remember he'd say: 'Resentment is taking poison and expecting the other person to die.' "

Walter thought about it, then laughed. "A volcanic moment?"

"His term, not mine."

"Women are supposed to have volcanic moments."

After she hung up, Sister didn't know how to take that.

CHAPTER 10

Driving into town on Thursday, Sister was glad she had canceled the day's hunt. Although it had been well ploughed, Soldier Road, a two-lane east–west road, proved slick in spots. The sun lit up the eastern side of Hangman's Ridge. It loomed a quarter of a mile to Sister's right. She was by the western side, still dark. Angled on a northeast, southwest plane, it rose one thousand feet above the rolling wild meadows surrounding it. With the sun behind it, shining through the black branches, she could clearly see the enormous old hanging tree.

Forever windswept, if foxes ran up the ridge they always gained at least ten minutes. Also, generations of foxes had expertly dug rangy dens up there, some impressive, others just places to duck into when pursued. She wondered if these present-day foxes were descended from foxes who had seen the hangings. In the early days of the Virginia colony, a corpse would be left up there to swing and decay as a warning. By the mid-1750s, the relatives were allowed to cut down the criminal and give him a proper burial. If he had repented prior to his hanging, his body could be buried in consecrated ground.

A rational person, seeing the hanged, eyes plucked out by greedy birds, might reconsider his plans to clean out a bank. But the impulsive human, probably not terribly bright, would blunder on, despite such gruesome public displays. There appeared to be no truly successful deterrent to crime.

Then again, why rob a bank? The easiest way to rob a bank is to own one.

Laughing to herself, she slowly made her way into Charlottesville, up 29 North to Seminole Shopping Center. Parking was no problem. Hardly anyone was there. She popped into Dover Saddlery for a gel pad, after which she decided to stop in the small tobacco shop.

The daughter of the owner, Elizabeta, an attractive woman with lustrous black hair, greeted Sister. "Hello. Are you looking for yourself, or picking up something for someone else?"

Leaning across the glass top counter, Sister admitted, "Actually, I'm hoping you can tell me about American Smokes."

"The murders?"

"Have other people asked? I suppose they might. It's been in the papers."

"Come 'round here and sit." She warmly invited Sister to join her behind the counter. "Given the weather, I suspect we will be uninterrupted." She sighed. "You'd be surprised at how weather affects sales of almost any product. Anyway, have people asked us about it? A few, but mostly we've read about the murders in the papers, too, and are baffled."

"Why? Because nothing was stolen?"

Elizabeta sat upright. "It's bizarre. If you're running the risk of committing murder, you might as well go on a spending blowout before you're caught."

Sister laughed. "That's one way to look at it. But it's also so odd that in each case a pack of American Smokes was on the victim's chest. Do you carry the brand?"

"We've never heard of American Smokes."

"What?"

"When I read about the murders, I thought American Smokes might be a new brand, but we've yet to get a sales call. The market has room for old-time cigarettes—by that, I mean premium tobacco. Everything mass-produced is made cheaper and the companies figure no one will notice the drop in quality. But no salesperson has called on us. Other stores in the county and in Richmond don't know anything about it either."

"You called around about American Smokes?"

"Both Dad and I did. If anyone knows anything, they aren't telling us."

"When you say cigarettes are made cheaper today, do you mean the grade of tobacco?"

"Well, some high-priced brands are still using the finest grade, but most aren't. What sends me into a spin is that cigarettes contain thirty percent less tobacco than they did years ago."

"I had no idea."

"That's why they burn so fast. A couple of deep draws and the darn thing's about to burn your nose off, even if you buy king size. It's such a rip-off. Same price. Less product."

"You think this is due to the high taxes on cigarettes?"

"Pfft." Elizabeta waved her hand. "Smoking has dropped in America, but it's booming in Asia, Africa, and much of South America. Booming." She lifted her nose, sniffed. "I think I can smell some exhaled smoke right now blown across the Pacific." She giggled.

Sister giggled, too. "Next thing, we'll be ordered to wear gas masks."

"Who knows what legislation will be passed next? But I can swear that tobacco is the most heavily taxed product in the country, even more than liquor."

Sister thought about this. She wasn't going to question a woman whose income depended on the plant. She expected it was true.

The younger woman continued, "It's not like beer, you know all those microbreweries? Cigarettes and tobacco are a whole different ball game. A brewery has a physical place. People can go in and sample the beer. I can't put out a cup full of sticks, like Dad did when he was young. You'd buy a cigarette for a penny, or maybe a few, and test them out at your leisure." She paused. "Like beer, there are so many different tobacco tastes. Well, anyway, there's no way to test a product unless you buy a couple of packs or you borrow a cigarette from a friend. Who is going to buy a bunch of expensive packs to see if they like the product? And for you, or any customer, a company needs shelf space. You come in here or you go to the supermarket or corner store for one of the huge brands, you can find it. A new brand from a start-up company would have to contact every single small outlet, as well as the people who run the big chain stores to beg for space. Obviously, the big boys want to hog as much shelf space as they can. Remember back when Coca-Cola and Pepsi had a soda war? It was all about shelf space."

"Fascinating," said Sister. "I've never worked in retail."

"What was your trade?"

"I was a geology professor at Mary Baldwin." Sister slyly smiled. "I got my rocks off." Then she laughed. "I think it would be funnier were I male."

The lady tossed her head, black hair shining. "Still, pretty good. Sometimes I wish I had gone to college. I'm not much for books."

"It's overrated. We're all born with special abilities, and college is only for some."

"Well, it wasn't good for me. But retail is hard, especially when the laws keep changing." She threw up her hands. "When Dad goes, I really don't know if I will keep the shop. I'll hope to sell it, but who knows?" She shrugged.

"Your father is Cuban?"

"Yes, he is. Did he tell you that?"

"Every now and then I come into the store with my gentleman friend and the two of them rattle on about cigars. Like every Cuban I have ever met, along with being incredibly courtly, he said there is no cigar tobacco like Cuban."

"God's honest truth." She thought for a moment. "Another reason why there are hardly any start-up tobacco companies. Too hard to learn about it and too hard to grow. People have no idea."

"That I do know," said Sister. "I remember when I was a kid we'd drive down to Charleston, passing huge fields of tobacco."

"Even today when they'll come along and cut the entire plant, it's not easy," said Elizabeta. "Someone still has to go out when the plant blooms and pick off the buds. It's sticky. The best of the best still do everything by hand. Take the top leaves first, watch the leaves change color, know when to pick and throw out the bottom sand lugs. Know whether to air cure, flue cure, all that stuff. That's why you pay a pretty penny for a premium cigarette. But it tastes like nothing else. There is no cheap way to grow and harvest good tobacco, even with so-called modern improvements."

"Who will do the field work?"

She raised then dropped her shoulders. "Not white people, I can tell you that. The only white people I ever see in a tobacco field are the people who own it, and a lot of them have to work it. The Mexicans smoke cigarettes, but they don't have a culture of growing tobacco like the U.S. used to have. The black folks that knew so much, well, most of them have passed on and a world of knowledge passed with them."

"We've lost years of hard-earned knowledge in so many fields," Sister said. She, too, felt the loss of the old people and the old ways. "Everyone is too good for fieldwork now. Hell, I cut my own hay. Have help baling it, but I get out there and toss those bales. Keeps a person strong and healthy. It's a lot less expensive than a cabinet full of pills and a trip to the doctor every time you get an ache."

"Dad says that, too. He says everyone is scared of their own body."

Both women laughed.

Sister returned to the topic of fascination for both women. "Since both murder victims were Cuban or second-generation Cuban, they might have been mixed up in some anti-Castro group. I mean, have you thought maybe it's political?"

"Could be, or maybe they just pissed somebody off." The pretty woman shrugged.

Sister paused. "It is strange. I was looking up stuff on the Internet, never a good idea. I waste so much time online, but I was shocked to find that since our country has demolished its tobacco industry the world's largest tobacco grower is China. The Turks grow a lot, as does Brazil."

"Inferior. All inferior. And if you really want to pass out, smoke an Egyptian cigarette. My God, the worst. Their most popular brand, Cleopatra, could kill a cow. If Cleo came back from the dead, she should throw asps at the manufacturers."

Sister laughed at the vision of a resurrected queen tossing snakes in a cigarette factory. She looked out the large windows.

"Sky's getting dark again. Well, I'd better head home. Thank you for your time."

They both stood up and the woman asked, "You said you come in with your boyfriend?"

"Gray Lorillard."

"The black fellow with the silver moustache? He's so handsome he could be a model."

"Please don't tell him that." Sister spontaneously hugged the woman, as it had been such a pleasant visit.

As she headed home, she mused about how her parents would have been shocked that she had just hugged someone she barely knew. Well, a lot of things would have shocked Mom and Dad, but they would have adjusted.

She thought, too, how strange that the equine business bounced back from nearly going kaput after the automobile became affordable. Horse numbers plummeted, then rose again. Albemarle County alone is presently home to fourteen thousand horses. The tobacco industry once appeared invulnerable, the horse industry seemed doomed. Now the reverse proved true. Odd. Even stranger was that no one seemed to know anything about American Smokes. Gliding past Hangman's Ridge, Sister wondered why. She had seen the cigarette soft pack on Adolfo's chest. Someone was making and selling the brand.

She pulled into the long unpaved drive to her house and then saw where she'd run over some brick walkways when plowing snow.

"Dammit. I bet I knocked off some bricks. Well, nothing I can do until spring." She parked the truck by the mudroom door.

The animal door flew open as Raleigh and Rooster rapturously ran out to greet her.

"You didn't take us," Rooster complained. *"You should never go anywhere without us."*

"And you were gone so long. Forever!" Raleigh leaned against her leg as she retrieved her everyday bag, the bottom wearing badly.

Golly stuck her head out the animal door to observe the dogs' thrill at Sister's return. *"Suck-ups."* She ducked back in.

Once inside, Sister removed the gel pad from the shopping bag, placing it on the kitchen counter.

She checked her messages, one being from Walter reminding her they could drive together to meet with Alfred, then Binky DuCharme.

"I really don't want to go," she said to her animals.

She thumbed through her All Saints calendar. Today was the presentation of Christ at the Temple, so it was a day dedicated to the Blessed Virgin Mother. Jeanne de Lestonnac (1556–1640)—another French saint named Jeanne—had nursed plague victims in Bordeaux. She'd also dedicated herself to the education of girls.

Raleigh nosed up at her, placing his paws on the table as she read from the calendar.

"Raleigh, get down."

"Tell me." The Doberman stared at her with soulful eyes.

"Théophane Vénard—1829 to 1861—was persecuted and killed when he was sent to Vietnam to serve as a priest. It was called Tonkin then. I look at this calendar and it always overwhelms me how some of these people suffered."

"That's why you need to take us with you wherever you go," Rooster said. *"So you don't suffer."*

Sister stood up, placing her hands in the small of her back, stretching backward. Then she noticed Golly curled up on the gel pad.

"Pussycat, that is not for you."

"Oh, yes it is."

CHAPTER 11

The old Gulf sign swayed high up on a sturdy metal white pole, while below the white cinder-block station from the 1930s sat on the north side of the crossroads known as Chapel Cross. The station's new and computerized pumps indicated some concessions to the twenty-first century. Binky DuCharme loved his old gas station. Inside, colorful nostalgic posters from the thirties, forties, and fifties hung on the walls.

Binky's wife, Milly, kept a tidy office: a counter and two small tables with oilcloth tablecloths. She had painted the wooden chairs orange and dark blue, the old Gulf colors.

Traveling east, this was your first shot at gas. Traveling west or north, this was your last because you'd run into the Blue Ridge, and the roads deteriorated into rutted dirt ones. I-64 and Route 250 gave the only good driving west to Augusta County. One would need to go all the way north up to Route 33 for a decent paved highway or south to Route 56 in Nelson County to get over the mountains.

The ancient Blue Ridge Mountains, while softened by time, were still mountains and not easily traversed. In their youth, they towered above the Alps, the Rockies, the Andes. Now, trees covered them so they blazed magenta from the redbuds and white from the wild dogwoods in spring. People journeyed from around the world to see their vibrant fall colors. The entire Appalachian chain dazzled onlookers from Maine down to Georgia, but Virginians nodded and smiled when people said they'd seen such lovely color in Vermont. Of course, it was, but it wasn't as sensational as the colors in Virginia. Not that a true Virginian would ever say that. Never wise to brag. But you can be sure they believed it.

Driving with Walter to the Gulf Station, Sister stared out the Jeep window at the sun in the western sky. Deep Prussian blue shadows filled the hollows. The spine of the mountains blazed with millions of tiny rainbows from the ice on the conifers, as well as the ice wrapping the deciduous trees. Creamy cumulus clouds in a turquoise sky completed the beautiful tableau at three in the afternoon.

Walter, behind the wheel, said, "Supposed to snow a bit Friday night, light, but continue on into Saturday."

"I know. I think we'll be able to hunt, though. The Bancrofts always get After All in shape even if it's a blizzard." She smiled, thinking of how much the Bancrofts had done for the club during her tenure as master. Nudging into their late seventies, Edward and Tedi were slightly older than Sister. They showed no sign of slowing down, despite a bit of a stoop when walking, but this is often the case with horse people. They go until they drop. If they drop during a hunt so much the better. They died doing what they love.

The two-century-old church for which the crossroads was named, Chapel Cross, came into view.

Binky's father had tactfully built the gas station just out of sight of the beautiful chapel. Old Francis DuCharme was a thoughtful fellow. His two sons usually were, too, so long as they were apart.

Walter pulled into the gas station. Milly opened the door to the office as they got out of the Jeep.

"Made hot chocolate," she called, waving them in from the cold.

Binky was behind the counter, a red greasy rag in his back pocket. He stuck his head into the garage, and yelled at his son. "Art, he wants a new muffler, too."

Up under a 2002 Ford F-250, Art grunted, "Okay."

Binky closed the door, grabbed two cups to help Milly, and sat down without ceremony. "Crawford."

"Yes." Sister gratefully took the hot chocolate.

"I hear through my niece that he's made big promises." Binky, mid-fifties, getting chunky, stared at his cup. He loathed Crawford, but the promises were tempting.

"He keeps his word," Sister replied. "I serve on the Custis Hall board with him. If he says he's going to do something or pay for something, he does it."

"He's so pushy," said Milly, unable to hold it in. "Driving around in that big red Mercedes. He certainly wants everyone to look at him."

Binky patted her hand lovingly. "He's all those things, Baby, but he's also filthy rich and we need the cash."

"I know, dear, I know." She sighed, then turned to Sister. "I hate this. We've been friends for over forty years and now Richie Rich wants to hunt our land."

Walter responded: "I can speak for Sister although she's known you longer than I have. Nothing will change our friendship, but it would help us if we knew exactly what Crawford has offered."

Binky cleared his throat. "He will put up new fences on our property, which means we can run cattle again. Cattle are bringing in top dollar."

"I estimate the fencing alone to be about two hundred thousand dollars." Having had to fence his own farm, Walter guessed roughly what the lower pasture land on the DuCharmes' five-thousand-acre estate would need.

"I don't know what the cost would be," said Binky. "We always cut and dried our own timber when I was young, but we can't do that anymore. The sawmill might could start up again, but Milly and I have to run the station with Art, of course. I hate to say it, if you decided to help out in a similar way with fencing, I don't know if I could run the sawmill equipment which would reduce the fencing costs."

"You could if you put your mind to it. You're still strong," Milly, still slender bordering on skinny, offhandedly mentioned, which Binky liked, naturally.

"Binky, you've always been strong," Sister agreed.

"Vitamins." He laughed. "Oh, Crawford also said he'd put in a new furnace in the big house, new plumbing, too. Now that sounds good for Alfred. Doesn't mean a thing to me."

The house, so imposing with its four white Corinthian columns, hadn't had heat for fifteen years. All the pipes had burst during the first hard winter. With reliable heat and hard work, the rest of the place could be restored.

"If Margaret marries, the place will be hers." Milly and Binky dearly loved their niece, a sports physician.

Margaret had acted as the go-between since the mid-eighties when the DuCharme brothers fell out over the disposition of the family estate, which neither of them could afford to keep up. There were other reasons, too—old emotional scores to settle, overheated and irrational—often the case in family disputes.

"Umm." Binky remained noncommittal.

"Milly, Binky, there's no way we can match that generosity. You must take it." Sister said this without rancor.

Binky looked down. "I hate that son of a bitch, too. He's only doing this to get back at you."

"He always wanted to be a master, and when he kept getting passed over, he left in a huff, started his own outlaw pack," said Sister. "Crawford is a man who has to appear to be on the top of the pole. He was very generous to Jefferson Hunt when he was a member." She paused. "I can't stand him either. I can see his good qualities, but they're overshadowed by his overweening ego. Yes, he's made a fortune. He's an astute businessman, but he doesn't know squat about hunting. He's one of those people who could ride for fifty years and never know what was really going on." She shrugged.

Walter got to the point. "It would be glorious if Old Paradise were reborn," he told Binky and Milly. "As you know, Kasmir Barbhaiya's land now runs up to your easternmost acres. We will be hunting his land, of course. Should the fox cross over into Old Paradise, however, according to the laws of the Masters of Foxhounds Association of America, we have the right to pursue it. Hard to knock hounds off a hot line anyway." He folded his hands together. "Will you be all right with that?" Walter asked.

"Sure," Binky said. "I don't care if you hunt it along with Crawford. He's the one with the grudge."

"Well, there's not a lot Crawford can do about the MFHA since he's an outlaw pack," said Walter. "He can't buy them off because he's not obedient to their regulations. Nor do they recognize him."

Binky remarked, "Bet he could buy his way in."

A long silence followed this, then Sister said, "As far as I know, that hasn't happened in my time but I can't say that it hasn't happened in the past. The beauty of the MFHA is that the founders and the board were always people of wealth. They couldn't be bought. But today, it sure seems that money can be a crowbar into whatever you want."

"Ah, hell, look at Congress." Binky's mouth turned down.

"Honey, don't start," said Milly.

"She's right. She's right." Binky cut off a brewing tirade.

"We are living through a time of complete corruption," Sister sadly remarked.

"Maybe it was always that way," said Walter. "Maybe now we just know it, thanks to constant media coverage."

"Hell, they're corrupt, too!" Binky nearly shouted.

Emerging from the garage area, Art closed the door behind him. "Sister, Walter, how are you doing?"

"Good. Yourself?" Walter inquired.

"Keeping body and soul together. Walter, do you still want me to drop off those big rubber water troughs?"

"Sure. Anytime. Just leave them outside the barn. Art, before I forget, if you need to add a surcharge since gas prices have gone up again, do it."

Art's face relaxed. "Thanks, Walter. Gas prices are killing me. Even just hauling stuff around the county. Both my trucks are diesel. Through the roof." He stopped for a moment. "A lot of people are putting off buying stuff, fewer deliveries."

"It's happening all over the nation," Sister chimed in. "Not that knowing other people are hard up makes it any easier."

"Misery does love company," Milly said.

"No, it doesn't, Mom," Art replied good-naturedly before returning to the garage.

Driving farther west to Old Paradise, Sister and Walter discussed the meeting. They passed the brick chimney, all that remained of the estate's old gatehouse.

"Glad I took the Jeep." Walter negotiated the packed snowy road.

"Wranglers can go through anything. You know what else is incredible, the old Land Rovers. Now they're so plush. I mean they still can go through everything, but I'd feel guilty taking a hundred-thousand-dollar SUV through two feet of snow or mud. Gray's Land Cruiser costs a lot, too. With a Wrangler, you don't worry about the expense."

"No, you just worry about the gas." Walter pulled his vehicle into the brick dependency where Alfred lived.

In the 1840s, over one hundred fifty people lived and worked on Old Paradise. Many were slaves, whose skills as wheelwrights, cartwrights, blacksmiths, and gardening experts proved useful. After the war, those Old Paradise people who stayed in the county began new lives as tradesmen. Those who stayed on Old Paradise, often less skilled, kept working the fields. That became tremendously difficult during these barren years, as there was no seed or horses to pull ploughs. But the DuCharmes and their former slaves kept plugging. Mostly, vegetables kept people alive. There was no meat. They finally scratched together enough money for two draft horses so a much larger area could be cultivated. By the 1880s, things improved enough that a decent future no longer seemed impossible.

Alfred also agreed to Walter's request, allowing Jefferson Hunt to stay on the trail of a hunted fox if he ran west onto Old Paradise's property. The two masters of that hunt tactfully did not mention their earlier meeting with Binky.

Alfred knew full well that Walter and Sister had to have seen him. "Heard Binky's lost weight," he said.

"Did. I think he's still working on it," Sister replied. "Alfred, you're the one who does your best to keep up the fields. Crawford's money has to be a big help to you."

"It's fencing that's the key. Cattle will turn this ship around. Fertilizer's come down from the original gas panic, still thirty percent higher than it was ten years ago. I tell you, well, I don't have to tell you, it's harder and harder to farm. But his money, the free labor, well, it's a godsend."

"I think it is, too, Alfred," Sister agreed.

Walter said, "What about corn? It's bringing high prices."

Alfred laughed. "Ethanol will ruin engines in about ten years' time. So the auto markets build these great engines, then we're forced to put in gas that will create problems. You mark my words. But, yes, if we grew corn, it should be profitable. I'd rather stick to cattle. Don't need to buy so much equipment. Can't afford the labor either."

"You're right," Walter agreed and Sister nodded. "Thank you for taking time to see us."

"I always have more time in winter and it's good to see you. I need to go out more. Margaret's been at me. She says her mother—and she always says her mother—wouldn't want me alone. You know, my wife's been dead seven years."

"Seems like yesterday." Sister had liked Alfred's late wife.

Alfred threw up his hands. "Where does the time go?"

"I expect cavemen asked that." Walter laughed.

"Yep."

Ever interested in stock, Sister asked, "Hey, what kind of cattle are you going to run?"

"Herefords. I like the horned ones, like their personalities, but I can't go through dehorning cattle. I'll get a few Polled Herefords, hope for the best. It will take time to get back into the game. The predictions from the ag magazines are the cattle market will peak in 2015, but it should stay high."

"Let's hope so," Sister said.

"I look at the unemployment figures and I want to say, 'Hey, we've got plenty of work but you'll get your hands dirty,' " Alfred simply stated.

Walter replied, "Even if a lot of those folks would be willing to do agricultural work, they don't know how. My old mill is in great shape. I could grind grain. People would be able to buy local flour. Everything still works."

"Wouldn't that be something?" Alfred's eyes shone. "I'd love to see that mill running again."

"Hey, I hear Art's back into his country waters business." Sister smiled.

"Now there's good money. No taxes." Alfred laughed. "I turn a blind eye. I get along with my nephew, but I don't want to know his business."

"Smart," Sister agreed. "To change the subject, when I was first married, I recall about one hundred low acres planted with tobacco, down there by the deep creek of your land, that bottom land."

"We had a good allotment," said Alfred. "Let it go when the shit hit the fan. And do you know, I never saw a dime from the Tobacco Commission to help against the losses?"

Virginia's Tobacco Commission, established in 1999 to disburse Virginia's share of the national settlement against cigarette makers, did give money away over time, but most of it found its way to Mecklenburg and Russell counties, those hardest hit by the destruction of the tobacco industry. Even today, most of the old 'bacca counties suffered the state's highest unemployment rates.

Sister nodded in sympathy.

Walter quipped, "Up in smoke."

Driving back to Sister's farm, the two hunt masters reviewed their list of other landowners who might fall prey to Crawford's machinations.

Sister reviewed those who might be in financial distress. "He can't buy them all off."

"He can," countered Walter. "Some people don't even drive a

hard bargain. The DuCharmes do, plus he had to satisfy both brothers. But other folks might be happy with nothing more than a new run-in shed." Walter bit his lower lip. "You okay with how we divided up the 'at risk' group?"

"Sure. I'll start my calls after Saturday's hunt. Oh, Tootie will be here."

"Good. Be good to see her."

"Do you mind if I put her on the hunt with Betty, to let her whip-in? She's always wanted to do that, and I could never really distribute one girl without offending the others, since her class had so many good riders. It was easier to keep them all in the field."

"You know a lot of people owe their hunting to you. When you think of how many youngsters started with Jefferson Hunt, me being one. Now they are adults and their children hunt with us. I love seeing that," said Walter, driving down the highway.

"I do, too."

"You know, Sister, I have a bad feeling that our troubles are just beginning." He switched the subject, as people who have known each other for years do.

She turned in the car seat to view his handsome profile. "Me, too, Walter. Me, too."

C H A P T E R   1 2

Reflected on the snow, the last rivulets of the setting sun changed from gold to pink to scarlet to purple. The colors announced a harsh winter's night ahead, a contrast before darkness, a brief blood-red splash in a cold world of white, beige, and gray. Winter's limited palette had the compensating grace of allowing one to see the true lay of the land.

Uncle Yancey, an older red fox, casually walked on top of the snow, the crust supporting his impressive thirteen pounds. This winter, he'd dropped, not significantly, only a pound so far, but by February pickings were getting slim. Much as he tried to fatten up in those rich months of autumn, he would lose that insurance fat by February. Up until now, the mild winter favored him, but his senses told him winter wasn't over yet.

Lifting his chiseled head, the setting rays turning his fur molten copper, he sniffed deeply. The odor of an old deer carcass greeted him. In another mile he'd arrive at the large heavy wooden feeding station built by the Jefferson Hunt Club. Why bother with an old carcass when good food could be found?

Uncle Yancey loved Sister's boxes. They had an entrance and an exit. He could slip in, eat, and even curl up if he wanted to. Years ago he'd gobbled himself insensate and fell asleep only to be startled awake by Sister Jane herself lifting the heavy lid. He froze. So did she. Then he finally scooted out an exit, but he didn't run. He maintained his dignity while she hoisted a fifty-pound bag of kibble, pouring it into the feeder.

Sister fed the foxes the same as she fed the hounds, changing the protein and fat content with the season. Before breeding began, usually in mid-December, she also drizzled wormer over the kibble. Uncle Yancey could always taste it, but he'd tasted worse. That wormer was one of the reasons he kept weight on as long as he did. His coat, two layers thick, caused humans to gasp when they spotted him during a hunt. He was handsome enough, maybe not as handsome as some of the younger boys, but still.

Passing the old family graveyard at the Lorillard place, the fox noticed Sam's battered heap and Gray's Land Cruiser. Uncle Yancey thought that even without proper claws if humans walked on all fours they'd keep their balance better. Resting underneath the Lorillard porch, he had overheard conversations where the two brothers decried the expense of gas, running trucks and cars.

"Poor people," he thought to himself as he trotted off in the sheer relief he was a superior creature.

When the hunt was on, the Lorillard place and After All, the big Bancroft estate next to it, along with Roughneck Farm, meant close to two thousand acres to run. When on a cracking long run while being chased by hounds, horses, and humans, Uncle Yancey could go to Roughneck, using thick woods, rock outcroppings, and the creek, to slow the field, and then he'd fly up to Hangman's

Ridge. The ghosts up there upset him, but not as much as the hounds on his trail. Arduous as that run was, he was fit and enjoyed fooling them. When he was in his prime, three to five years old, he could run all the way west, turn, and come back to the Lorillard place, where he kept a den.

His mate, Aunt Netty, had her den at Pattypan Forge. She drove him out last year when she saw how nice Pattypan was. She had previously thrown him out of their joint den because he was a slob, then she moved into Pattypan where she ran him crazy with her incessant demands. She rarely had a good word to say about him, even though he shared his food. The old girl was turning into a first-class nag. *Yap Yap Yap.* Drove him crazy. So what if chicken bones were on the floor of the den? He moved back to his old home place, his childhood den, which rested under old boxwoods where once a cabin must have been, before the Lorillards had the money to build the clapboard four-over-four Virginia farmhouse. No frills, clean lines, big porch, as many windows as they could afford back then, the old house was inviting for human and foxes. For safety's sake, Uncle Yancey also had a den in the graveyard itself, as well as another under the Lorillards' front porch. The humans could smell him under the porch, but they didn't bother him. As for the graveyard, it too was inviting, though he'd regularly have to run off invasive skunks and groundhogs—mostly skunks, never a pleasant exchange. The two human brothers often fell behind in sprucing up the graveyard, which only encouraged wildlife to inhabit it. They'd get to it at least once a year and, as the brothers foxhunted, they left his den undisturbed.

The smells from the house enticed him. Often on warm nights, he'd prowl around the back door. You never knew what they'd drop or throw out. Over his lifetime he'd noticed how inattentive humans could be. While walking, they might juggle a cup and a plate of food, their toe hits a rock and some food falls off! Other times, the two fellows rocked on the front porch chairs, unaware Uncle Yancey was sitting below, listening in.

Humans fascinated Uncle Yancey. He liked to listen to the sounds they'd make. Their vocal range from high to low, interested him. He especially liked to hear them sing. Each voice sounded different. He liked it best when men and women sang together, but at the Lorillard place it was mostly the two brothers singing spirituals their mother had taught them.

Now that he was closer to the old abandoned farm road, the deer carcass smell hit him again. He detected something else: an old tang, something different.

Curiosity got the better of him. He took a slight detour from his direct route to the feeder a quarter mile away, following his nose.

Turning north on the abandoned road, packed hard with snow, he trotted along, soon finding the deer remains. She must have been shot in late November. Little was left of the doe except skin and fur. This infuriated Uncle Yancey. If a human kills an animal, they should haul it off and eat it. Then again, many humans weren't good shots. They'd wound a deer, try to track it, lose it. The suffering animal would then die a protracted painful death. Much as he liked to eat fresh deer meat, Uncle Yancey believed in a swift death. When his time came, he hoped it was mercifully fast. Most of all, he hoped to outlive his nagging spouse.

He noticed another jawbone protruding through the collapsed rib cage. Uncle Yancey reached over to push it. The whole jaw was now exposed, the bottom of the teeth away from him. He pulled his paw back. This was a human skull. Wisps of red hair were now visible.

Uncle Yancey claimed no expertise on studying humans, but he knew they killed one another, whereas foxes rarely do. If a fox kills another fox, it's usually while still in the den before they emerge as adults. The parents allow their cubs to kill any diseased or weak ones, then haul the dead kit out.

The four in Uncle Yancey's birth litter survived this early time, as they were strong, healthy little things. Later, one brother, fully adult, was killed on Soldier Road, distracted by mating season. Uncle Yancey's other two brothers moved far from the home territory. Being the strongest, Uncle Yancey claimed this area for his own, although he had to get away from his father once he was half grown. Not that his father would kill him, but the message had been clear: You're on your own, son.

That was most of what the clever old fox knew about interspecies murder. Humans excelled at it. But he also knew they generally buried or hid the body. This human must have been killed about the same time as the doe. They may even have been killed together. The killer didn't have the time or inclination to better dispose of the corpse. Hiding it under a deer during deer season showed some thought.

He left the sorry tattered remains of two creatures, heading back toward the feeder box. Once there, he easily slid inside, sat down, and enjoyed the kibble.

A noise outside stopped him mid-chew. He heard a side-to-side walk on top, then a familiar voice.

"Throw some out," St. Just, the crow, demanded in his horrid voice.

As the crow and the fox hated each other, this request surprised Uncle Yancey. The bird must be hungry indeed.

"I'll push some out, but first you have to tell me what you know about the deer carcass with the dead human underneath maybe a fourth or a third of a mile, a touch more, from the Lorillard place."

The large blue-black bird hopped onto the ground so he could peer inside—not so close that Uncle Yancey could snag him. He knew how quick foxes were.

"I don't know anything."

"But you know they're there."

"Sure."

"How long have you known?"

The crow cocked his head from one side to the other, *"Mmm, second generation of maggots."*

"Long time back. Did you ever see a human go back to check?"

"No. You know as well as I do that road isn't used much. It's a good place to dump trash. Okay, I told you what you wanted to know, push out some food."

"You did and I will, but before I do: Did you get a look at the dead human while the face was still distinguishable?"

"No, he was under the deer. The only reason I knew he was there is human carrion smells different. Okay? Food."

Uncle Yancey threw out enough kibble to satisfy the bird. *"Food supply down?"*

"Yes, it is," the bird said dropping a piece out of his beak, which he then quickly scooped back up. *"Usually people put out plenty of food for us, but this winter has been different—even worse than last year's. It's milder, but not much food."*

"Hard times. For them, I mean."

"Uncle Yancey, bird food can't cost much."

"Most of them are trying to save every penny. I hear the brothers talking."

"Plenty of food in these boxes," said the crow.

"Sister never forgets us. I don't understand money, do you?"

"No. If you can't eat it, build with it, or hatch it, it's not real."

"Pretty much, I agree," said Uncle Yancey. *"Do you need more? It's half full. Sister will fill everything back up soon. It's a big job. You know she has these at her farm and at After All? And other foxes have told me wherever the hunt goes, boxes follow."*

"You're lucky."

"Know what I'm going to do?"

"I have no idea," St. Just replied with a hint of sarcasm.

"On the next hunt, I'm going to run right by those bodies. When I hear the horn, I'm going to show myself, get them all excited, and run the whole pack, human and hounds, over there."

"There will be hell to pay." St. Just half fluttered back onto the top of the box.

Uncle Yancey emerged. The crow, no fool, flew onto a bare branch overhead. *"Not for us."*

CHAPTER 13

The darkness of the covered bridge enveloped them, shafts of light shining through the high opening following the length of the roofline. The heavy wood floor clattered underneath the Jeep, then pale light greeted Sister and Tootie at the old structure's other end.

"I'm glad you've kept up your riding at Princeton," said Sister. "I think you'll need a tight seat today."

"There are a lot of stables around, but they're all show jumping. No one has the land to really ride up there like we do here." Tootie felt her heart skip a beat at the sight of all the trailers for Saturday's hunt. "I miss this so much."

"Hope you got enough sleep. You didn't get in until late. I heard you, but then fell right back asleep. You know your way around the house. I wasn't too worried, and I shut the bedroom door so the dogs wouldn't carry on."

"Rooster's gotten a little fat, hasn't he?" teased Tootie.

"Never let a hound sit around." Sister nodded. "He'll run it off in the springtime. He's too spoiled now to hunt in winter. There's Ronnie Haslip waving to you," Sister said as they looked for a spot to park at today's fixture, the Bancrofts' After All.

Ronnie was the club treasurer and already wore his heaviest scarlet frock coat. He grinned when he spotted Tootie in Sister's Jeep. He yelled something to the others, and the longtime members of the Jefferson Hunt turned, greeting Tootie in one way or another.

Ben Sidell, the sheriff, was tacking up Nonni. He turned, saw Tootie, and smiled.

"It's a little homecoming," Sister remarked. "Some of the Custis Hall girls are here, too. Ava Dubrovsky, Emmy Rogan—well, you can see for yourself. There's the Custis Hall van." Sister pulled in next to the hunt's hound trailer, which Shaker drove. The club's horse trailer was driven by Betty and parked next to that.

Tootie lifted her leg over the high Jeep doorwell, gracefully stepping out of the vehicle as Betty rushed up to make a fuss.

Much as one wishes to visit before a hunt, there's little time. Tootie called to the girls who had been one and two classes behind her, then hurried with Betty to tack up Iota.

"He looks fabulous." Tootie's eyes shone at the sight of the beautiful horse. "Oh, Betty, I've been riding some other horses up north, and they've sure taught me what a great horse Iota is."

At the sound of his name, he turned his dark head.

Tootie threw her arms around his neck.

Sister, being master, looked for Walter. She saw the joint-master was greeting those people capping—riders who came as guests of club members. She walked over to do the same.

A member is to bring their guest to the master for a formal introduction. That's it. Hello. Good to meet you. Brevity at this point is not for a lack of curiosity or delight in the newcomer, but if one is staff, those crucial moments before a hunt are often freighted with decisions. There are yet many factors to be weighed.

For example, the landowner whose fields and forests you are hunting is under no obligation to inform the master of conditions. However, if something is radically changed—an entire creek crossing torn up, a huge sinkhole opened—usually the landowners will tell the master, who then passes the information along to the staff.

Added to that, sudden changes in the wind and the weather is always a reality this close to mountains. A shift in the wind usually means a shift in the first cast. The strategy planned by the master and huntsman the night before may need to be adjusted to the new conditions.

No matter how much a master and huntsman map out their hunt, of course, the fox schemes otherwise. Nevertheless, like many masters, Sister preferred to start with a plan.

Today she hoped to perform the introductions, make changes to the hunt plan as necessary, and then take off right when it said on the fixture card, mailed earlier to today's riders. This informational card listed the fixtures, and times were printed next to them. In the old days, a few reminders, such as "We hunt at the kindness of landowners," might also be on the card. As per tradition, the size was to be such that it would fit in a gentleman's inside coat pocket. Where a lady placed hers was up to her. These days the card size and the card weight changed. The old heavy card stock—good paper, true printing—gave way to some long, narrow fixture cards, others that folded over, and few were still truly printed. Most clubs ran their fixture cards off of computers, a task performed by a blessed volunteer if not the hunt secretary. Since the Franklins owned a large press, they did the Jefferson Hunt's printing as a gift to the club. The last two years, Sister had insisted on paying for the costly proper card stock.

When one picked up a Jefferson Hunt fixture card today, it was nearly identical to those first ones back in 1887, including the ink being in the club's color: a true hunting green.

Sister cared deeply about tradition, decorum, and above all, making people feel welcome. Everyone at After All that day rose early, pulled their horses, tack, and themselves together in 22°F weather. Some drove all the way from Fredericksburg to hunt with the pack; others had only to rumble down a country road. They all deserved as good a time as possible. Hopefully, bracing runs would be part of that but, if not, a glorious ride in smashing territory would suffice.

All these manner of things raced through Sister's head as she mounted Rickyroo, her eight-year-old, flaming-chestnut, Thoroughbred. Always excited by a crowd, Ricky danced a bit.

Shaker rode over to Sister on Kilowatt, a talented horse bought by Kasmir as a gift to the club last February.

"Boss, still as the grave," he said, looking up at the sky.

"Sure is, but the clouds are low, gray; we might rouse someone." The first cast keyed up Sister.

"All right then."

"Hounds please," she said in a clear voice. This let the field know it was time to go.

So many people had shown up today. Kasmir, his friend High Vajay, Ronnie, of course, and Henry Xavier—who had hunted with Jefferson Hunt since boyhood. Charlotte Norton, the headmistress of Custis Hall, accompanied the girls, along with their riding coach and Tariq Al McMillan. Those from Custis Hall had arrived in two big horse vans. Sister smiled when she saw Felicity next to Tootie. Felicity, whose son had turned one year old on September 14, made a point of hunting weekends. Sister gave up counting when she reached sixty people. Tariq and Donny rode together.

Felicity's husband, Howie, was a nonrider and thus pressed

into service. He stood by the hound trailer. When Shaker nodded, Howie lifted the heavy latch and out poured the eager hounds.

They stood by Shaker. Not that they wanted to but they knew this mattered. Like Sister, they followed tradition.

"All right then," Shaker quietly called to them. He turned Kilowatt and rode north along Broad Creek, the covered bridge behind him.

Gray rode with his brother, Sam, to whom Sister lent a good horse. Sam was a gifted rider and might have had a good career on horseback had he not fallen into the bottle. At fifty-eight, Sam might still ride in a point-to-point or a local show, but the glory that might have been his would never come his way again. At the top level, a person only has one shot at an athletic career.

It was Sam's day off from work with Crawford and if he wanted to hunt with Sister, there was not much his boss could do about it. Truth was, Crawford couldn't run his stable without Sam.

The hounds patiently trotted along Broad Creek. Deep in parts, it was mostly two feet in a normal year. It had many crossings, though occasionally its banks were high. The creek drew a variety of wildlife to it, as its clear waters refreshed all.

In the far distance, a bobcat picked up his head, listened to the horn calls and the hoofbeats, then wisely climbed a tree.

Reaching that spot, the pack stopped for a moment.

"Move along," Shaker advised. "Move along."

Shaker's philosophy, not always shared by his master, was that if the hounds didn't open and just milled about, he would push them on. If the scent was good down the line, they'd open.

Sister favored a slower draw, just in case the scent scattered, or maybe the fox had walked across a fallen log. But as Shaker got good results, she did not interfere. Though it was true that if those hounds feathered, their tails moving, and Shaker pushed them, Sister just might chide him about it later. Sister rarely corrected staff in the field. They had enough on their minds without fearing they'd upset the master.

As junior-master, Walter left all hunting matters to Sister. She knew more than he did. He'd ridden in the field for years before becoming a joint-master. The more he learned about hounds, quarry, etc., the more he learned the old girl possessed a sixth sense.

They'd trotted, then walked for a half hour. Nothing. Broad Creek forked up ahead, jutting eastward.

Pattypan Forge, deserted decades ago, rested near the right fork. The going was better on the left. Shaker paused, looked back to his master.

Sister pointed right. Sure, it was rough in there, but this wasn't a trail ride. You go where there's a chance to break out your quarry.

The trail narrowed. Hounds surged ahead, reaching the forge, its brick overgrown with vines.

Young Pansy readily picked up Aunt Netty's scent. *"She left about six this morning."*

"There's another line over here." Giorgio, a hound from a new cross Sister was trying, spoke up. *"It's not too faint."*

Aggressive and egotistical, Dragon put his nose down on the second line. *"That's Target. We'll follow him."*

Diane didn't argue with her brother. His nose was good, his drive unimpeachable, though his manner left a lot to be desired.

The pack swung toward Dragon, moving on now, but they did not open. A yip here, a yap there to keep other hounds in the back notified, but the fox scent stayed touchy.

Vines hanging off a few old trees just about strangled some riders. Sister picked her way through old deer trails. Finally she cut a bit south to the old rutted trail, the ruts having been made for over two centuries as workers brought iron, copper, even silver to be melted down and worked at the forge.

Bobby Franklin, with Second Flight, was still fighting the tangle when the last of First Flight reached the old road. Suddenly the entire pack opened. Sound ricocheted off trees, seemingly off the old forge now behind them.

Sister would lose time if she tried to follow directly behind the pack in the thicket. Instead, she galloped along the road, snow and mud flying under Rickyroo's heels. The road fed into a better road that ran east and west. The snow hadn't been plowed, but it had settled down a bit so horses could run in it without overly tiring themselves. She veered east. Rickyroo put on the afterburners, for the determined hounds were pulling away.

Scratched to bits by brush, Shaker fought his way out of the damned mess, found the road farther down than Sister. Thanks to a long stride, Kilowatt effortlessly covered ground. He never looked as though he was trying hard, but rather gliding. Shaker made up the distance.

On the left, her usual side, Sybil ran at the edge of the thick woods. She was well away. Betty moving through corn stalks was also well away, meaning moving fast and up with the hounds.

Target was a good half mile between himself and the pack. The fox didn't linger because the "D" hounds and Sister's new "G" line were a tad faster than Jefferson hounds used to be.

He ducked into a narrow woods, ran across moss and running cedar to mess up his scent. Then he popped out at the corner of the Lorillard place at an old falling-down shed. He blew by that dilapidated structure, then by the big newly refurbished woodshed.

Target paused, turning his head toward the sound. A more beautiful sight than this fox on the snow would be hard to find. He breathed hard, but he was far from blown.

In his prime, Target could have run for hours if need be. However, he didn't want to run that long. Snow drifts, not always easy to spot, could slow him down or he could fall too deep into a hole to get out in time. Better to duck into the main entrance to Uncle Yancey's graveyard den.

Nimbly, Target leapt up on the drylaid stone wall, two and a half feet high, then dropped onto the other side upon an infant's tomb, the little angel on the tombstone announcing a baby lay beneath.

Ducking into the den, he awakened Uncle Yancey, curled up, fast asleep.

"What in the hell are you doing here?" the older fox growled.

"Hounds."

The den had numerous tunnels, as well as various sitting rooms.

"Let's move farther back. If Trinity is out today, he's a digger. No point in putting up with that." Uncle Yancey led Target farther along to a pleasant space lined with sweet hay. *"I overslept,"* said the older fox. *"I meant to give them a hard run today. There's something I want them to find."* Uncle Yancey paused, but before Target could say anything, he sighed. *"Are you still at Pattypan Forge?"*

"I go between here, there, and Hangman's Ridge. Depends on which food boxes are full and well; it depends on Aunt Netty."

Uncle Yancey laughed a high, dry laugh. *"My bride will run you crazy. Why do you think I'm over here?"*

"Her version is you refuse to pick up after yourself and she's not doing it anymore." Target added, with a hint of sarcasm. *"She says you're too tired to mate."*

"Me! She's the one who says she's not running after cubs anymore. Furthermore, she needs to fix that tatty tail. She looks like a goddamned muskrat." He puffed out his chest. *"While we're on the subject of vixens, where's Charlene?"*

"My mother's at home," Target replied. *"I'm checking these other places for her because there's too much traffic at Foxglove. Not the farm itself, but they paved the road by it."*

"He's in here!" Dragon bellowed as the pack quickly caught up with him outside.

The two dog foxes listened.

"I'll dig him out." Trinity started frantically digging.

Shaker, off Kilowatt, speedily pulled the handsome young hound out of the den. You can't allow a graveyard to be desecrated.

"Hold up now," Shaker commanded the hounds.

He walked Kilowatt to the stone fence, hopped up on it, then stepped into his stirrup. Why swing up if you don't need to do it?

The field reached the graveyard in time to see hounds jumping back over the stone fence.

Grateful for the moment to catch their breath and take a swig from a flask, there wasn't much chatter among the riders.

Sister rode up to Shaker. "Let's go back on the road toward After All. If we parallel the woods we'll eventually get into Tedi and Edward's big back pasture. We might get another run."

"If we don't, I'll keep pushing."

They turned, walking out of the Lorillard farm.

Target and Uncle Yancey popped out of the den to watch them ride off.

"I'll flank them and draw them to the deer and human carcass."

"What human carcass?" Target asked.

"There's a dead person under a doe at the end of that old road that goes north," said Uncle Yancey. *"Doesn't really go anywhere, but I suppose way back when there must have been something over there the Lorillards used."* Uncle Yancey thought of the decayed corpse. *"Most of the flesh is off. I could only see the jaw and part of the head. Might be a lot left under the doe, although she's caved in."*

"Don't go, Uncle Yancey. If the footing were sound you'd be safe, but the snow is treacherous. Dead is dead, human or deer. It's not worth the excitement." He thought for a moment. *"Do you know who it is?"*

"No."

"Well, it doesn't matter. One human is as bad as another."

With the field reversed, Sybil rode on the right and Betty was now on the left. Their task, difficult in heavy woods, was to stay on the shoulder of the pack. If you think of the hunt as a clock, the huntsman is the button where both hands come together. The pack is at twelve o'clock, and the whippers-in are at ten o'clock and two o'clock ideally. And it is merely an ideal.

Due to the heavy woods, Sybil moved closer to the pack. She picked up deer trails and stayed in good order. Coming out on the dead-end road, she glanced behind her, a habit born of years of whipping-in. Many was the time she looked back only to see the fox sliding behind her.

She saw a few deer. Turning her head to go on, she looked again, as she glimpsed a tatter of cloth.

Curious now, the tall middle-aged lady walked over on Bombardier. A piece of torn coat flapped in a light breeze. Nearby, an upturned jaw was unmistakably human.

She knew not to "Tallyho." That would bring the entire field to this spot as well as the hounds, who would joyfully tear apart the bodies or what was left of them.

She kicked on Bombardier, shot out of there to speed down the dirt road.

"Staff," she called. The Second Flight, then the First, moved to the right so Sybil could shoot by. This was exactly what they should do: Hounds always have the right of way, followed by staff.

Sybil pulled up beside Sister. "Master, there's a dead person on the Lorillard service road, that road to nowhere."

CHAPTER 14

S heriff Ben Sidell knelt down. He didn't touch the corpse, waiting instead for his team to arrive. Saturday was supposed to be his day off, but his hunt day was turning into something else. Gray and Sam drove back with him, all three men leaving their horses at the trailers. While among the other riders of the hunt, all three, plus Sister and Sybil, had kept their mouths shut.

Ben parked his battered Explorer about fifty yards from the Lorillard's cul-de-sac just in case there might be any evidence in the road. No point driving over it, pushing it farther into the snow.

"When's the last time either of you came down this way?" he asked.

"October," Gray replied.

"About the same for me," said Sam. "Once the old shed disintegrated back here we have no reason to come down."

"Occasionally we check the road to see if poachers have parked here," said Gray. "With all the thick pines and creepers, it's easy to hide a vehicle even in winter. Now that Sam and I both live here,

— 113—

though, we've taken care of that problem. They know we're watching."

"Could you hear a vehicle from the house?" asked the good-looking sheriff.

"Maybe in summer," Sam volunteered. "In winter, everything in the house is closed up—plus I've usually got a fire going. Damn, whoever dumped the body and the deer probably was one of the old poachers or someone who hunted alongside them. Course, most of those old boys are gone now. Hell, they got so old if they did kill a deer they couldn't drag it out." Sam shook his head.

"Who in particular among these old poachers might still be alive?" asked Ben, wishing the crime team would get there.

Sam thought a bit before answering. "Well, and you probably know this, back about three years ago Art DuCharme was poaching everywhere he could. Course, he's not old. Why he did this I don't know. Oh, and Donny Sweigart. Donny stopped all that once he started dating Sybil, but Art, who knows?"

Puzzled, Ben asked, "Art DuCharme has thousands of acres to hunt. Why come over here to poach?"

Gray's moustache twitched upward slightly. Good as he was, Ben was from Ohio. He missed a few deep layers at the bottom of the seven-layer cake of Southern life.

Sam looked at his brother, then the sheriff, to whom he owed a great deal. When Ben first took over the job, he could have roughed up Sam and his fellow drunks. Instead, the young sheriff tried to get them into the Salvation Army programs. He acted as though, even as low as they might be at that moment, they were still human beings.

Sam then said, "If Art could shift focus away from his still, good. Why hunt there, risk others hunting there with you? People talk. Why let anyone see where he hides stuff? Then again, if he actually poached a deer without getting caught, he wins twice.

Some people always have to have their hand in." He used an old phrase, which Ben didn't know, but he understood the meaning.

Standing around, no longer on horseback, the cold felt colder.

The crunch of tires on snow drew their attention back up the road. Ben had specifically told his crew not to hit the sirens. The arriving vehicle parked behind his Explorer. Four officers stepped out of the county-issued SUV, two in uniform. One of the cops wearing civilian clothes was the police department photographer.

Joylon Hobbs, the chief investigator, took off his warm gloves, then wiggled his fingers into thin rubber ones. He knelt down carefully before leaning over and opening the collapsed rib cage of the deer. Now visible, the human wore a heavy wool coat.

"Pennsylvania tuxedo," Joylon said.

"And what is that?" Gray didn't mean to intrude, but the description piqued his curiosity, already high.

"That's the old name for his kind of wool winter jacket," said Joylon. "Black plaid over red. Usually hunters will wear them, or at least country hunters. The city and suburban fellas wear four-hundred-dollar Gortex stuff with all kinds of linings, zippers, reflecting tape on the camo."

"Ah," Gray simply replied.

The two uniformed officers, both of them somewhere between thirty-five and forty-five, were stringing up crime scene tape. After securing a perimeter, they began scouring the snow. All they found were Bombardier's tracks and then human footprints belonging to Ben, Gray, and Sam. Anything of potential value would be under that snow. They reported back to their boss, Ben.

"We don't usually see this," Luke uttered laconically.

"Yeah," Jake agreed. He looked over at the Lorillard brothers, then back at the sheriff. "Murder around here is almost always domestic violence or drugs. Luckily, we don't have much of that, but this, smart. I mean, the killer was smart and country."

"Don't jump to conclusions," Ben chided him, but not with rancor.

"Yes, sir." Jake straightened up.

"Your hands getting cold?" Ben asked Joylon.

"Yes, they are. Hard to tell what's left of the body. Won't know until we get him on a slab. With any luck, we'll at least know how he was killed. Used to be when we found a body, which was not often—back in the seventies or eighties—we'd know them. Now there's so many new people, we don't." He asked Ben, "Did you call in a retrieval vehicle?"

"I did. And I told them no siren, too. After All is full of people. No point getting them stirred up and no point dealing with curiosity seekers."

"Why would anyone want to see this?" asked Sam, appalled at the thought.

"You'd be amazed at what people want to see," said Joylon. "Years ago back when I first started, we had a killer from just down the road from here that was insane. No doubt about it. He strung up his cousin, whom he hated, tortured him and put his eyeballs out with a ballpoint pen. For whatever reason, a local newspaper reporter included all the grisly details of the murder in his story, and our office was flooded with requests for the pictures." Joylon stood up, peeled off his surgical gloves, gratefully putting back on his warm, woolly ones, knitted by his wife.

"Sick," Gray half spat.

"World's full of strange people," Joylon replied simply.

"Gray, Sam, I'm sorry to keep you all out here in the cold," said Ben. "Why don't you take my Explorer back to the trailers? I'll have Luke and Jake drop me off when we're finished here. Just leave the keys in the ignition. No one's going to steal that barge."

"Funny," Sam mused to his brother, "no worry about theft, but we've got a killer out there somewhere."

Back at the After All gathering, a few people who had noticed the Lorillard brothers' absence asked where they'd been, to which they replied noncommitally. But most folks, happy with the hunt, with the wonderful party, continued gabbing away.

Gray finally made his way through the crowd to Sister, who raised her eyebrows in question.

He took her by the elbow, steering her clear of the other exultant hunters for a moment, never easy at such a hunt breakfast. "Sure enough, a body under a deer," Gray told Sister. "Been there quite a while."

"Years?" she asked.

"Months. Four, maybe five, according to Joylon. The mild winter accelerated decay. I don't know how those guys can do that work. Turned my stomach."

When Sybil joined them, Gray informed her of the gruesome developments on the road to nowhere.

"Ugly," Sybil said tersely.

"You were so wise to come up to me." Sister said, praising Sybil's impeccable instincts to maintain order during the hunt.

"How many years have I whipped-in to you? Twelve, I think," she answered her own question. "You taught me if something goes wrong, don't broadcast it. If I can, fix it. If I can't, find you."

Gray exhaled. "I don't think you can fix this."

"No," Sister responded. "Once we know cause of death and identity, if they can find that out, who knows what we might do? You know we generally assume that someone who has been murdered was an innocent victim. Then again, has it ever occurred to either of you that some people need killing?"

Both Sister's boyfriend and her whipper-in stared at her for a long moment. Neither said a word.

CHAPTER 15

After Rickyroo had been wiped down with a little Vetrolin rubbed on his back and legs, he munched alfalfa in his stall while drying. Next, Sister would throw an expensive but excellent Irish turnout blanket on him. The lightweight but warm lining and an exterior that could resist ripping justified the blanket's price.

Cleaned, with fresh water in their stalls and a bit of food, the three horses happily chatted.

Sister, Betty, and Tootie were busily cleaning tack in the warm tackroom. Surrounding each woman was an array of saddle soap, clean water, dirty water, a jar of saddle butter from a company in Grangeville, Idaho, small sponges, old washcloths, and fresh soft dishtowels to finish the process.

In the background, the radio stayed permanently tuned to the classical radio station. Sister and Rickyroo liked Tchaikovsky.

"Someday I'm going to roll the dial to heavy metal and watch you pitch a fit," said Betty, wiping the browband of the bridle, which hung from the cleaning tack hook. The tack hook looked like a small version of the grappling hooks used to board enemy ships back in the days of sail.

Sister squeezed out the small sponge full of saddle soap. "Takes more than that to make me pitch a fit."

She then filled in the others about what had transpired at the Lorillard place when Sybil found the dead deer and human.

"You waited this long to tell me?" Betty threw her rag on the floor.

"You were in the truck with Shaker." Sister held up her hand for peace. "And I wanted time to sort this out. I have."

"Maybe I should keep away from you. First, that man in New York. Now another. That's two bodies."

"I didn't find the second one. Sybil did." Sister turned to Tootie, who had finished with her bridle and was wiping down her saddle. "You're not saying anything."

"It's creepy." The young woman lifted up a stirrup, tossing it over the seat. "I don't know what to say."

"It is that and it will be in the papers and on the radio and TV tomorrow. We should enjoy this period of grace." Sister wrung out her washcloth. "I'm glad none of us had to see such a sight. Sybil said she couldn't see much except an upside-down jawbone but once she looked hard, she knew it was a human. Gray and Sam saw more, but Gray said there was no way to tell who it was." She glanced at the wall clock, big and round. "He should be coming home soon."

"Sam okay?" Betty paused. "I always worry when there's something dreadful."

"Gray said he's fine," answered Sister. "I really believe he won't drink again."

"He's in my prayers." Like Sister, Betty had witnessed Gray's brother, so bright and gifted, excel at self-destruction.

"How do you know when someone's an alcoholic?" asked Tootie. "I mean everyone drinks at Princeton on the weekends. Some during the week. The only people who don't drink are the ones on varsity or those like me who don't like the taste."

"I suppose people tend toward alcoholism early, but because our culture accepts rowdiness in college or at least up through the mid-twenties no one can separate fish from fowl," mused Sister. "Tell you what, though, by thirty it's plain as day. And each generation has to figure it out all over again. No one young wants to believe their sister, brother, or best friend is on that slippery slope. The hardest part is there's not one thing you can do."

"You can tell them," Tootie said to Betty as she worked on the other side of her saddle.

"You can," Betty said, her tone measured. "And once in a blue moon someone will listen. Mostly, they deny it and will hate you for it. Friendship with an addict of any kind will tear you apart." She stopped. "I don't talk about it much, but my oldest daughter destroyed her life with drugs. Now she sits in jail, which is probably the best place for her. Bobby and I tried everything."

Jennifer, the Franklins' youngest daughter, was an exceedingly lovely young woman now in her third year at Colby College along with Sari Rasmussen, Lorraine's daughter. Lorraine was Shaker's lady friend, a fairly new romance.

"I'm sorry, Betty," said Tootie. "I can't imagine anyone not listening to you." Tootie meant it. "I wish my mother were more like you."

Betty was touched. "Tootie, thank you. Your mother tries. She thinks she's doing what's best."

Sister chimed in. "Both your parents are so proud of you. They're proud of you, Tootie."

Tears welling up as she finished her cleaning, the pretty college student mumbled, "Only as long as I do what they want me to do." She picked up her saddle, sliding it onto its home on the rack that had her name on it. "Maybe I don't want to be what they want me to be."

The tears ran freely now.

Betty rushed to put her arms around Tootie's waist. "Is it as bad as all that?"

Tootie nodded. Betty walked her to one of the director's chairs where she sat. Betty sat opposite.

Sister hung up her bridle, then joined them, taking a seat. "Do you still want to be a veterinarian?" she asked.

"I do. An equine vet. My father says it's a waste of my life. He'll cut me off if I pursue my career with animals. He says I'm smart enough to be an investment banker and I'd make millions. I don't need millions." She wiped her eyes with the Kleenex Betty had fished from her vest pocket. "I just want to be happy and I want to help horses."

Sister took a deep breath. "Parents take a long view. Your mother and father are thinking about how hard that profession can be, and it's not especially lucrative. You'll struggle sometimes, Tootie, and so far in your life all you've known is wealth. I say this because I love you. You really don't know what it is to do without. You're only a freshman. There's a lot of time to make a decision."

Tootie worshipped Sister. "That's what Val says. I know it's true, but maybe I need to find out for myself."

Betty said, "Tootie, you might be right. I admire your dream and we'll find out about the grit."

"You have it on the hunt field, why not off?" said Sister, reaching over to wipe Tootie's tears. "What can we do?"

"Let me stay here with you, Sister. I'll get a job. I'll pay rent. I hate Princeton."

Sister, who thought Princeton both beautiful and demanding in the best academic fashion, folded her hands. "You will never get a better education anywhere else."

"That may be so, but I can't concentrate there."

Having raised two girls, Betty took a different tack. "Honey, I never could either. I made it through two years at Randolph Macon before throwing in the towel, but I don't have your brain. Why don't you finish out this semester? Come back after that."

"That gives you the time to figure out expenses as best you can," said Sister. "You know I don't want any rent, Tootie, but you'll have your car insurance and other expenses, like gas. It adds up. Your father's threatened to cut you off and I believe he will if you drop out of school."

Betty pursed her lips, unsure of the wisdom of what she was about to ask. "What kind of work do you think you can do?"

"I can work horses," said Tootie. "I can clean a vet clinic. I'm not proud. I can do anything with a computer. And I can learn. If I don't know something, I'll learn it." She looked straight at Betty. "I know finishing out the semester makes a lot of sense, but I'd rather drop out now so my grades don't suffer. At least my first semester grades were good and I can transfer those later. If I have to go to night school like Felicity, then I will."

Sister unfolded her hands. "You know your own mind. I can't change it. Of course, you can stay with me, but you have to talk to your parents before you come on down. Tell them they can also talk to me. I know I'm going to be on their shit list along with you. Your father has never liked me."

"He doesn't like too many people. Too competitive."

Yet Sister admired the African American media mogul. "That's what made him millions at a time after LBJ pushed through the Voter Rights Act. Didn't he start his magazine business in the seventies?"

"Did. He waited until he was in his forties to marry because he said he didn't want to worry that he couldn't support a wife. All my father thinks about is money. Every single decision he makes is about money. He tells me the first question I should ask whenever I make a decision is 'What is this going to cost me?' Not, will I learn anything? Will I love what I'm doing? Will I do good for anyone else? I can't live like that. *I won't live like that.*" Her voice rose and she was no longer crying.

"Millions do," Sister simply said. "Men think their money obsession is merely being logical. Women think it's the new way to think now—in other words, they're imitation men. I'm afraid most people only wake up and realize what's truly important when death brushes by them or someone they love. Tootie, who knows what will happen tomorrow to any one of us? But at least we've lived, truly lived. Betty's had a harder time than I have with money. I've been lucky there, but I've endured other painful lessons. I wouldn't trade one minute of it. Not one. So you talk to your parents and best you do it before you go back to Princeton to pick up your gear."

Leaping from her chair, Tootie hugged Sister and kissed her on the cheek. Then she bent over Betty and kissed her.

"Thanks," said Betty rising painfully from the stool. "My leg hurts."

"Betty, what'd you do now?"

"Knocked a tree when we were at Old Paradise. My feet were so wet and cold I didn't pay attention until later when it started to throb. It will go away."

They heard the big Land Cruiser churning up the driveway, Gray at the wheel.

Sister looked out. "Here comes Mr. Wonderful, and the lights are still on in the kennels."

"I'll go see if Shaker needs a hand," Betty volunteered.

"Me, too," said Tootie.

"All right, then," said Sister. "See you up at the house. Betty, would you like some supper?"

"No, thanks. I ate enough at the hunt breakfast and Bobby will be wanting his supper. I've got him on a new diet. It's working, but very, very slowly." She pushed open the tackroom door and headed to the kennels, Tootie in tow.

Sister cut the lights in the tackroom. She walked into the center aisle to cut the lights there. Darkness fell so early in February, or so it seemed, even though a minute of sunlight was added each day after the winter solstice.

As he was dry, she threw on Rickyroo's fancy blanket. Tootie and Betty had already put their horse blankets on. As the night promised to be another bitter one, she decided to bring in the other horses. Walking out the barn's big double door, she whistled. Up ran Lafayette, Aztec, Matador, and Keepsake. Opening the gate for them, they all four entered the warm barn.

Aztec ducked into Lafayette's stall for a second, just to see if his feed was better.

Lafayette bared his teeth as the younger horse hurried out. *"I'll bite your hindquarters."*

"Yeah, but your teeth are getting worn down," the six-year-old sassed back as he trotted into his stall.

Sister shut each stall door after closing the outside doors. She rechecked each stall, even though she had filled the water buckets. She hoped it would stay warm enough inside the barn that the buckets wouldn't freeze overnight. Usually the horses gave off enough body heat that the enclosed barn hovered above freezing, but on the coldest of nights those buckets could freeze—meaning more work in the morning.

A squawk drew her eyes upward. Bitsy hopped from a rafter into her nest. Sister waved to the little owl, then left the barn, closing the door tightly behind her.

Twilight turned the sky royal blue, then the blue darkened. A thin line of gold traced the top of the blue mountains. The evening star glittered brilliantly. The clouds of the morning's hunt disappeared. Tonight, bright and clear, would be particularly cold.

The kennel door creaked opened and shut, and Sister waved to Shaker and Betty. Tootie ran up to Sister and the two walked up to the house.

The dogs greeted everyone. Gray had made a pot of green tea for Sister and Tootie. He kissed them both, then sat down at the kitchen table with the Sunday *Richmond Times-Dispatch*.

"Still a good paper, even if it is one quarter the size it was in my youth."

Sister decided to tell him about Tootie later. She sat down next to him as the young woman brought over the teapot, then the cups.

"Thank you." Sister knew how Gray liked to read the paper undisturbed, but she had to interrupt just for a moment. "Where'd you find this tea?"

"Tea Forte Citrus Mint," he answered with a smile. "Harris Teeter. They make a Lemon Ginger, too. That has a bite. This is more soothing. For me, anyway, and I am chilled to the bone. I bet you two are as well."

"You were out in the cold longer than I was," Sister said.

Golly sashayed into the room, her tail straight up, waving grandly. *"I'm here,"* the cat announced.

"We know," Raleigh barked in reply.

Golly jumped into Tootie's lap. *"From here, I can see everything on the table,"* she bragged.

"I can smell everything on the table and there's nothing to eat." Rooster hoped for a dog treat.

Sister gratefully sipped the delicious tea. "A hot shower after this tea and I'll feel good as new. Tired but good."

"You first." Tootie smiled.

"Thanks. I sort of want to pull off my boots and I sort of don't. My toes are so cold." Sister then patted her deep yellow vest, removing the cigarette case she'd bought from Adolfo.

Gray glanced over from the business section of the paper. "Isn't that heavy over your heart like that?"

"A little bit. I suppose I could put it in a lower pocket but I like it close to my heart. Silly." She drank another deep draft of the hot tea. "I promise I'll let you get back to the paper, Gray, but we didn't get to talk much at the breakfast. You said the sheriff's department couldn't make an ID. Could you see the body at all?"

"I saw the man's jacket. One of the officers called it a Pennsylvania tuxedo."

Sister sat up straight. "A Woolrich jacket? Heavy, red with a black plaid over it?"

"Yes."

"You don't see too many of those anymore, but there was that new fellow, hadn't lived here long, who sometimes hauled odds and ends with Art DuCharme, he wore a really old one. Can't remember his name, but you know who I mean?"

Gray thought. "Short fellow, kind of heavy, not too bright. Art would use him to help move stuff once in a while."

"Yes, I can't remember his name, but I remember he had such red hair."

Gray put down the paper. "He did, didn't he?"

"Bright red."

"There's still some left," Gray said, remembering the scene.

CHAPTER 16

Sunday, February 5, was a playoff Sunday. That meant sports dominated all forms of media. Sister liked football well enough although she wasn't obsessed by it. Baseball was her game.

Gray had driven back to the Lorillard place so he, Sam, and a few of their unmarried, divorced, and temporarily single friends could watch the game. A big flat-screen TV filled the wall in the Lorillard brothers' living room. Due to his past, Sam lacked close friends except for Rory, a fellow he'd met on Charlottesville's Skid Row. Rory had also cleaned up his act. Gray, on the other hand, enjoyed many friendships, quite a few of them men from the hunt club.

Sister and Tootie helped Shaker with the hound chores so he, too, could go.

The two women, having finished the horse and hound chores, happily returned to the house.

Once in the kitchen, teapot boiling per usual, Sister said, "Why don't you get it over with?"

Tootie slumped at the table, which brought the two dogs over to comfort her. "I know. First, I'll call Val."

"Don't be surprised if she tells you you're crazy."

Tootie smiled. "Oh, she will. Val and I have been roommates for four years. Well, four and a half counting Princeton. We're so used to each other and now"—she looked at Sister—"I'll have a new roommate."

"She already has a roommate. Me." Golly announced from the window over the sink where she was drooling over the cardinals eating at the bird feeder.

Sister laughed. "Oh, Tootie, with Val you draw double the number of handsome young men. You aren't going to get that with me."

Tootie plucked her cell phone out of her jacket, which she'd draped on the back of the ladder-back chair. "You know, it gets tedious. I don't care about that stuff. I really don't. Val lives to be the center of attention." Tootie hastily added, "I'm not criticizing. Just a fact, and it's one of the things we had to learn about each other."

"Go in the den and sit by the window. Better reception."

"Thanks."

"And Tootie, then call Mom and Dad. Get it over with. Steel yourself."

"Yes, ma'am." Tootie rose, removed her coat from the chair, and walked down the hall to the den.

Rooster followed her while Raleigh stayed with his beloved Sister. The Doberman hated it when she wasn't within eyesight. Occasionally he wangled his way to a hunt where he would patiently wait in the truck, windows cracked. Usually, he was left home, convinced something dreadful would happen to Sister. Being a dog and therefore sensible, he imagined wolves, frenzied buck, mountain lions, or other dastardly humans. Trouble usually came in an official government letter in the mail or via a phone call. He couldn't imagine that.

Tea steeping, fingers warming, the tall woman sank into a kitchen chair at last, Sunday paper before her. Reading the paper was a ritual she enjoyed as much as Gray. She could pull information off her DROID or from the computer, but it wasn't the same as spreading out the paper, reading and listening to the rustle of the pages as she turned them.

The budget crisis soaked up ink, as did another sex scandal involving a married senator, one who had much publicized his virtue. Laughing, she flipped the page, suddenly finding an article of interest.

"Raleigh," she told the dog, "the report on the body found at Gray and Sam's say it is under investigation. Foul play may be involved, or it may be a hunting accident. A hunting accident? You shoot the deer, it falls on top of you? Come on." She read further. "Cause of death is not yet determined. The remains will be sent to the medical examiner in Richmond." She looked at the dog. "If anyone can find out what killed him, they can. Hmm, this is a curious report. Obviously, Ben and the department want to downplay violence. Oh, he's been identified as Carter Weems. Couldn't think of his name to save my life." She lowered her voice, confiding in Raleigh, "He's the only person I know who wore a Woolrich coat—the old kind, the heavy-duty, lasts-forever kind that people wore when I was a kid. It says Weems had been arrested in the past for hauling illegal guns and illegal whiskey in North Carolina. Also asks if he has any next of kin and will they come forward." She took a long drink of hot tea. "Can't stand it."

She rose to call Betty.

"Betty, did you read the paper?"

"I was just going to call you. I vaguely remember him. Well, he must have been up to no good."

"That or he crossed the wrong person. The little reference to him hauling moonshine, well, he knew what he was doing, but if someone wants to pin something on you that's all too easy."

"True." Betty thought for a moment. "Who knows what's being brought into the county or carried out of it? Albemarle is rich. Loaded with cocaine. Meth in the county, but for all those people with money to burn, cocaine is the drug of choice. And yes, we all know 'shine is driven out of our county, out of any county that has runoff from the Blue Ridge Mountains. That water is pure. Well, we think it's pure."

"I sure was glad that Sybil wasn't mentioned. We don't need the hunt club in the papers, even though finding the body is no reflection on any of us or any other foxhunter."

"Why would that matter?"

"Crawford," answered Sister. "He could find a way to use it against us."

"Now, Janie, that's a far stretch. Don't let him get to you that way. He wouldn't stir up the anti-hunters because he's hunting. Finding a body shouldn't arouse our other landowners."

"You're right." She sighed deeply. "I'm jumpy. It's a strange time."

"Yes, it is. Oh, Bobby's over at Gray's watching the game. Actually, I'll watch the playoffs by myself. He screams, jumps out of his chair, throws popcorn. Tell you what, girl, wears me out."

Sister laughed. "It's odd how men identify with teams, with other men who have athletic ability. It's like they're in love with them."

"Bobby can still get misty-eyed over Bear Bryant," said Betty, and they laughed.

"For Gray, it's Roberto Clemente," said Sister. "Here's what gets me, all this focus nowadays on head injuries in football. Of course, they're responsible for the early dementia and suicide of some of those retired players. Don't you think?"

"Hell, yes."

"But would we watch football, would it generate as much cash, were it not violent? See, I think we are violent by nature. We repress it, but we are thrilled to watch it in others, most particularly in sports. And I'm part of it, too. Not saying I'm not."

"Too deep for me." Betty laughed. "We've had violence enough. The man you and Tootie found in New York and now Carter Weems." Betty paused. "Have you read through all the paper yet?"

"No, called you as soon as I read the article about finding the body."

"Go to the business section. One of the Philip Morris warehouses was burned Saturday. That's never happened before."

"No." Sister thought. "No suspects for that? Well, I'll read it."

"No. Could be one of the antismoking groups. I mean a lot of these organizations are becoming really radical like PETA, things like that. Now, the antismoking crowd could be going that route."

"I sure hope not."

"These days everything seems upside down," Betty said, voice rising. "People say they believe in the sanctity of life, then blow up an abortion clinic killing everyone in it. Other people say there's only one God, theirs, and they fly airplanes into buildings. I understand hate, I truly do. What I don't understand is double-think."

"Me neither, but why assume that humans are rational?" said Sister. "I've done enough stupid things in my life to make me realize we can all be irrational. Mix in politics, power, profit, sex, or religion and the insanity goes global, doesn't it?"

"Sure seems to. Well, this is a happy Sunday conversation."

Sister laughed. "Sometimes you just have to get it off your

chest. Then I think of our friends, those in the hunt club, those in church, those at Custis Hall. We know so many people and most of them are straight up. So if we have good people here, there have to be good people everywhere."

"You're right."

After ending the call, Sister returned to the kitchen table. Sitting down, she tried to concentrate. From down the hall, she could hear Tootie's voice while she spoke on the phone, louder than usual. Sister drummed the tabletop with her fingers.

"That is most irritating," Golly said. Clamor of this sort really got on the cat's nerves.

"You're such a priss." Raleigh walked over to the sink and stood on his hind legs to reach Golly on her windowsill perch.

She exposed one sharp claw. *"Don't you dare come closer."*

The Doberman didn't, but he opened his jaws as though to clamp down on the cat. *"You'd be so tasty."*

Furious hissing drew Sister's attention from the paper. "Raleigh, leave her alone."

The dog dropped back to all fours, returning to his master. *"You always take her part."*

On her feet again, Sister walked to the phone. Even though the phone was close by, Golly ignored her. The cat licked her paw as though she hadn't a care in the world, and pretty much she didn't.

Pulling up a chair by the counter, Sister sat down after she dialed. "Ben, it's the old lady."

"Sister, good hunt yesterday, despite all."

"Yes, hounds did well. The youngsters are stepping up to the plate. You can cuss me for this, but my nosiness got the better of me. Who identified Carter Weems?"

"Art DuCharme."

"Funny, because Gray and I were talking last night, late, trying to figure out who it might be. Gray told me about the jacket and I remembered, sort of, a fellow who sometimes helped Art haul stuff. Couldn't think of his name, plus that fellow can't be the only person in the area to wear one of those jackets. They're just about indestructible."

"They are, but the body wasn't. One of the men who helped extract the body from under the deer recalled the man. I got hold of Art and he came right down to the morgue."

"I don't wish that job on anybody. Identifying remains."

"Poor Art passed out. When we revived him, he said it was Carter Weems. He'd wondered where he'd gone, but Carter was a drifter. Only worked when he had to. Art said he never suspected anything like this might have befallen him. Those were his words, befallen."

Art passed out because Carter was a grisly sight. Sister wondered whether Art also feared what might befall him.

CHAPTER 17

The day's hard hunting outside in the cold finally caught up with Sister. She leaned back in the kitchen chair to stretch out her legs.

Golly sprawled out on Lafayette's equine gel pad, heard joints pop. "*Getting old,*" she said, reveling in the cozy spot.

Raleigh remarked, "*You're no spring chicken.*"

"*I'm no chicken.*"

"*A birdbrain, then?*" Rooster laid his head on his paws.

"*I'd have a battle of wits with you, but you're unarmed.*" Golly shifted on the gel pad.

"There's an awful lot of noise in here," Sister said to the three animals, then added, "and not much in the den."

She rose, stretching her arms over her head before walking down the hall to the den. The dogs followed. Golly remained on the gel pad for it was comfortable, so comfortable that Sister, grumbling, let her have it. She'd buy another for Lafayette.

"Well?" Sister inquired of Tootie, who sat on the cushioned sofa, deep in thought.

"You know what he said? 'You made your bed, you lie in it.' Then he handed the phone to Mom. She recited all the reasons why it's a bad idea, but she knew my mind was made up. It could have been worse." Tootie looked from the fire to the deep darkness outside the window. "I'm not doing this to disappoint them. If I don't follow my heart I'll make a bigger mess later. Haven't you ever noticed that the people who don't do what they should—you know, don't find the right work or follow their dreams—turn on themselves eventually or turn on everybody else?"

"Or both." Sister sat next to her on the sofa. "You're right, Tootie. It really could have been worse."

"The first thing I'm going to do when I get back to Princeton is try to get Dad as much of his money back for this semester as possible." A long pause followed. "That's all he cares about."

"Honey, that's not true," Sister said, taking the distraught Tootie's hand. "Really. He loves you. He wants what's best for you. He can't see beyond what he believes is right. So everything comes out sounding like a financial transaction. You might say it's your father's metaphor for life."

Turning her beautiful face to Sister, she said, "Well, he is right about one thing: I'm going to find out the value of money. Felicity sure has, but she has that kind of brain. You know she invested our kitty at Custis Hall? I don't think like that, but I can pay bills. I can check my balance online. Like I said, I'll learn."

When Tootie, Val, and Felicity were students at Custis Hall, their senior year, each time one of the girls swore she had to put a dollar in the kitty. By graduation time, the sum neared one thousand dollars. Instead of having a party, the girls voted to let Felicity invest it. She had, and even in these hard times, she was making about fifteen percent on their investment.

"You'll figure it all out," said Sister. "In time, your father will see that you made the right decision."

"I don't know." She paused. "Felicity should have been his daughter."

"She's had her own troubles with her parents," Sister reminded Tootie.

"Getting pregnant before graduation—yeah, guess she did. The funny thing is, I think Mom and Dad would have handled that better than this. I'm in my freshman year, already Mom keeps talking about a suitable boy, graduation. I can't think about that stuff."

"I didn't either until I met Ray. Once married I thought, well, an unmarried woman is incomplete. When she's married, she's finished." She laughed.

Tootie laughed, too. "But you always knew what you wanted to do, didn't you?"

"Not as clearly as you do. I loved geology, loved teaching, but when RayRay was born, I loved being a mother. Beyond that, I didn't have much direction in life."

"Hunting."

Pondering this, Sister finally answered, "Now I see that hunting provided the framework of my life, but I wouldn't say it gave me direction. I'm not complaining. It's all worked out and it will work out for you, especially if you don't make a big drama out of it."

"Do you think I am?" Tootie worried.

"No. I think you're remarkably self-possessed. I know you're strong under pressure, I've seen you in the hunt field. And in New York, you handled finding a murdered man. But that's not quite the same as something inside the family or with romance. A lot of people, young or old, blow everything out of proportion, making matters ten times worse."

"No time to be dramatic," Tootie said, nodding. "Val's dramatic enough for both of us." She laughed a little.

"Yes, well, if she wants that political career she keeps talking about, she'd better learn to squelch that. What time do you want to leave in the morning?"

"I don't have a class until the late afternoon so I thought seven."

"All right then. I'll make you breakfast."

"Sister, you don't have to do that. You're doing so much for me."

"I have to eat, too. Oh, before I forget, the body found during the hunt has been identified. Carter Weems. A drifter from North Carolina who picked up odd jobs, mostly hauling."

"I'm glad I didn't see that."

"Me, too," Sister agreed. "It has to be murder. Human bodies don't wind up under deer. No word from the authorities about how he was killed, or they aren't saying. Actually, I think Ben would tell me."

"Sometimes I think about dying," Tootie said, then quickly reassured the older woman: "Not doing it to myself, don't you worry. I'm just glad I don't know when I'm going to die. Would you want to know?"

"Takes the fun out of it."

"Death?" Tootie was incredulous.

"No, it takes the mystery out of life. It is possible to know too much," stated Sister. "Most of it doesn't matter anyway. I think of that line in Ecclesiastes, 'all is vanity.' Still, finding a body in my hunt territory makes me want to know who did it and why. Maybe I want to know too much."

She did.

CHAPTER 18

"Do you think they'll try to kill you?" Crawford asked, voice emotionless as he leaned back in his cozy den chair.

Dismay crossed Tariq's face. "No. I'm not that important." He paused. "At least I hope I'm not."

"You're important enough for Congressman Rickman to accuse you of fronting for the Muslim Brotherhood." The older man, well dressed even at home, twisted a half smile. "He is, of course, an idiot hoping to get publicity, which he has, claiming this whole hullabaloo is for the sake of national security. All right, you've come to me for help. You owe me the truth."

"Yes, sir." From his perch on the edge of a Morris chair, Tariq lifted his deep brown eyes to Crawford's light ones.

"Are you a member of the Muslim Brotherhood?"

"No. I am a Coptic Christian. There are twelve million of us in Egypt and we are under great stress. Churches have been burned. You may not remember but a little over a year ago in Cairo the military publicly abused some of our women. Pushed them around. Mocked them and roughed them up."

"Rape?"

"No one is saying that, including the victims, but our women were attacked publicly by the military in Cairo because they aren't Muslim and don't follow the dress customs of that faith. As for the Muslim Brotherhood, I fear them more than the military. I fear anyone eager to impose their religion upon another."

"Hmm." Crawford smiled as his wife Marty came in with a silver tray holding tiny china cups, a small pot of espresso, delicate little plates—upon which rested curled orange peels, lemon peels, and both white and natural sugar cubes—and a large plate with chocolate swizzle sticks. "Thank you, darling."

Marty kissed him on the cheek, then said to Tariq, "I know we don't make coffee like you get at home, but I think I've come close—and oh, would you like some clotted cream?"

"Clotted cream?" Tariq's eyebrows rose. "How I loved that when I studied in England. No, thank you. But with great good fortune, I will visit you in the spring with fresh strawberries."

She clapped her hands without making much noise. "And I'll have the clotted cream. That's perfect." She then looked to her husband, whom she understood and loved despite all. "Anything else?"

He reached up to run his hand down her forearm. "Not a thing."

She left the two men as her husband poured the coffee.

Tariq nodded slightly as he took the proffered cup. "You are a fortunate man."

Crawford looked at his wife's back as she moved down the hall. "One of the reasons I am where I am today is because I found her. I'm not exactly a warm and fuzzy guy. She makes up for it, and she rightly reprimands me for missing things about people."

Tariq smiled. "My mother's version of that was to say nothing to my father but to throw up her hands, roll her eyes to heaven, and leave the room."

The two men laughed, then Crawford continued his interrogation. "For you and your people, it probably doesn't matter who governs Egypt."

"Yes and no," said Tariq. It wasn't often that he discussed Egyptian politics, even these days with his country in such a tumult. "Coptic Christians will always be a minority. Holding office, getting government or military jobs will be difficult if not impossible. Intermarriage, especially in places that are"—he considered his next word—"unsophisticated can bring death to young women or men. Oh, yes"—he looked at a surprised Crawford—"there are still people like that. Honor killings."

"We don't have honor killings in America, but we still have plenty of people that are narrow-minded."

"Perhaps all countries have extremists," said Tariq.

"Egypt baffles me. Like most Americans, I thought ridding yourself of Mubarak would solve the problem. It seems to have opened a very large can of worms."

"That is always the case with dictatorships. Look what happened to Yugoslavia after Tito died. All the Balkans in chaos."

"You're right." Crawford was beginning to appreciate this young man. "I suppose that's another mess that will never be resolved."

"And again, religion is a part of it. I remember when the Muslims were killing the Christians. I was just a child, but my father told me it could happen in our country. He said that when the Muslims killed the Christians they cut off the two fingers of their right hands, the index and middle fingers. That image stuck with me."

"Why on earth would they do that?" Crawford was incredulous. "I mean I've heard of giving the finger but—"

"Because when Catholics and other Christians make the sign of the cross they use those two fingers."

"So they do," Crawford murmured.

"As I grew up, I learned there had been barbarism enough on both sides, but as we are only ten percent of Egypt's population, my father's fears propelled me."

"Your father must be a rich man to send you to Harrow and Oxford."

"He was the first Egyptian to import semiconductors. My father is an engineer."

"And a businessman. And you?"

"He sent me to get the best Western education possible. And then to consider—in the fullness of time, as he would say—is there hope for our people? If not, is there a way out?"

"I see. So Congressman Rickman imperils more than your tranquillity."

"Yes. I'm at Custis Hall, a place I very much like, to learn more about America. There are plenty of well-educated Egyptians in your big cities but not many in the countryside of the South. I want to know what they think."

"In hopes of arousing us to help Coptic Christians in some fashion?"

"That may be too much to hope for, but if I have a good understanding of America, perhaps I can help raise money to send back home."

"So you think your peoples' circumstances in Egypt will get worse."

Tariq nibbled on a swizzle stick, measuring his words. "I pray they will not. But I fear deeply, especially if tensions explode in the Arab world with Israel. We are the leader of the Arab world. A war is not inconceivable and often, when such a situation occurs, people look for a scapegoat in their own country. In Egypt, the Coptic minority is made-to-order."

"I suppose you are. Why have you come to me?"

"You are on the board of Custis Hall. You are powerful and rich. You know how to get things done. I ask your help in neutralizing Congressman Rickman. Can you stop him from saying such untrue things about me?"

Crawford smiled broadly. He made a steeple out of his hands as he rested his elbows on his chest. "Let me take care of this, but I have a price."

"Yes?"

"You no longer hunt with Sister Jane. You hunt with me."

Seeing Tariq's surprise, Crawford added, "I never forget or forgive an insult."

"Yet you serve on the board of Custis Hall with her."

"I do, and we work well together for Custis Hall," said Crawford, frowning. "We're both practical and can put things aside, but I will get even with her. Everyone thinks of her as the Artemis of our time. I'm sick of it. Sick of watching people kiss her ass in Macy's window."

"Macy's window?" asked a puzzled Tariq.

"An old expression about obsequious public display. Anyway, it will cut her if you hunt with me."

"I can but bring myself," said Tariq. "Custis Hall has its own arrangements with Jefferson Hunt."

"I know that," Crawford said, a hint of irritation in his voice.

Tariq inclined his head slightly as if a small bow. "I will do as you ask."

"Dumfriesshire hounds," Crawford boasted. "I have Dumfriesshire hounds."

"I know them well. I have hunted in England and Scotland, sir. Before the ban."

"I suppose you have." He laughed loudly. "I hear more people in England hunt now with the ban than without."

"It is amusing and so very English. They love tradition—and the chase is thrilling, even if no blood is shed."

Crawford raised his voice. "Honey."

"Yes, dear," his wife called from her sunroom.

"Will you bring a fixture card?"

Within a few minutes, Marty handed a fixture card to Crawford, who passed it to Tariq.

"He will be hunting with us now," Crawford informed his wife. She smiled. "How wonderful."

Tariq studied the fixture card, correctly printed on ivory stock, the ink a rich burgundy, two crossed foxtails at the top.

"A fixture card properly given." Crawford beamed.

That same February 6, the day Jeb Stuart was born in 1833, Donny swung by the Gulf station. He found Art working in the garage on an old carburetor.

"Wonder how many mechanics know what to do with a carburetor these days?" Donny asked.

"Every one of them, if they have any sense." Art stopped working, wiping his hands on a red rag.

"Know what happened?"

"No," Art answered.

"Think he shot his mouth off?"

"How in hell would I know? Even when he was loaded, Carter knew what side his bread was buttered on."

"Well, he pissed off someone."

Art tried to hide his fear. "That doesn't mean it has anything to do with business."

"You've got a handgun, right?" asked Donny.

"Sure I do."

"Carry it. I'm carrying mine."

Art was about to say more, but then his father walked into the garage.

"Hey there, Sweigart," said Binky DuCharme.

"Good to see you, Mr. DuCharme."

"I think it's finally winter."

"Me, too."

"How's business, apart from hauling with my boy?"

"Not so good." Donny shrugged. "People don't want to spend money on landscaping or maintenance in a depression."

Binky nodded, his eyes a little watery. "But they have to spend it on car repairs. Business is booming here. Folks are hanging on to their old cars. Now, we aren't sitting in high cotton, but it's not bad."

"I can see that. The lot is full. Saw Betty Franklin's old Bronco. The yellow jacket." He laughed.

"It is yellow." Binky shook his head and laughed. "You can always see her coming. Luckily for Betty, it only needed a tune-up, new plugs, nothing major. The Franklins are really having hard times."

"Yes, they are. They're good people." Donny liked hunting with Betty and Bobby.

"Ever think, Sweigart, that the real shits of this world make it big while the good guys finish last?"

"Yeah, the thought has occurred to me."

Art piped up. "Well, Pop, I guess that means we'll all finish last."

The old man folded his arms across his chest. "Who said you were a good guy?"

"Me," Art replied.

Binky walked over to the tire rack ready to work. Art and Donny knew they couldn't speak freely.

Under his breath, Donny said, "Carry a .347 if you have one."

"That's a lot of firepower."

"You never know when you might need it."

CHAPTER 19

At Foxglove Farm, a small waterwheel designed by owner Cindy Chandler sent water from the upper pond to the lower pond. Even in winter, the delightful sound of the splash on the wheel, followed by the emergence of a stream of water from the pipe just above the lower pond, was refreshing. The ponds, though frozen, rarely froze six or seven inches thick, so the wheel could always pull up water. Only once in twelve years had the ponds frozen so thickly that one could safely skate across.

As the crow flies, Foxglove lay eight miles true north of Roughneck Farm and the kennels. Soldier Road created an obstacle between the two farms. If one drove around from one to the other it added another three miles to the journey. Riding on horseback from Sister's farm road, one could climb up to Hangman's Ridge and come down the north side, well crossed by deer trails, traverse a large meadow, much of it trappy, cross Soldier Road, dropping down a well-graded bank (courtesy of the state of Virginia) and thence onto Foxglove's southernmost fields, which Cindy did not use for pasture. Instead, these meadows exploded with wildflowers, which remained colorful until mid-November. Adding further aesthetic pleasure to the bucolic scene were the occasional huge old walnut, locust, or willow trees near the stream.

Foxes liked the spot, too. The barns and outbuildings backed to the northwest, providing shelter for horses, two cows, and foxes scooping up dropped sweet feed.

Clytemnestra and Orestes, her son, both frighteningly huge beef cattle, now luxuriated in their own living quarters, built extra large. Mother Clytemnestra, evil-tempered at times, moved faster than one supposed. Even the foxes gave this Large Marge a wide berth. She didn't stray far from her cozy paddock in winter. All the gates were closed today, as it was Tuesday, a hunt day.

The two bovines raised their heads as they heard the horn a mile away. They'd grown accustomed to fox hunts.

Sister to the black fox, Inky, Georgia, a young gray, was running for her den at the schoolhouse. Georgia thought the building, built in the mid-1800s and lovingly preserved, was the best place ever. She knew how to get inside.

On February 7, the temperature was 37°F at nine-thirty, but it was rising. For those on a hunt, this made for a good day for scent, especially where the sun struck the earth. In other spots, patches of snow still hugged northern slopes and creases in the land.

Not terribly worried, Georgia ran along. She planned to scurry along the raised bank between the two ponds because that's where some hounds always slipped into the water. It amused the fox and slowed down the horses, too.

Today's ground was a bit slippery. On Matador, Sister kept at a good trot, breaking into a gallop when conditions appeared more favorable. However, as she approached the fenced-in higher pastures, the hounds picked up speed, singing louder.

Glancing behind her, she saw that everyone followed in good order. The Tuesday and Thursday crowds tended to be hard riders. As with any sport, Saturdays added many weekend warriors.

A well-set, simple, three-foot-three-inch coop punctuated the fence line. Matador, an ex-steeplechaser, smoothly cleared the obstacle. Fortunately, the ground was tight on landing. Once the sun hit either side of these jumps, footing might be sloppy on top, yet hard underneath. You prayed because there was nothing else you could do about it.

Shaker, ahead on Gunpowder, stretched out. Georgia put on the afterburners. True to form, she bolted across the high twelve-foot-wide bank between the ponds.

Shaker crossed the bank. Betty veered into the woods as she ran ahead of the huntsman while Sybil easily took a hog's-back jump into an open pasture on the left.

Georgia, brush flat out behind her, ears pricked up, ran neck and neck with another fox she'd never seen before. He'd joined her on the other side of the pond. No time to talk, but the dog fox stuck right with her. She sensed he was green to hunting.

Sister's stride was lengthening. Matador ran over the bank. Everyone made it except one Custis Hall student, mounted on her own majestic Warmblood. While the animal could jump the moon, he wasn't quite as sure-footed as the Thoroughbreds and quarter horses, and he slipped as the earth churned up. Both slid down the embankment, the horse's hind end cracking through the ice.

To the riding girl's credit, she didn't panic. She leaned far up on his neck while the animal scrambled out. Cindy Chandler, riding tail for First Flight, stopped for them. She checked the horse to see that he hadn't gotten cut up by the ice, then the human and horse continued on, wet.

Georgia used the woods to her advantage, but Pookah, a

second-year hound, displayed her own talents by picking up the line where Georgia had dashed through an old hollowed-out log. The smell of wood and moss had somewhat disguised her scent.

Cora, running up with the youngster, said, "*There are two foxes.*"

Pookah asked, "*What do I do if they split?*"

"*Stick with the hotter scent.*" Cora offered no guidance if the scent was equal in strength, which it would be today.

The pathways through the hardwoods, kept open by Cindy, made for easy going. Shaker burst out of the woods in time to see Betty on his right and Sybil on his left both flying along, caps off. The women pointed in the direction the foxes ran. He shot up a slight rise, then came out on the thirty-acre back meadow, which contained the schoolhouse, saw both foxes in tandem racing for the structure, hounds perhaps fifty yards behind.

Sister emerged from the woods just as the two grays ducked under the schoolhouse.

Georgia dove into her den, the young fellow behind her.

"*Follow me,*" Georgia commanded.

He crouched behind her as she moved along, then climbed a few paces upward at an angle to wiggle through a hole under a desk set against a wall.

"*Wow. All this is yours?*" Inside the schoolhouse, the gray fox looked around as the hounds carried on underneath.

"*All mine.*" She advised, "*Stay under the desk until they go. You never know if someone will peek inside.*"

Outside, Shaker on Gunpowder, blew "Gone to Ground," as there was no way to crawl under the schoolhouse. One by one, the hounds emerged, congratulating one another for their good work.

The Custis Hall girl who'd gotten the icy dunking, Kylie Engle, shivered.

Hearing her teeth chatter, Cindy rode up to Sister, "I'm going to take Kylie back, get her into some dry clothing."

Sister agreed, then turned to the field. "Cindy is heading back, if anyone wants to go with her."

A few people in both First and Second Flights followed Mrs. Chandler.

Sister rode up to Shaker. "The ground is getting filthy, but that's hunting. Let's pick up another fox."

"Righto." He tapped his cap with his crop.

As Shaker led the hounds to the back farm road, Sister turned to count heads. Six left, eight in Second Flight. Her eyes alighted on Donny Sweigart, a slight bulge on his left side. She didn't remember giving Donny permission to carry a handgun. Well, no matter. She'd talk to him about it later. It was probably a good idea: Shaker and the two whippers-in had pistols loaded with ratshot, rarely used, but someone in the field should be able to put a suffering animal out of its misery if necessary. Fortunately, in her thirty-odd years as master, she'd had only two hounds and one horse die in the hunt field. Wounded deer, however, were another matter, and it made her sick when the hunt came across one.

They walked along the road heading south. The sun, a welcome sight, raised the mercury to 42°F, a wonderful temperature for hunting. Robin's-egg skies mitigated against good scenting, but the great thing about hunting was you never knew. A high-pressure system might not presage a bad day.

Sister noticed a mob of crows sitting in barren tree branches. Cackling and gossiping, they stared at the riders, hounds moving toward them. A flash of blue signified a blue jay darting toward his home base. The crows called out abuse and, saucy fellow that the jay was, he answered in turn.

As Sister laughed at this drama, all of a sudden the hounds opened with a roar. This puzzled her: If a fox was about, surely the crows would create an uproar, but they stayed put while the hounds thundered down the farm road before turning sharply right.

A stacked row of hay bales made for a temporary jump until Cindy could design one to her liking. This pierced the fence line and Sister was soon over. The electrifying pace kept her and everyone focused. Clods of mud flew from hooves. Seeing the hounds ahead, she could see bits of mud flying from their paws. They ran tightly together, throwing their voices.

The grasses, high, were down slightly from the snow that had been weighted on them. Sister still couldn't see the quarry. Within minutes, she'd dropped into pines. The hounds turned right again, and Sister found herself slowed by the lowlands along Soldier's Road. The thin ice on top cracked as Matador ran through it.

Thank God there was no traffic on the road. The hounds crossed into the meadows, at the base of Hangman's Ridge, now a half mile away. Although a low meadow, it had no standing water but the going was tough. Sister headed for a deer trail she knew and happened to see a large flash high up. Hounds, well behind a coyote, pushed as hard as they could.

Once on the deer path, she climbed. At times, the earth slipped under Matador. Gamely, he pressed as fast as he could because the hounds were pulling away. Breathing hard while Matador wasn't, they finally came out on the top of Hangman's Ridge, a long flat expanse, its black tree in stark contrast to all around it. She paused for a moment to listen for hounds and to figure out the best way down, depending on where they were. The field came up behind her. Everyone remained silent.

A slight gust made the tree moan, or so it seemed. Then Sister heard the hounds. She took the farm road down, which, while slippery, wasn't as rough as the deer trail. At the bottom she kicked on, took the coop into her field with the old ruins, and flew, flat-out flew to the edge of her field, where she soared over the hog's-back jump into the woods of After All. They ran the mile and a half to Broad Creek where the hounds lost the scent.

Everyone was grateful for the breather, all the more so since bad footing took a toll on the horses. Shaker cast both sides of the creek. Nothing.

He looked to his master on the opposite side of the swift running water. Sister waved him in.

Once over, she called to him: "Lift them, Shaker. It's been a decent day."

"Yes, ma'am." He called the hounds to him. "Caught a glimpse. Coyotes."

"He certainly ran in a straight line." Sister nodded.

Pookah mumbled to Cora, *"We could have picked him up again."* The talented young hound was disappointed.

"Yes, and we could have run to Main Street, Charlottesville, too." The older hound smiled.

"At least to Roger's Corner." Pansy, Pookah's littermate replied, referring to a convenience store in the opposite direction. *"Do coyotes always run like that?"* she asked.

"Usually," the older hound answered. *"They go straight as a stick, just go, go, go, but they aren't clever like a fox. There's not much to figure out, although this one did manage to throw us off."*

Diva joined them and said, *"All he had to do was run in Broad Creek. Because he's bigger, about sixty pounds, he can stay in the water a lot longer than the fox, who will hit a deep spot and have to swim. Some coyote are as big as we are."*

"Ah," said Pansy. *"What happens if we corner one?"*

"It will be one hell of a fight," Cora replied.

That gave the youngster something to think about as they walked all the way back to the kennels. Sister would have someone drive the kennel trailer back from Foxglove. No point in walking the hounds or her horses all the way to Cindy's. She bid everyone to go on and she'd drive over once horses and hounds were put up.

Betty, who had borrowed one of Sister's horses, and Sybil put the hounds in the kennels. Sister took both her horses to untack, clean up, and get water.

Hunt staff runs like a platoon. It's a small unit and everyone knows their job, ready for abrupt shifts in task.

After, they all jammed into Sister's truck, reaching Foxglove just as everyone was going into the house for breakfast. Perfect timing.

Sister found Cindy. "How's Kylie?"

"Dry and warm." Cindy smiled. "And she fits into my clothes. I don't know if I'll see that sweater again."

Sister noticed Kylie in Cindy's jeans and a dark green turtleneck sweater. "You'll never see it again because you'll give it to her. I know how you are, and I regret I'm not your size."

"You'd have to shrink a few inches." Her dear friend laughed as they headed for the hot drinks.

Hot tea in hand, Sister walked over to Donny and Sybil, who were deep in conversation.

"Sybil, I am stealing your boyfriend."

Her whipper-in laughed, turning to chat up the schoolgirls who hunted today.

"Donny, I noticed you were carrying a gun."

Surprised, he said, "Yes."

"That's fine with me, but you should have asked me first. The last thing I want is someone armed in the field who can't hit the broad side of a barn. You can shoot. Why are you carrying a sidearm and what caliber?"

"I'm sorry, Sister. I didn't mean to break a rule." He inhaled. "Two reasons. I saw a wounded deer when we hunted in January and I couldn't do anything to help it. And well, I know this is—" He paused. "Anyway, a dead body was found in our hunt territory. Just in case, you know?" He looked at her.

"Well—"

"Sister, he had to be murdered. No way that's a natural death."

She sighed. "I know. I'm not so worried for the club, Donny, but he was found on Gray's farm. The only people who know about that abandoned road are poachers, and if you think about it, us."

Glass held high, Kasmir approached them.

Donny quickly said in a low voice, "It's a .38. I keep a rifle in the truck."

"All right." She put her hand on his shoulder, squeezing lightly, then turned. "Kasmir, my very own maharaja."

He kissed her on the cheek and they instant-replayed the morning's hunt.

Later, riding back to the farm as Sybil drove the hound trailer, Sister thought, *What you see coming is not what you see going.*

Funny that popped into her head. Her father used to say that when life was confusing.

CHAPTER 20

Gray stamped and wiped his feet on the heavy sisal doormat inside Sister's mudroom door.

Raleigh slipped through the dog door on the kitchen side to greet him. Rooster remained with Sister in the den, where she was at her desk paying bills. Golly was nowhere to be found, never a good sign.

The handsome man stepped inside the house and placed *The Washington Post* on the kitchen table, calling, "Where you at?"

"Den!" she called. She always smiled when he used the colloquialism.

Picking up the paper again, he walked down the hall and dropped in the den's big leather club chair. "Hell Road. Honest to God, the drive home from Washington, never good, was a goddamned mess today."

"Traffic."

"Where do all the people come from? Remember when we

were kids and the road to Washington was two lanes of pitted asphalt?"

"That was because they still feared we'd march on them again." She teased him.

"Not my people."

"Do you know that for sure?"

"Not really. When Great Aunt Tinsley died, she took most of the family history with her. She was the one who knew about all the Lorillards in the War Between the States. Now I wished I'd asked a few questions, but we sure did hear about the time she met Booker T. Washington. A thousand times."

"A great man." Sister nodded.

"Don't you wonder how many people who did a lot for others were never recognized? Or who died at nineteen in war?"

"Yes, I do." She pushed aside her checkbook, stood, and walked over to the recessed bar in a bookshelf.

She poured Gray a stiff Blanton's with a splash of water, a pinch of bitters. He liked his bitters, a twist of lemon. After handing it to him, she said, "I'm glad you're home."

"Me, too. Oh, read the first section of the *Post*. Where there's a little recap of news from other places."

She dutifully took the paper, sat opposite him in her own club chair. She found the section, her interest now piqued.

"What in the hell is going on?"

He shook his head. "I don't know, honey, but you can tell everyone you were in on the first murder. I don't think this is a personal vendetta anymore."

She read aloud as Raleigh put his head on the chair arm to listen. "Oliver Frontenac, proprietor of the exclusive Chicago Tobacco Emporium, was found shot through the head, a pack of American Smokes on his chest. Police believe nothing was stolen from the store, et cetera, et cetera." She looked at her Doberman, then at Gray. "This gets under my skin. It really does."

"It's getting under mine, too, and maybe that's because two dead bodies we sort of know is two too many, even if Carter Weems has nothing to do with any of this other stuff going on."

"Right now, I'm ready to consider anything, no matter how fantastic." She folded the paper in quarters, smacking it on her knee. "And let's not forget that an Altria warehouse burned up."

Altria was the parent company of Philip Morris. "Which brand?" asked Gray. "Do you remember?"

"Marlboro."

"That's one of Philip Morris's biggest moneymakers," he said. "It is possible that fire was in some way connected, although I don't see how."

"What baffles me is why would anyone kill these days over tobacco? Savaging the industry seems to be a done deal." Sister frowned. "Seems un-American to bedevil an industry that served as collateral for loans from France. We'd have not won the War of Independence without France. Do you have to kill these few people who still sell tobacco products? Or burn out a warehouse?" Sister petted Raleigh, who closed his eyes in pleasure.

Sprawled on the rug, Rooster opened one eye, then closed it again.

"I don't know, honey, there's a lot of crazy people in this world. If they're killing over tobacco at least that's a dispute over a real thing. You can hold a cigarette or a tobacco leaf in your hand. It's killing and persecution over ideas that seems to raise human cruelty and perversion to new heights. And you know, this is creeping closer to home. The Henrico County Board of Supervisors approved construction of a mosque, perfectly reasonable, we have freedom of religion in this country, and some of the locals got all up in arms about it, doing their best to show off their intolerance."

"Midget minds."

He took a long drink. "I wouldn't kill for a bottle of Blanton's, but I might consider it on a bad day."

She laughed at him. "Bourbon is so sweet. Smells good, though."

"That it does. I watch myself. You know how that one glass at the end of the day can get bigger and bigger? Or the other trick is you start with one glass of wine or one shot of whiskey, yet the glass is never drained."

"Gray, you're not going to turn into an alcoholic."

"I hope not, but I'm vigilant. Sam certainly provided me with a dismal example and Momma could knock it back, too, when the mood took her." He smiled at Sister. She always looked so pretty. "How was today's hunt?"

"Good." She smiled. "Ran two foxes under the schoolhouse and then picked up a coyote heading south on Cindy's back farm road. That was wild."

"*Two* foxes?"

She nodded. "It is mating season. Looks like our schoolhouse fox has a boyfriend. And Kylie Engle, the sophomore at Custis Hall, slipped in the lower pond. Horse scrambled out. The kid kept her head."

"Speaking of kids, what have you heard from Tootie today?"

"She was able to get some money refunded to her father. Now she's packing up her room at Princeton. Val is pitching a fit—Tootie's version. I'm sure Val's is a little different."

He leaned his head back on the chair, stared up at the ceiling for a moment. "Tough call," he said, and she knew he referred to the right course of action for Tootie.

"Yes, it is, but I think she's right."

"I hope she's able to make an arrangement so if she wishes she can return to Princeton," said Gray sensibly.

"I don't know. Oh, you know what else happened today? I noticed that Donny Sweigart was carrying a pistol. Happened to notice the bulge at his side. If he falls, he'll break his ribs and oh, that will hurt."

"Why is Donny carrying a gun?"

"He says we can't be too careful after the corpse was found at your homeplace."

"Seems a little extreme."

"Does, but I gave him permission after the fact. Never hurts to have a good shot in the field."

"True." He heard a thump upstairs.

Sister looked at the ceiling. "Now I know where Golly is. I'll find out what she's done later. I've been paying the bills and that's trouble enough."

He laughed. "Damn cat."

"How true. So very true," Raleigh solemnly intoned.

Sister returned to the large desk, rolling her chair to the computer. "I just had an idea. The American Smokes murders were in New York, Boston, and this latest, Chicago."

"Right," he said skeptically, unsure whether to encourage her.

"Okay, give me a minute here. Here we go." She peered at the screen. "Just the taxes on a pack of cigarettes in New York City with federal, state, and local taxes is $6.46. That's just the taxes. The rest of the cost is determined by the brand, et cetera. Okay, now, Chicago has the second highest tax rate at $5.67 per pack, which will go up another dollar, and—" She kept looking. "Can't find Boston, but the Massachusetts state tax per pack is $2.51."

"What's Virginia?"

"Ummm, thirty cents. Which makes sense. Let me look at another tobacco state here. Kentucky, sixty cents. North Carolina, forty-five cents. South Carolina, fifty-seven cents, uh, Georgia, thirty-seven cents and Tennessee, sixty-two cents. Those are the to-bacco states."

"Connecticut." Gray finished his drink.

"Three dollars and forty cents." She raised her eyebrows. "It's not really a tobacco state. I mean it grows cigar wrapper leaf, but that's not the same."

"Right." He rubbed his chin. "Those are today's taxes. As this depression we're in deepens, some states will raise what they call 'sin taxes.' Never works."

She turned off the computer, returning to the cozier chair opposite Gray. "Exactly." He looked at her puzzled, so she continued, "Contraband. The murders are in the states with superhigh taxes. It's no different than moonshine. Bring in a high-tax product and sell it with no taxes—people will snap it up. I'll bet there are studies on lost revenue because taxes have climbed too high."

Gray, as a CPA, chuckled in appreciation. "A good accountant can help the state or the nation figure that out, but I promise you the state or the federal government isn't going to make those statistics readily available."

"Why the hell not?"

"Because then they'd have to admit their programs aren't working."

"But that's so stupid," she blurted out. "If you're losing revenue, why not fix the problem?"

"Honey, I ran campaign finances, remember? There are people whose entire purpose in life is to vilify a candidate. They have got to find something wrong. Why give them the ammunition? My job was secure. No elected official's job truly is, and it's when they think they're invulnerable that they blow it. Look at George Allen. He became a little overconfident in 2006."

"George." She grimaced for a moment. "One of the most likable fellows I've ever met. More to the right than myself, but you know all that's bull, too. You throw red meat to the nutcases in your party, and both parties have them. It's always a mistake to cater to extremists."

"True," said Gray. "And then later people simply can't admit they're wrong."

A long pause followed this. "You did. You divorced your first wife."

He threw back his head and laughed. "Touché."

She laughed, too. "And am I ever glad you did."

"Yeah, well, so am I." He smiled at her, loving how the light shone on her silver hair. "I'm trying to think of any politician who has admitted he's been on the wrong track."

"You'd be thinking for a long time." She then asked, "So what do you think about my idea?"

"Tell me your idea again."

"Did you not listen to me?"

"I did, honey, I did, but I may be missing something."

"Maybe these murders are about contraband cigarettes brought in and not taxed."

"Ah. So someone could steal cartons from a warehouse or even a store here and carry them up north?"

"Why take that risk?" she said, puzzling it out. "Why not make a pact with growers who hold back some tobacco for you? I mean if people can make moonshine, why can't they cure tobacco and make cigarettes, or shred the tobacco so people can roll their own? That's a lot safer."

Gray studied the woman he loved for a time. "Janie, did anyone ever tell you you could have made a good criminal?"

Upstairs, another good criminal knocked over Sister's silver tray with a brush, comb, and small perfume bottle on it that had been given to her by her mother. Golly evidenced no interest in perfume, she wanted to nestle in the alpaca sweater her human had put on the bureau instead of in it.

Sister had been in a hurry when she left the sweater there, which she would regret. In kneading the sweater, for Golly loved the cool feeling of the alpaca wool that then turned warm, the cat tore a big hole.

Later, when they went to bed, Sister spotted the damage and saw red. She likely would have stayed mad, too, if Gray hadn't reminded her that it was mating season. He never failed to make her laugh.

C H A P T E R   2 1

Sister and Shaker walked fifteen couple of hounds, thirty hounds single, on foot. Hunting hounds are counted in couples, a practice dating back to ancient Egypt. Sometimes after a rousing hunt, huntsman and master would walk out those hounds that had not hunted the day before, as well as a few who had. Mostly, the hunted hounds relaxed while the others enjoyed some exercise.

Pookah and Pansy had hunted, but their youth invited a bit more instruction from their trainers. Hounds being pack animals, as are humans, need to learn to work together. Veteran hounds, Dragon, Diana, and Diddy also walked out to give the youngsters some ballast.

It was 31°F under clear skies at nine in the morning on February 8 as they headed for Hangman's Ridge.

Sister liked long walks. She felt they worked out the kinks. Also, walking didn't pound her feet as did running, although she and Shaker would trot with the pack in bursts. Fearing old age was not in her nature, fearing laziness was.

Dragon led, Diddy's nose on his flanks.

"*If I'd been out yesterday, we would have brought down that coyote,*" said Dragon.

"*Right.*" Diddy agreed, although she didn't believe him.

"*He could run,*" Pansy exclaimed. They hadn't been there, how could they be so confident?

"*I'm faster than any ugly coyote.*" Dragon puffed out his chest.

Raleigh chortled. "*Dragon, you're a conceited ass. I'm faster than you are.*"

The house dogs accompanied the pack walks, serving as canine whippers-in. Hounds knew the Doberman and harrier would enforce the huntsman's commands.

"*If I didn't have to walk with everyone, I'd take you down,*" the well-built American hound threatened. Dragon followed that with a low growl.

"*You and what army?*" Raleigh laughed, as did Rooster on the other side of the pack.

"*Shut up, you miniature foxhound,*" Dragon snarled at Rooster.

Medium-sized, Rooster did appear to be a smaller version of the foxhound, but then most scent hounds bore some resemblance to one another, even a beagle, an especially engaging animal.

"That's enough." Shaker quietly reprimanded Dragon, who shut up.

The hounds behind Dragon wished the huntsman would have smacked the braggart hound with the butt of his crop, but Shaker rarely struck a hound, and he wouldn't do so for chatter. Dragon would push in front of other hounds, most of whom ignored him. Sooner or later a young, strong male would gain enough confidence to challenge him. The fight would no doubt be ugly.

The slippery and steep climb to the top of Hangman's Ridge had everyone puffing. Minks, on their hind legs to observe the humans and hounds, scurried into their dens.

"All these minks. Years ago there wasn't a one," Shaker noted.

"There were always a lot at Pattypan Forge," Sister recalled. "Small though they are, they can be ferocious. They're weasels."

"Apart from dinosaurs, I reckon we have just about everything in our territory."

"Give it a few years. The elk released in the reclaimed mining lands in southwest Virginia will be here, too." Sister swept her eyes over the long flat ridge, the hangman's tree moaning in the breeze. Up here, there was always a slight wind, even on a calm day.

"Repent," a ghost whispered, but only the hounds and dogs could hear.

"Don't they know there are spirits up here?" Twist shivered.

"I think they can feel them," Rooster answered the youngster. *"They deny it."*

The tricolor, Twist, was surprised. *"Why?"*

"Quirk of the species." The harrier stuck with the humans, covering the large expanse of ground.

"Coyote tracks," Shaker called out. "Fresh. Not from yesterday."

Sister walked over and took a look. "Very fresh." She put her gloved hands on her hips. "The coyotes are using this as a crossover. Pop over Hangman's Ridge and hit up Foxglove or us. At least they can't get into the feeder boxes. We've got plenty of fox tracks by the feeder boxes, which is a good thing."

"No, but they can stick their paw in and pull out food." Shaker pulled his scarf tighter around his neck. "It's always colder up here. I've read too many horror books. Spirits. Makes it colder."

"Well, who knows what's in this world that we can't see?" asked Sister. "But we sure can see coyote tracks. Shaker, if there's one, there's a family and probably a couple of families."

"Yep." He took a deep breath. "The air's good though, isn't it?"

"'Tis."

"I wouldn't be surprised if the coyote found Carter Weems first. Didn't Gray say there wasn't much left of the doe?"

"Meat gone. Then the carcass collapsed. But if the coyotes ate the deer, you'd think they would have pulled out the second corpse."

"I don't know." Shaker headed toward the path down. "It's funny. You don't think about stuff like that. Something happens and I try to come up with answers based on what I know. As to why he was killed, I'm not going to figure that out."

Moving to the other side of the pack, Sister stated, "Doubt I will either. You know, Shaker, I have this feeling more's to come or something. I don't know why. It's probably this place giving me the willies. God knows, there are, what, eighteen unquiet souls up here?"

"You really believe in ghosts?" he asked.

She thought about this, then said, "Of course, no one can prove an afterlife, but throughout history so many inexplicable events have happened. What about the apparition of Joan of Arc to the French soldiers in the trenches of World War One? Thousands saw her and described her the same. Was that her spirit? Was it some mass delusion? Sometimes when I come up here to check for tracks or to see if there's a new fox den, I could swear I hear whispers from that tree. I'm just suggestible, perhaps."

"I don't want to hear them," said Shaker.

"Who does?" Raleigh sensibly said.

Shaker, unusual for him, murmured to Sister. "Are you afraid to die?"

Without hesitation, she replied, "No. I'm more afraid of not living, I mean really living: full gallop, devil take the hindmost."

He laughed. "You have nothing to fear."

"Want to hear something really silly?" She patted the left side of her chest. "I stick that cigarette case from World War One over my heart when I can. Makes me feel good."

He brightened. "Well, if you believe in spirits, then each man who signed that old cigarette case and the officer to whom it was presented, they're all watching over you."

Back at the kennels, each hound eagerly received a treat as his or her name was called, then the happy animal walked into its particular run.

Raleigh and Rooster needed a treat, too. After all, they whipped-in.

Raleigh dropped his treat upon hearing a vehicle. *"Stranger."*

Rooster considered stealing it, but then thought, *"Perhaps not."*

Hearing the vehicle later than the dogs, Sister glanced out the kennel office window. "Shaker, Tariq Al McMillan is here."

He looked up from checking Thimble's paw. "Did he drive up to the house?"

"Did. Let me get on up there. All's well here."

It was in the kennel, it wasn't at the house.

Sister trotted up there as Tariq turned back to his car after knocking on the door, Golly bitching and moaning inside about the noise.

"Tariq! Hold up," she called to him as though he were a hound.

"Sister." He smiled. "Forgive me for coming here unannounced."

She opened the back door and took his coat, hanging it up on a peg as well as her own. "Please come in. I can offer you all manner of libation."

The dogs checked him out as he gingerly stepped inside while Golly turned her back on the kitchen counter. Her morning beauty rest had been disturbed.

"I don't want to put you to trouble and I should have called or emailed," said Tariq.

"Sit down. You look a little peaked."

"Beg pardon?"

She motioned to a chair. "You look a bit pale. Peaked. How about if I make you some coffee, tea? It's early in the morning, but I can rope coffee with the best of them."

Tariq again looked puzzled. "Rope coffee?"

"An old Southern expression for when people lace their morning coffee with whiskey, bourbon, or scotch. God knows, you can't use gin or vodka for that."

"People really do that?" He sat down, amazed.

"Every day. I don't, but I rarely drink. I actually like the taste, but I never saw that it did me or anyone else much good." She paused. "How stupid of me. Tariq, if you're Muslim, please forgive me."

He smiled at her. "I'm not. I'm Coptic Christian."

She put up the pot of water for tea, placed bone china before him, and quietly remarked, "Egypt can hold an election each year. It can bounce between the Muslim Brotherhood and the former regime, but you'll always lose, right?"

He appreciated her insight. "To a greater or lesser degree. It's not easy being a Christian in Egypt."

She put out various sugars and honeys. "It's not easy being a Christian here either, but for vastly different reasons. Have you ever considered what a difficult religion it is to practice?"

He nodded. "That I have."

"What can I do for you?" She sat down, waiting for the water to boil.

"I suppose you read about the attack on me by Congressman Dave Rickman, where he accuses me of being a member of the Muslim Brotherhood, stating he will protect America from the likes of me."

"I did," said Sister, concerned. "There's no trouble at Custis Hall, is there?"

"No, though I must go up to the embassy in Washington."

She rose to pour the tea. "Why?"

"Well, for one I'll need their help if Rickman keeps this up. He's made more recent statements about municipalities refusing to allow permits for mosques."

"It appears he has found his issue."

"Yes." Tariq gratefully accepted the tea. She put out cookies, too.

"It's a cheap shot," Sister forthrightly declared as she sat down.

"I still must present myself at the embassy because I have been personally named. I received a call yesterday from our vice-ambassador. My father knows I have a good relationship with the embassy and the New York consulate. I hope they will help me."

"Is there a possibility they won't?"

"Yes."

"But why?"

"I am a citizen of Egypt. I'm here on a work permit. The government doesn't wish any embarrassment. There are enough"—he paused—"sensitive areas with your government."

"I see. You could be recalled?"

"I don't work for Egypt's government. They can't recall me, but your government can cancel my work permit and deport me. The reason I have come to see you is that I have been promised help. Help that, uh, insults you."

At this, Sister's eyes opened wide. "What do I have to do with the Muslim Brotherhood?"

He smiled at that response for a moment. "Crawford Howard buys up elected officials like, what do you call them, ah, jelly beans?"

Sister was getting the picture. "Yes, he does. He is a shrewd man and he pulls many strings."

"I sought his help. He knows Congressman Rickman and he promised to neutralize him—I don't know if that's the right word, but he promised to get him off my back. In exchange for which, I must hunt with him and not you."

"You have no choice." She instantly replied, knowing she had said the same thing to the DuCharmes.

"I am deeply embarrassed."

"Don't give it a second thought. Your Middle Eastern studies course at Custis Hall is so important. Young people—well, old people, too—need to learn about this misunderstood part of the world. All we ever hear are the bad things."

"There are many bad things and many good people. One of the reasons I came to America was to learn about religious tolerance."

She exhaled through her nose. "This may not be the ideal time to learn it here."

"It is so much better than in my country or other places. I love history, I study it all the time. Whenever a person or a group comes to power with the idea of cleansing the human race, not only is there failure and bloodshed, there is long-term economic suffering."

"More unrest."

"And bloodshed. I suppose bloodshed can be justified if it ultimately brings stability and a modicum of freedom. I'm thinking about the two world wars. We aren't short of examples."

"No. But then I think of the Inquisition."

He nodded. "We can justify anything, but I'm not sure that the Inquisition brought long-term economic damage. Now, Edward the First running the Jews out of England? Long-term damage."

"You do read your history." She noticed a soft pack of cigarettes in his shirt pocket. "I didn't know you smoked."

"I don't at school. The girls are ferocious about not smoking, but I'll smoke off campus. Most Egyptian men smoke. It's considered effeminate not to do so."

"Used to be that way here until the twenties when women smoked as a badge of liberation."

"Odd." He leaned back in the chair, glad to be able to speak with her. "It's somewhat the same in my country. It's considered improper for a woman to smoke, especially if she's from the lower classes. But educated women, rich women, they do it. Perhaps not in public, but they do it and it is considered daring, rebellious."

"Maybe because it's easy to take out a little stick and light it up as a form of protest. I suppose it is a badge of bravery despite the harm it ultimately does." She finished her tea. "More?"

"Oh, no thank you. I am grateful for your understanding and I don't look forward to hunting with Crawford. I think only his wife, Sam's brother, and possibly one or two other people do so."

"Yes. He's a generous man, but a weak one. No matter how smart he is, how rich, he's weak. He wastes a lot of time and money propping up his ego and it's a full-time job for his wife. However, if he promised to, Crawford will put the screws to Congressman Rickman. He'll enjoy that."

Tariq changed the subject. "I did not expect you to be a student of tobacco."

"Virginia, it's a tobacco state. But when I found that gentleman, Adolfo Galdos, murdered in New York City, the tobacco shop owner, I became intrigued. Since then, there have been more murders."

"Yes, I read about that."

"And each murder occurred in an area where cigarettes are highly taxed. As you know, Illinois raised its tax another dollar—and that's where the last murder took place. I have to believe there is a connection." She threw up her hands. "Not that I can or would do anything about it. Who is going to listen to a Virginia country-woman?"

"I am." He smiled. "Thank you again."

As she walked him into the mudroom where he put on his coat, she asked, "Please don't take any Custis Hall girls hunting with Crawford."

"I will not," he promised. "Also, I don't think their coach would allow it. You mentioned that Crawford will put the screws to Rickman. He's also putting them to you."

She nodded slightly. "He is, but Tariq, never underestimate a foxhunter, a real old-time foxhunter."

CHAPTER 22

The huge waterwheel at Mill Ruins gently slapped the stream that ran strong in the deep mill race, ice at its edges. As the hounds cast behind the mills, Sister and the field waited by the impressive structure built in the late eighteenth century. Generations of Virginians had driven their wagons to the mill, left their grain behind only to return later. Though no longer in use, the waterwheel still demonstrated to visitors how much could be accomplished without electricity. Hunting here at Mill Ruins had inspired Cindy Chandler to build her own much smaller waterwheel.

Filling up the field were Cindy, Gray, Donny Sweigart, Kasmir, his best friend High Vajay, Ronnie, Xavier, the regular hardcore hunters, of course, along with the Saturday folks. Sister counted twenty-three in First Flight. Bobby shepherded a bit more than thirty in his.

The chill settled into their bones as they waited by the water. Walter Lungrun—on Clemson, his most reliable horse—was glad he could help out this Saturday by having the Jefferson Hunt at Mill

Ruins. It was to have been at Mousehold Heath. Although established in 1807, Mousehold Heath was a new fixture owned by a nice young couple, the Jardines.

Unfortunately, a sinkhole opened up in the Jardines' driveway, followed by more caving in. Jim and Lisa frantically called Sister at eight on Friday night. She drove over. She stood on one side of the hole, the Jardines on the other. It was too late in the evening for road work from a paving firm. She called Kasmir on her cell, as he was always repairing, building, doing something handy. By ten that night, Kasmir and a few of his men brought over two dump trucks filled with riprap. Afterward, the Jardines' drive was still relatively impassible, although Jim could jolt over with his old Land Rover. Kasmir would finish up on Monday, and then the Jardines could call a paver to cover it up, smooth it over.

Lucky for all, Walter stepped in with Mill Ruins. On every Jefferson Hunt fixture card, the club member had been directed to go to Mousehold Heath. A last-minute change meant everyone would need to be notified. The hunt club secretary, Adelaide Merriman, sent emails. However, a few members did not get Adelaide's emails, so Walter and Sister divided up the names and called to make sure everyone got the message.

Being a master meant one handled events both on and off the field. Most clubs did their best to help landowners, too, and Kasmir actually would have been upset if Sister hadn't called him to help out the Jardines. This was one of many reasons why Sister loved her people and why she loved being a master. She liked to solve problems.

Next to High, the Bancrofts and Kasmir watched the water spray off the wheel. As the sun hid behind clouds, it looked like diamonds instead of rainbows.

Damn, I hope they hit soon. Sister thought.

Asa must have read her mind. The old hound walked out from

behind the mill, a few other old fogies with him. Coming out on the farm road to the back acres, he lifted his head, deeply inhaling. He put his nose to ground, sounded out with his basso profundo voice, and they were off!

As Sister crossed the wooden bridge, hoofbeats reverberating, she patted herself on the back for not retiring Asa.

The light gray clouds hung low. To the west, the sky darkened. Although sloppy, the footing wasn't too bad, as Walter kept most of his roads in sterling condition, regularly bringing in loads of crusher run. Alongside, white-streaked fields showed all the snow had not yet melted.

Five minutes beyond the bridge, the brisk trot turned to a gallop. Staying together, the pack ran parallel to the road in an open field. Betty kept up with them. Sybil did, too, but once she reached the end of the northern meadow, she jumped into a woods out of sight. The pasture on the right continued on. Hounds stuck to the line on the larger right pasture. They easily jumped its stone fence, which had been laid in 1780. These days a stone fence costs a bundle. In 1780, it was one way to clear the fields—but once laid, those stones held forever. If a few became dislodged, you put them back up. Nothing compared with them.

Sister's six-year-old Thoroughbred, Aztec, a handy 15.3H, popped over the fence. He'd started the day fussy but settled in with the run. Like most Thoroughbreds, standing around bored him. And like most Thoroughbreds, he saw no reason to keep his opinion to himself.

Bisected by the farm road, the hounds split. One group veered toward Sybil while the larger group stayed straight on. Both groups picked up speed. Sister stuck with the larger goup.

Shaker blew them on, but right now the hunt was in the hands of the whippers-in. Sybil needed to send the splinter group back to the main group. The problem was both groups were running hard on hot scent. They'd come upon two foxes. As it was mating season—the time of the best runs, usually—a huntsman wanted to keep his hounds on the dog fox.

However, you had to see the fox tracks together, before guessing who was who. The male's prints were usually slightly larger.

Sybil was deep in heavy conifers and hardwoods. She rode to cry, as it was difficult to see. Betty, still out in the open, moved closer to the main pack, based on cry as well. Her job now was to keep the main pack together. If they shot out toward her, she'd stay right with them.

By definition, a whipper-in is either sitting still, freezing their butt, or running for Jesus.

With the small splinter group of hounds, Tootsie heard Shaker blowing them back.

"*What do I do?*" The young hound worried. "*This scent is scorching.*"

Trinity—one year older, with the same bloodline—advised, "*Keep on. How do we know the others won't lose their line?*"

"*But aren't we supposed to obey the huntsman no matter what?*" asked Tootsie.

"*Listen, kid, if they lose that line, that whole bunch will come over here, as will Shaker.*" Trinity laughed. "*We will have saved the day. He'll take credit for it.*" Trinity laughed again.

Steady on with the main group, Asa felt a shift in the wind, then he sniffed in a kaleidoscope of scent. The pack had come up on a crossroads, a meeting spot for deer, fox, and bear. They had all been here recently. The dogs stopped for a moment to tease out the fox scent line.

DeDe, a young hound from the "D" line, circled the crossroads. "*I don't know what I have.*" He inhaled another snoutful.

Asa hurried over. "*That's the scent of boar. Ignore it, and pray we don't run into the damned pig.*"

"Over here." Diana called, and once again they were running their fox.

The path through the rightward woods opened onto a high meadow. Here, an old three-board fence sagged in parts. Some boards were missing, but the coops held up.

Sister and First Flight jumped in, while Bobby looked for a low place to step over.

The hounds moved along more deliberately than before, but they stuck to it, even while Sister and the two fields of hunters could hear the splinter pack of hounds just screaming.

"Should we go to them?" DeDe asked.

"No, we should not," Asa firmly replied.

Sybil, riding next to those hounds, was having one of the best hunts of her life. The red fox burst out in front of her, crossed a narrow path in the woods, then crossed back up ahead. Fox, hounds, and Sybil found themselves out on that same high meadow as the main group but a good half mile farther down.

All of a sudden, the sky filled with crows flying low over Sybil's fox. The crow called St. Just hated foxes. He led the squadron of birds, but the fox easily evaded them, dropping into the sunken farm road. Crossing the old rutted mess, the red fox shot out on the other side of the road, circled partway and then, at last, took refuge in an old shed.

Within five minutes, the fox hunted by the main pack also ran into the shed.

Fortune smiled on Jefferson Hunt this day. If the foxes had not come back together, who knows when or how the pack would have been reunited?

Riding up to the shed door, Shaker saw it was locked.

Walter dismounted, and pulled a heavy key ring from his pocket. He tried the key that was to fit this lock. Didn't work.

"This isn't my lock," Walter said to Shaker.

"It's okay," said Shaker. "I don't need to get in there. I'll blow 'Gone to Ground' out here."

Walter swung back up on Clemson, riding over to Sister as Shaker blew the magic notes.

Once done, Walter said, "Sister, something's wrong here. I'm going back, and I'll take someone with me if you don't mind. I need to cut the lock."

"Fine. Take Gray." She turned, calling to her boyfriend. When Gray heard the request, he rode back with Walter.

Shaker smiled at Sybil, picked up the hounds and the two whippers-in, and the pack walked down the rutted road to the creek. Whenever there's a mill, there's water for miles—certainly more than enough to satisfy a pack of thirsty hounds.

Walter and Gray reached the stables in twenty-five minutes. They untacked their horses, wiped them down, threw down some hay, and hung up fresh water buckets.

"You've got bolt cutters?" Gray asked.

"Yeah, I do."

Once equipped, the two men piled into Walter's Jeep, drove out the main drive to head west toward town. Close to a mile down the state road, they came to the bumpy farm road at the edge of Walter's land. Bouncing and sliding back to the shed, they reached it without too many head bruises. A seat belt could only do so much.

Walter was large and powerful like Sister's Big Ray had been. He easily snapped the hardened lock throat. He swung it around, dropped it out of the lock slot to open the door.

The two men stepped inside the cavernous space.

At the end, two large den openings announced good living for foxes.

Gray lifted his head and inhaled much as the hound Asa had done at the beginning of the day's hunt. "Tobacco," he declared.

Sniffing, Walter shrugged. "Yeah, but why?"

Gray looked down to where it appeared boxes had been stacked. A few little squiggles of shredded tobacco dotted the floor. He knelt down, took off his gloves, and pinched the slivers between his thumb and forefinger. He stood up, dropping the meager find into Walter's hand.

Walter smelled it, then held it under Gray's nose.

"It's pretty good tobacco." Gray shrugged as he faced the physician.

About twenty years apart in age, the two fit men stood in the large space, pondering the possibilities when a vixen carefully peeped out of her den.

Neither man noticed, so she remained still to better study this oddly built species. Why they all didn't fall flat on their faces she didn't know.

Walter again smelled the tobacco. "I don't get it."

"Contraband," said Gray. "Sister's been doing research since that fellow was murdered in Manhattan. There are millions of dollars to be made—that *are being* made—on contraband tobacco. Smuggling cigarettes into states with high cigarette taxes appears to be a profitable black market."

"Jesus Christ." Walter whistled. "Why the hell are they using my shed?"

Gray replied, "For one thing, it's far out here and you don't use it. The road testifies to that. As to how long they've been using it, who knows? But I would figure the tobacco is prepared in one location, rolled, packed, brought here. When a seller needs more, I guess it's shipped to them. They are likely finished here or we'd find more evidence: shredded leaf or empty packs, stuff like that."

Walter scraped the concrete floor with the toe of his boot. "Keeps the moisture out."

"Right. This is a good place to stash goods."

Walter dropped the shards of tobacco into his pocket. "Well, it's someone who knows the territory."

"I'm thinking it's someone who hunts," said Gray.

"This isn't a poacher," said Walter. "Like what happened on your place—that could have been the work of poachers. I don't have poachers."

"Actually, Walter, I was thinking this is the work of someone who foxhunts."

CHAPTER 23

"Are you sure?"

"Of course I'm sure," Donny growled at Art, sitting behind the wheel of his truck.

"But you said you all moved off."

"We did," said Donny, shifting in the passenger seat. "We got on another fox, but Walter and Gray rode back to the house. I know they came back to the shed. I told you this."

"I'm not stupid!" snapped Art. "But I want to make sure. That big shed is perfect. You didn't see anyone there."

"No, and I couldn't very well ride back there by myself and make sure, could I? Come on, Art, think. I also couldn't ask Walter and Gray what they were up to. We'd better find another place."

Art, sitting inside his truck, Donny in the passenger seat, fiddled with the vehicle's radio, tuning in a twangy song about bad luck. "I hope the boss doesn't find out," he said.

They talked in Art's truck, motor running, at Roger's Corner. People often bought fried chicken, potato salad, and brought it back to their vehicle to eat. There was no place to sit at the convenience store. Donny's half-ton 1992 Ford F-150 van was next to Art's Topkick.

Donny reached over to turn down the country-and-western station. "Listen to me. Shut up. If he finds out anything, it will be because Walter and Gray talked. Then we can say we didn't want to bother him about it, he's got a lot on his mind. Listen to me, Art. Don't turn up the goddamned radio station! Shut up. Act normal. We need to find another place to store the cigarettes until it's time to ship them. Let me think."

"Kasmir Barbhaiya has so much property he doesn't know what to do with it, and it's close. Or there's Tattenhall Station."

Donny stroked his chin. "Tattenhall Station is vulnerable."

Art was getting surly. "Why?"

"Too many people drive by," said Donny. "It's a crossroads and the railroad tracks slow them down. If we're seen there too many times, it might tip off someone. Also, sometimes Jefferson Hunt is allowed inside."

"Walter and Gray don't know what's going on. They'll forget this in time."

"I hope so. We have a couple of choices. We can rent a large storage unit. People come and go in those places all the time. The problem is that tobacco in such large quantities even though boxed throws off a strong odor."

"Where else could we put it?"

"We could buy up some rolls of insulation. It's light, easy to lift. The main barn at Old Paradise is in good shape. Maybe Margaret goes in there, but I doubt it. Alfred doesn't bother it either. That road's so-so. It's passable. Better than the road to Walter's shed. Also, people expect you to be on the property."

Art shrugged. "Yeah."

"So we put the cigarettes there in the barn after we pick them up down in Russell County. Put them up in the hayloft and place rolls of insulation around them, or heavy canvas. Crawford's promised to pump money into your parents' farm so it will look as though you've started work on the barns—especially if you leave a few rolls of insulation still wrapped up inside in the center aisle. That should work, at least until we find a better place."

Art squinted, placing his hands on the steering wheel. "I can bring in some two-by-fours. Might work. We'd only be in and out about every two weeks. I don't know. Let me think about it."

"People think you're making 'shine. Your family won't look too closely. They'd rather not know. And it is your property."

"Not as long as Mom, Dad, Alfred and Margaret are alive."

"You know what I mean. Once Crawford writes those checks to your folks, we'll have to look elsewhere because your father will get workers to put up fencing out there pronto."

"Can't do that until spring." Art relaxed his grip on the wheel. "Sounds like a plan." He took a deep breath. "I just don't want any trouble with the boss. The money's good. He can be touchy. I think about Carter, you know."

"Mmm. Bullet lodged in the back of his rib cage. They think he was shot through the heart."

"When did you hear that?" asked Art, agitated again.

"Today's paper. Report from the medical examiner's office."

"You think the boss had him killed?" Art's throat tightened.

"What I think is that Carter shot his mouth off to the wrong person. Might not have been the boss. How do we know he didn't trash-talk some of the guys down in Russell County? That's a hard bunch."

"Mmm." Art rolled his tongue over his front teeth. "They might be a hard bunch, but I don't think they followed Carter all the way to Albemarle County to shoot him."

"Maybe not." Donny took his point.

"The boss is playing for much higher stakes than we are."

Donny sighed. "You're right. All I want is enough money to buy a good engagement ring and put some aside. I'd like to start my own business someday."

"You? I never thought of you running a business."

"People fool you."

Art half smiled. "They do. Look, I don't want to wind up like Carter Weems. We've done a good job. It's just bad luck that Walter and Gray got into the shed."

"Foxes got there first," said Donny.

"Think Walter will call Ben Sidell?"

"I don't know. None of his property was harmed."

"Nothing we can do but wait it out." Art frowned.

"And buy insulation and two-by-fours," added Donny.

Gray hadn't wanted to tell Sister about the shed at Walter's breakfast. He waited until later. She listened with great interest.

"We're one step closer," said Sister. "Though to what I couldn't say."

"I'm not sure I want to know," said Gray. "It isn't our affair. And we don't know for sure that tobacco contraband is stored there."

"Why else would tobacco be in Walter's shed? It's a tight shed, too, even though it looks like hell." A thump upstairs drew her attention. "I am going to catch that cat at her mischief. She's put a hole in my alpaca sweater, torn up every piece of paper she can find. This cat needs a serious talking-to."

As Sister climbed the stairs, Raleigh and Rooster lifted their heads from their paws, then put them back down again. So many times they'd been blamed for the devious cat's depredations. This time, she would be caught red-handed.

Gray turned on the television, but before he could settle down,

Sister came back down the stairs with a black hair dryer, long nosed, in her hand. Golly had knocked it on the floor. Now it didn't work, not even a tiny whir.

"Can anyone tell me why a cat wants a hair dryer?"

Gray started to laugh, then Sister did, too.

The dogs barked, hearing a car pull up outside.

"I'm home," Tootie called out a minute later, as she came into the kitchen.

Smiling, Sister leaned down and kissed Gray. "Everything happens at once."

CHAPTER 24

"Where were you yesterday?" Sister said over the phone to Ben Sidell. She'd called the sheriff to check in, and just maybe troll for information.

"Nonni threw a shoe," he said. "Couldn't get the blacksmith out late Friday. I hate to miss a Saturday hunt."

"I guess you heard what happened?"

"Heard it was a good hunt. Walter called me and told me about his shed."

"What do you think?" she asked, twisting the phone cord and looking out the kitchen window.

"What do you think?" He teased. "Used to store tobacco." He continued in a more serious vein. "I've already checked with the tobacco shop in Seminole Square, the one in Barracks Road and the one up Route 29 toward Ruckersville. I asked them why they don't sell contraband."

"That's an interesting question. One would think as an officer of the law, your question would be the reverse."

"For that, Sister, I would go into the shop with a deputy and a search warrant, but I don't think any of those folks are selling contraband."

"Why not?"

"For the very reasons they told me," said Ben. "Virginia has the lowest cigarette tax of all fifty states. There's a little profit to be made, but not enough to court the risk. They were all pretty straightforward about it."

"But the tobacconists know about some illegal activity of that sort?"

"How much they know is up for question. I called the biggest shop down in Richmond; that owner estimated the black market profit is in the millions."

"Crime does pay," Sister mused.

"It does, sometimes even when you get caught," said the sheriff. "With that kind of money, a man can buy the best lawyers there are. Maybe he serves a short term in a minimum security prison. More than likely the fellow pays a fine, which seems huge to us but is a pittance compared to what he's hidden away, usually out of the country."

"I won't repeat your answer to this, but these kinds of crimes—selling illegal tobacco or moonshine—do they really hurt the state?"

"No. They hurt the corporations that abide by the law, especially the smaller ones. Those entities are so huge, often international, they can afford to abide by the law. It's the smaller companies or the start-ups that get squelched, as they often lack the funds to comply with the latest regulation. It's hard for us in central Virginia, for instance, to think of moonshine as a small business, but it is. The larger profits from moonshining are due to no taxes, but who does that hurt? Well, our wonderful delegates in Richmond tell us this hurts the state because of reduced revenue. If they'd get out of people's way maybe they'd be motivated to create revenue by other means and I wouldn't be risking my men, blowing the county's money on wild goose chases."

She appreciated that he was direct with her and she genuinely liked the man. "Where would you rather put your energy?"

"Sister, I want to bust every child molester in this county. What I'd really like to do is kill them, but I can't do that. I'd like to reduce personal abuse, much of it directed toward women, children, and animals. And given the time, I would love to focus our department on fraud, especially at the corporate level."

"Banks?"

"Banks, yes, plus, there are a few companies we've kept our eye on. We can't catch them, but I'm convinced they are cooking the books. I just don't have enough people on the force. And you'd be surprised at how much theft goes on inside a bank. When the person is caught they are usually released. It is not reported as a crime because it will shake client confidence. I want to nail 'em. Also, there's plenty of white-collar crime right here in Albemarle. You don't have to go to New York City to find it. And they're a lot smarter, way smarter than the people who commit crimes of impulse."

"Ben, if you do catch them, they'll get off with a slap on the wrist, right?"

"Every now and then justice really is served, but it is frustrating for me and the team. I've got good people in this department. They put up with a lot and they aren't exactly well paid."

"Why do you do it?"

"Because I really believe in law enforcement. If we are equal before the law then we have a stable and fair society. People can deal with pain better than injustice. I believe that."

"But you must pursue this contraband case, right?" asked Sister. "Well, I guess it's not a case yet."

"I think it is," said Ben, surprising her.

"You do?"

Ben trusted his master. "I'm pretty sure Carter Weems was part of it. We checked out his past convictions, all of them in North Carolina. Transporting illegal liquor, transporting tobacco up north. He got off over and over with a decent lawyer, and I know he couldn't afford the lawyer. How could he? He blew his money. But whoever he worked for helped him out, and I expect his contacts were wide. If Weems hadn't been a drunk, he could have been a real player."

"Networking." Sister laughed.

"Works in every business," Ben said.

"I'm so glad I talked to you," said Sister. "You make me think."

"Back at you. You know this county better than I do. You know all the skeletons in those closets."

"Some, but when I think about it, they are all skeletons of personal pain, the desire for social approval. For my generation, such events as a child out of wedlock, infidelity, or being homosexual oppressed people terribly." She laughed again. "Well, not everybody."

He laughed, too. "Hey, two fox dens in Walter's shed? Why?"

"It's not really two dens. It's two entrances and exits and there will likely be more outside. Foxes aren't the best architects in the animal kingdom, but they see the possibilities. For instance, when we draw down Broad Creek over at After All, have you ever noticed the den openings right above the creek, two or three feet above the water? They're dug right into the creek bed."

"I have," said Ben. "I always wondered what the foxes did when the water rose."

"That's a fire exit, sort of. If a fox is besieged, he or she can always go through one of the tunnels, come out and jump into the creek, which will wash away scent. Foxes adapt, not just to weather and food conditions, they adapt to the hounds. My hounds possess drive, so the foxes around here need to be resourceful. They adapt, and far more quickly than we do."

"You don't say?"

"You'd better believe it," answered Sister. "The fox isn't hampered by any belief system. He or she reads nature exactly as it is. And we are part of nature. I swear to you, Ben, they know us better than we know them."

"Perhaps if you're the hunted you have to."

She considered this. "Yes. That's why I think criminals in the upper ranks are often smarter than the rest of us."

"They certainly aren't hampered by morals." He waited a beat. "Actually, that's not quite true. In many cases, there really is honor among thieves. It's unreasoned violence that captures our attention. Maybe because if we admit it, we are all capable of it."

"True. Well, this has been a refreshing morning phone call. I am wide awake, alert, and ready for life." Sister loved a challenging talk, especially with someone she respected.

"That it is. Now I need a promise from you and it's not about foxhunting."

"Shoot."

"Don't go down to Walter's shed and don't go to where we found Carter's body."

"Umm. If you tell me where the speed gun is today, I won't."

Ben feigned shock. "As a public servant, I can't do that. I do know, however, that you suffer from lead foot, especially on Soldier Road."

"Ben, you'll make a Virginian yet." She laughed at this Ohio transplant. "I promise. Do you mind telling me why?"

"The perp or perps could go back. I'm less worried about the shed than that abandoned road at the Lorillards'. We've scoured both places thoroughly, but Weems' body lay a long time on that old road. The killer could have dropped or left behind some evidence, and it is driven down in the mud. Say you're that person, you put your hand in your jacket pocket you wore when you killed Carter. You discover a lighter or a trinket is missing. Even a match pack. But you can't look for it while the corpse is fresh. He may have gone back, but if he did lose something and he didn't find it, he'll be worried now."

"What about Gray and Sam?"

"I told them to steer clear, too. Our budget is so tight I can't spare anyone to watch it full time, but I sent Jake over there, to sit in that road out of the woods, oh, maybe once a week. It's a long shot."

"Ben, you have a lot on your mind."

"Everyone does." His voice was warm. "The people who coast in life are the ones I feel sorry for."

"Well, you and I will never need sympathy then."

After bidding him goodbye and hanging up the phone, she tossed on her old flight jacket and went outside to the kennels.

Shaker was in the boys' big run while Tootie was with the girls.

"Everyone okay?" Sister asked Shaker.

"Asa's a little sore. He's taken his canine Motrin." Shaker smiled, mentioning Rimadyl.

"This really is his last year, isn't it? Thought it was last year, but he's so tough and he keeps up." She opened the gate into the enormous run, dotted with large pines and oaks. "Asa, you've got some aches and pains. No hunting Tuesday and Thursday. I need you Saturday."

"I can go all day every day," he bragged.

She looked into his soulful brown eyes. "Saturday's tough territory." Then she said to Shaker, "I think a few of our 'P' and 'D' girls are due in season, maybe March."

"They are. A couple of 'T's,' too."

"Give them another year. I don't like to breed a hound until he or she has hunted two full years, as you know."

"Right."

"No hurry, but think about the 'D's' and 'P's' you've hunted over the years. I'll go back through the bloodlines. Way back. We should breed this fellow."

"All right. We should breed Dragon, too."

"No, his brother. Dragon is too much trouble." She knelt down to pet Asa, then stood up. "I'll go check our new kennelman," she said, meaning Tootie.

She walked around to the girls' yard, separated from the boys' yard by a twelve-foot-wide path, easy to mow in summer.

"What are you doing in here?" Sister smiled at Tootie.

"Cleaning up, getting to know everyone," said Tootie. She might be a college dropout, but she was far from lazy.

"I didn't expect you to come work in the kennels."

"I know, but I like it and I'll do as much as I can on the farm until I get a job. And even then, I'll still do chores in exchange for my rent."

"All right then. I'll leave you to it. I'll be in the barn."

As it was Betty's day to help in the barn, the two friends knocked the chores out in no time.

"Looked at the weather?" Betty asked.

"Did. Looks like it's going to stay cold with some snow on Saturday. We should still be able to hunt this Saturday." She closed a stall door. "Course, you never know."

"Well, we hunt Skidby on Tuesday, Little Dalby on Thursday, and Tattenhall Station on Saturday. I wish I knew Skidby better," Betty said of the newer fixture.

"Yeah, we lose it during deer season, and it takes years to really know a place. This will be our second year, but you know, that's hunting."

"I know," agreed Betty. "Mill Ruins turned into a good day."

"It's full of foxes over there. We can thank Peter Wheeler for that." The fixture's former owner, also a former lover of Sister's, was a bold rider who bred foxes because he loved them, then set them free.

"Walter's done a lot with that place, but it's so much for one person to keep up," said Betty. "That's one of the reasons his shed could get used." Betty had seen Walter ride off with Gray and assumed that a horse had thrown a shoe, taken a wrong step, or that Walter or Gray had injured themselves. Naturally she asked him about it at the breakfast. Walter probably shouldn't have told her or others what he'd seen, but he was furious about being locked out of his own shed and then discovering it had been used.

"Walter has a lot of land, and it costs a lot of money to hire help these days," Sister said, walking the center aisle, making a last-minute check of the barn.

Betty looked up as Tootie slipped in through the center aisle doors, closing them behind her. "Hey, girl."

Tootie hugged Betty. "I'm really home now. I'm going to live in central Virginia."

"Our gain," Betty said, refraining from asking about details.

Sister checked the big round clock over the tackroom door. Another big clock was in the tackroom. No master ever wants to be late for a hunt club function.

"Girls," Sister said. "Let's go on down to Roger's Corner. I need milk and I don't want to go into town."

"Are you buying milk for that worthless cat again?" Betty teased.

"She drinks half-and-half," said Sister.

"When I die, I want to come back as one of your cats," Betty joked.

"I'll go first." Sister smiled.

"Oh, come on. Your mother's family lives until they're national treasures." Betty brushed straw from her coat.

"Well, are you two coming along or not?" asked Sister. "Truck?"

"Sure." Betty strolled past Sister. "There's more room in the truck for my big butt."

Minutes later, the three of them cruised out to Soldier Road.

"Miss Franklin, I've been thinking about your printing press," said Tootie, from the backseat. "You've said people aren't printing up invitations like they used to, and business is bad."

"Tootie, sometimes they don't even properly print up wedding invitations. I find that shocking."

Sister kept her eyes on the road. "Well, Betty, if that's shocking, I've got some stories for you."

"Mostly from your past, Madam." Betty loved Sister and loved to torment her.

"Were you really bad?" Tootie leaned forward; her hands on the back of Betty's captain's chair.

"She was awful," said Betty. "She won't tell you, but I will."

Sister glanced in the rearview mirror. "Let us just say I did not walk on water, but there were others who were worse. At least I was discreet."

Tootie smiled, wondering what Sister and Betty really were like when they were young. "Want to hear my idea about your business?"

"Yes," said Betty. "It will greatly elevate the conversation."

Tootie leaned way forward into the space between the two front captain's chairs. "Everyone I know texts, Skypes, stuff like that. It's great, but it's not special. What if you allowed people to design their own cards and stationery?"

"Don't they do that on computers? They do." Betty responded, although intrigued.

"It never looks professional. The color is never saturated—I think that's the word graphics people use. What if people could come to you and really design cards? I know they can select paper colors, typefaces, stuff like that, but that's kind of cut-and-dried, too, isn't it? I mean, what if they want to use rice paper or paper of an odd size?"

"Well, I never thought about it, but guess it is pretty formulaic." Betty twisted in her seat to better look at Tootie.

"At Princeton, I'd go into the shops and a couple of times Val and I went into the Village. There are stores with really funny greeting cards, cards with like wheat stalks on them. Really original."

"A letter press. What you're talking about is a letter press."

"Do you have one?"

"We do. It's rarely used." Betty thought about this. "But yes, one can do some creative things."

"Maybe you could start by doing stuff yourself, getting it into shops, use the Internet to advertise. And make the ads funny."

"Tootie, you just might have something," said Betty, her enthusiasm growing.

"I think she does," said Sister. "This is such a conformist time; everything is mass-produced. Anything personal is just about revolutionary." She thought out loud. "Take a lot of work. Not just doing it, but getting stuff into stores."

"We can sell some online," said Betty. "You'd be surprised at how effective e-commerce can be, and Bobby and I haven't taken advantage of much. We don't really understand it and as Tootie has pointed out, we haven't been thinking in new ways."

"It's hard to think in new ways when your back is against the wall," Sister remarked.

"That's when you should take the biggest chances," said Tootie, who had taken the biggest one of her life to date.

As they thought, Sister kept her eyes on the road.

"Aha," Sister half shouted.

"What?" Betty couldn't see what was provoking the comment.

Sister pointed toward an SUV at a crossroads, parked to the

side. They were one mile from Roger's Corner on Soldier Road. The speed gun was handheld.

Betty looked at the speedometer. "You're okay."

"Ben told me someone would be out on Soldier Road."

"Did he now?" said Betty. "I wish I had that cozy a relationship with our sheriff."

"Well, I had to make him a promise that I wouldn't go to Walter's shed, nor where Carter Weems was found."

They turned into Roger's Corner. Betty said, "Janie, Ben wouldn't ask you that if he didn't think there was some danger."

"I know."

"What in the hell is going on?" Sister's old friend asked.

CHAPTER 25

February 13, Monday, promised light relief from the cold snap. At 6:00 AM the mercury was already touching 32°F.

Dressed in a handsome navy blue with chalk pinstripe suit, Gray kissed Sister on the cheek. "You know it's already bumper to bumper on Route 66 outside of D.C."

"Crazy. What time is your meeting?" Sister, like Gray, was already dressed for work.

"Eleven. Then lunch at the Press Club, which I truly enjoy." He sighed. "I'll be home Tuesday night."

"Here." She handed him a Tupperware container filled with pasta, just as he liked it. "In case you wind up working late."

"Thank you, sweetie. You make the best tortellini. Sure you're not part Italian?"

Gray tried to limit his time in Washington to one or two days a week. Although nominally retired, his old firm kept summoning him to solve sensitive problems with huge clients. Skilled at mathematical sleight of hand, accountants could bury profits, hiding them from other accountants' scrutiny. Gray, well paid for his brilliance, kept a small condominium in a high-rise near D.C.'s Kennedy Center. This way, if there were a performance at night he could attend, and as he had many good friends in D.C. his time spent there was convivial. What troubled him was the work, which just lately involved an uptick in campaign finance malfeasance on the part of clients. Given that it all was confidential, he kept these qualms to himself, but at times the weight of it bore down on him. What also bore down on him was the confusion of those campaign finance laws.

Never asking for details, Sister invariably knew when he needed a lift. She respected his loyalty to the firm and the confidentiality of many of his cases.

No sooner did Sister watch his car rumble down the drive than Tootie appeared in the kitchen with her laptop.

"Good morning," said Sister. "What will it be?"

"Sister, I can make my own breakfast."

"I know that, but I do a better job than you." Sister enjoyed taking care of someone young.

Tootie smelled the enticing aroma of fresh oatmeal. "Whatever's on the stove," she said.

Sister puttered around as Tootie devoured real oatmeal: steel cut oats, the kind that takes forty minutes to make. The dogs, bored that no bacon was frying, slept at her feet. At the window, Golly hungrily eyed the birds outside at the feeder. Every now and then, the big cat emitted a kitty cackle.

"Dream on, Golly," taunted Raleigh.

"You just wait until spring," mused Golly. *"It will be a feathery mass murder."* She sighed in contentment at the thought.

Sister sat back down with her second cup of coffee, black, her broken black hair dryer on the table before her.

Tootie stared at the hair dryer for a moment saying nothing. She returned to her oatmeal.

"I'm thinking about opening a hair salon," said Sister, patting her impressive head of hair.

Spoon poised midair above her oatmeal, Tootie asked, "With one hair dryer?"

Sister smiled. "It's broken. Circumstantial evidence suggests Golly had something to do with it."

"I didn't know Golly's fur needed styling."

"Thank you," Golly called from the window.

"The last two weeks she has been on a tear," said Sister. "She's a one-cat terrorist operation." Sister unscrewed the side of the handheld dryer, poked at the wires. "It's easier to buy a new one. I will lose my temper trying to fix this thing. If I put it on the front seat of the truck, I'll remember to get one and get the same brand. It was a good dryer."

"Did I ever tell you about the time my mother took me to the most expensive place in Chicago for cornrows?"

"You did not."

"The weight of it. All those beads."

"I bet you looked so pretty."

"I guess, but I don't want to spend my life doing my hair. All I have to do now is take a shower, dry off."

"You're lucky. Now may I ask why you brought your laptop to the kitchen? You can work in the den."

"I want to show you some handmade cards from a hand press in Washington. This lady is making money."

"Really?" Sister shoved the broken hair dryer to one side.

On the kitchen counter, a small TV had its sound turned low. After the weather report came local headlines. Tootie happened to look up and see a familiar face on screen.

"It's Mrs. Norton!"

Sister turned around and saw the headmistress of Custis Hall in front of a microphone, crowded by reporters. Sister turned up the sound.

"Custis Hall is not in the habit of hiring enemies of the United States," said Charlotte Norton. "We are not amused by these allegations."

A young female reporter, asked, "Will you take legal action?"

"First, we need an emergency board meeting, but if the board approves it, yes, we will." Charlotte Norton looked utterly displeased by the prospect.

The TV journalist turned back to the camera, and then the report played video of yet another allegation by Congressman Dave Rickman.

Standing in front of the national Capitol building in the cold, he warmed to his subject. "We have been attacked by terrorists. Just because this happened in 2001 doesn't mean we can let down our guard. They are here. They are undercover and I want a full investigation of Tariq Al McMillan of Custis Hall. I am convinced he is, shall I say, 'a person of interest.' "

"Why is that?" a male interviewer asked, tone flat.

"He is an Arab. They all hate us."

"Congressman Rickman, are you saying that all Muslims hate us?"

"Haven't they proven that?" Behind him, the top of the Capitol dome shone rosy as the sunlight just touched it. Rickman had perfectly staged this moment.

"Congressman Rickman, Mr. Al McMillan is a Coptic Christian," the interviewer stated.

The well-groomed Rickman paused, gathering his thoughts as it were. "I don't believe any Arab is a Christian. I will root out every enemy of this country. Every single one."

The station then cut to Tariq in his campus office, sitting at his beautiful new desk. Composed and handsome, he quietly countered the congressman's spurious allegations, also remarking that he had been in close contact with the Egyptian embassy and he sincerely hoped this would not be blown out of proportion.

"Is he out of his mind?" shouted Tootie. "That congressman?"

"No, Tootie, though Rickman appears to have studied a long-dead and very notorious senator from Wisconsin, a mean drunk who upended this country for a while, accusing everybody and his brother of being communists."

"How can he get away with this?" cried Tootie. "I took Mr. McMillan's class. He's a good teacher."

"You didn't call him Al McMillan?"

"He told us McMillan was fine. I learned so much in his class. Like I didn't know that places like Iran and Iraq were created after World War One. Or how the British divided up territory with no regard to the different peoples, and the big split between Sufi and Sunis. He's a really good teacher. He's not some terrorist."

"For some people, anyone with dark skin is suspect."

"But he's a Christian."

"Rickman isn't," said Sister, "though I bet he parks his sorry ass in a pew every Sunday with wife and children, and then makes sure we all know about it." Sister had witnessed enough hypocrisy in her life and was no longer shocked by it. If anything, it was amusing—until it hurt others.

"Can't we do something?" asked Tootie.

"I'm sure before the day is over I'll have both a call and an email about that emergency board meeting," said Sister. "All I can do at this point is to go to the meeting, if it's called. Apart from Tariq himself, accusations like this open the door for all manner of miseries inflicted upon schools. That Custis Hall is private and exclusive ups the ante. Rickman gets to kill two birds with one stone.

He looks like he's putting America's national security first, but it's also a sly attack on the so-called elites."

"Because they hired Tariq?"

"Because they experience more freedom than the state schools, even though they adhere to state regulations. What I have learned about education sitting on your alma mater's board has been eye-opening. You know, I don't know if I could teach today even at the college level. I don't think I could swallow the bullshit."

Tootie, rarely hearing Sister swear, just looked at her.

At seven-thirty that morning, Tariq phoned Crawford at home.

"Mr. Howard, did you see the news this morning?" The young professor's voice trembled.

"I did." By contrast, Crawford's voice was strong and confident.

A brief silence followed. "Do I no longer have your support?" asked Tariq.

"You will have my support when you show up in my hunt field."

CHAPTER 26

"How can we be sure?" asked Lucas Diamond, hands folded on the glossy long table. In an elegant room off the campus president's office, the eight board members gathered at the mahogany table, none looking happy to be there.

"Our procedures for hiring are rigorous." The head of personnel, Isadore Rosen, felt hot under the collar since he and the department were both under fire.

Setting aside ego, President Charlotte Norton stepped in. "Luke, the process takes time and starts with a curriculum vitae. Once we've sifted through that, we narrow the field down to usually four candidates whom we interview. But even before that, we call for references and of course, one's friends can be helpful."

For the sheer joy of tormenting him, Sister sat right next to Crawford at the table. Neither had spoken so far. With the exception of board members Lucas Diamond and Nancy Hightower, none of the others present took Congressman Rickman's charges against Tariq seriously.

Isadore took his cue from the headmistress.

He breathed deeply and calmed down before speaking. "We called the Egyptian attaché in New York City, an associate of our mayor. He knew Tariq's parents. The report was good so we pursued more conventional lines: former employers, one private school, and one small museum in London. Again, exemplary reports. Then we checked into those three people he cited as references. Excellent. By the way, one of those references was the Bishop of Winchester."

Charlotte again stepped in. "You all are aware that Professor Al McMillan is a Coptic Christian? As an undergraduate, he was part of a group at Oxford who worked in the summers at various churches—Anglican, of course."

Nancy Hightower blurted out, "Then why on earth is he accused of belonging to a terrorist Muslim group?"

Crawford finally said something: "Because Rickman is a jerk who wants publicity. The Muslim Brotherhood is not a terrorist organization. That's like calling Baptists terrorists. The organization is strict concerning religion, basically they want to turn back the hands of time, but many of its members are well-educated professionals."

"Doesn't Rickman know Tariq is a Christian?" Lucas, who should have been a bit more worldly, was surprised at the congressman.

"Even if he knew what a Coptic Christian was, he would go on the attack," said Crawford. "He's looking for people who can't fight back. Anything to keep his name in the media. He'll keep beating the drums because he thinks its a ticket to higher office."

"We can fight back," Charlotte firmly stated. "We are one of the few schools who have a Middle Eastern Studies Department and it is second to none. Furthermore, we have a summer program abroad and this year ten of our students will study in Oman."

Lucas was not one to give up his position easily. "Wouldn't it be easier to let Al McMillan go at the end of the school year, with a bonus and a good recommendation, and then hire someone, uh, American?"

All eyes stared at the sandy-haired man.

Finally, Sister quietly replied, "Lucas, we need people from that part of the world. At some later date, I think we should discuss expanding the department and perhaps hiring gifted people living in dangerous countries like Syria, for example."

"We're not an asylum," Lucas shot back.

"No, we are not." Crawford found Lucas tedious beyond belief. "But many brilliant young people around the world have no future in their homeland, especially women. Mrs. Arnold happens to be right. Custis Hall should lead the way on this issue and we need to study and better understand the Middle East, free of media hysteria or government policy."

Sister smiled a bit at Crawford. He could see the big picture. It was the big ego that was the problem.

"Lucas and Nancy, I'm sure that Isadore would allow you to see Tariq's curriculum vitae as well as the recommendations," said Charlotte. "He was hired before you came to the board. I assure you we were very thorough. We always are because as a private school, we come under a fair share of scrutiny. Many parents are, shall we say, especially vigilant about their children's education. And well they should be." Charlotte privately thought all helicopter parents should be shot down, but it was one more thing she and her staff had to deal with.

And they did.

"Of course." Isadore nodded to the two nervous board members.

"First, let me say that Sister Jane and Crawford have expressed an interesting initiative we should entertain another time," said the dean of students, George Jacobs. "If you don't mind, Frances, what do you suggest regarding the media?"

Frances Newcombe was the six o'clock news anchor at a big network station in Richmond and also a Custis Hall graduate. She clearly spelled it out. "Give as many interviews as you can. Contact the stations in Washington, Richmond, Lynchburg, Roanoke, Charlottesville. Try to get the reporter here because a shot of Charlotte—and it should be you, Charlotte—in front of the old administration building or out on the main drive, will generate more interest than a talking head. Hit hard that the accused is a Christian, and that this is still the land where one is innocent until proven guilty as well."

"I don't know if stations from D.C. will send reporters but it's worth a try," said Charlotte. "Frances, what about radio?"

"Any way you can get the word out, do. Custis Hall should go on the attack."

Crawford, who certainly liked the way Frances looked, tempered this plan. "That sounds like a great deal of work. Of course, local radio and TV are good. Big cities would be a boon. But if the board and our headmistress will allow me, let me see if I can fix the problem. Give me one week."

No one moved a muscle.

Finally, Charlotte asked, "Is there anything we can do to help you, or is there anything we need to know?"

Crawford smiled. "If Rickman has not publicly recanted within one week, then I believe Custis Hall should follow Frances' wonderful suggestions."

Sister drove to the old brick dorm behind the administration building, the prized dorm in which to spend one's senior year. She beeped the horn and Tootie soon trotted out, jumping into the truck.

"And?" Sister raised an eyebrow.

"Everyone is great. And there are so many people coming to hunt on Saturday that they need two trailers. Actually, Leslie said they might have to call around for help."

"That is good news." Sister smiled: the more, the merrier.

"It's a great fixture."

"Tattenhall Station really is, and Kasmir always opens it up for us to have a breakfast." Sister pulled out of the campus drive, and headed toward Roughneck Farm.

"I love having a breakfast in the old railway station," said Tootie. "Don't you wish it was used again?"

"Yes, I do, but I think it will be a cold day in hell before passenger service really comes back. Solve a lot of problems, though."

"How was the board meeting? I know you can't really tell."

"Pretty interesting," said Sister. "Everything may yet turn out all right for your former professor. We'll see."

The truck lights illuminated the curving main drive, the huge cast iron lampposts throwing halos of yellow light against the February darkness.

Coming from the opposite direction, Sister could just make out an old Saab thanks to the lamppost light, which showed the car's outline. She flicked her lights and slowed down.

Tariq stopped, rolling down his window as Sister rolled down hers.

"Master," he greeted.

"Hang in there, buddy," Sister encouraged him.

He smiled, then acknowledged Tootie. "You can't stay away from Virginia, can you?"

"No," she replied.

"Education is a passport." He had heard about her dissatisfaction with Princeton as some of his students, seniors, stayed in contact with Tootie.

"I want to be a veterinarian," she called over the running motor.

"I see." Deciding to address that another time, Tariq asked Sister, "I know you can't discuss the meeting but did you ever see *Lifeboat?*"

"Yes. I watched the original with Tallulah Bankhead and Walter Slezak. What a powerful film."

"I hope I'm not going to be thrown overboard." He looked up at her as the truck was higher than his Saab.

"I don't think so." She smiled.

The teacher in him emerged. "Is it not an impossible problem? The sum is greater than any of its parts, which means some people must die so many can live."

"Impossible," Sister agreed.

Tariq frowned for a moment, then pressed on. "In my country if an elected official made a statement such as Congressman Rickman he would be being supported by the state. It would be an opening gambit to prepare public opinion for more reprisals against the person defamed."

Sister, in a strong voice, said, "Rickman does not speak for the government although he obviously speaks for repressive elements in his district. They keep reelecting him."

"I pray you are correct." Tariq smiled weakly as he rolled up his window, then waved goodbye.

Sister rolled up her window. "Poor fellow. He's having a helluva time."

Tootie wondered aloud, "How do people like Rickman get elected?"

"Honey, that's a long discussion for another day. I'll give you a preview: It's much easier to be against someone or something than for it. Quirk of our species."

"I looked on your calendar," said Tootie to lighten the moment. "Today it says Catherine dei Ricci. I like knowing the saints' days—not that it has had anything to do with the board meeting or hunting."

"Let me see, I read it this morning," Sister mused. As the car headed up the hill, she recalled the Florentine lady. "Born in the sixteenth century and lived a good long time."

Tootie had the dead black hair dryer in her lap, which she fiddled with. "What I don't quite understand is why, in the calendar, do they give her name and other saints, too, and after the name, it says 'Virgin.' I mean, how could they know?"

"That's a good question." Sister laughed and so did Tootie.

CHAPTER 27

Art and Donny both grumbled that they wished they had a narrow hay elevator. Art had backed the truck into the Old Paradise barn as Donny closed the doors. The floor, packed dirt, would ruin the bottom cartons of cigarettes so they carried them up the heavy wooden ladder to the hayloft.

"Damn, when we come back for 'em, let's throw these things down." Art removed his heavy jacket, since he was sweating.

"Can't do that. We'll crush the cigarettes." Donny stepped off the top rung.

Art passed Donny as he headed for the ladder and a trip down. "Was this my idea or yours?"

"Mine." Donny thought he should take the blame. "But it's a good place and there's no reason we can't come up with a hay elevator later. That would make this job easy. Just put the carton on, give it a push, and up she goes."

"Used to have one," said Art. "Like everything else on this

damned farm, it broke. Christ, I hope Crawford and Dad and Alfred sign those papers soon."

Donny just nodded as he, too, headed back down the ladder for another carton.

Although light, a man could carry but one carton at a time. He needed one hand to hang on to the ladder.

For all the huffing and puffing, the job took only an hour.

"Hand it up." Donny, on his stomach, leaned over the top of the ladder as Art pushed up a heavy brown canvas tarp.

Four more of those and the cartons were covered. The problems weren't the elements, but bird poop, as quite a few winged creatures inhabited the barn.

The two men put rolls of insulation in front of the tarp.

Roger, a gray fox, also used the barn, but neither man knew of or discovered his den in a back stall. No reason for them to look in the stalls. The fox was fascinated with the men's cussing, the smell of tobacco, and the noise of feet on the ladder. Wisely, he kept his head down.

Finally, the two finished upstairs, climbed down, took some two-by-fours off the truck bed, and laid them on the floor. They leaned for a moment on a cobweb-covered stall door.

"When do we have to drive up to New Jersey?" Donny asked Art. He had contact with the boss whereas Donny did not.

"Next week."

"Wouldn't we get more money if we made the drops in the city?"

"We'd be sitting ducks with our Virginia license plates. It's bad enough we drive into New Jersey or up to western Massachusetts. Takes forever using the back roads, but we can't risk a weigh station," Art said.

"I guess you're right, but the weight of the tobacco is so much less than the stuff they're really looking for at those stations."

"Can't take the chance," Art said. "This is a good gig. Besides, there's always a state trooper at those stations."

"Fat, too." Donny laughed.

"Do you know some states are setting weight rules for cops? Bet the gym owners are glad about that."

Donny smiled. "Bet the troopers' wives are, too. Man, can you imagine having some three-hundred-pound guy smashing on top of you?"

Art shot him a dirty look. "No. Why, can you?"

"Oh, sure." Donny grinned as a little part of him enjoyed setting off Art, a man of limited imagination.

"Perv."

Donny changed the subject back. "Have you ever seen the trucks that smuggle the stuff into the city?"

"Once when Carter drove with me up to Massachusetts, three vans—plumbing company logo painted on them—off-loaded straight from my truck. These guys are pros. Any city we go to, I mean the actual delivery men, they don't just deliver smokes, they drop off 'shine, probably weed, and some of the trucks are outfitted so guys can actually cook meth on the road."

"That shit is nine miles of bad road." Donny looked up at the roof beams, hand-hewn and tremendously thick. "Would have liked to see this barn getting built."

"1816. Used saw pits and muscle power. Works as good as anything we do today, it's just slower."

"Yeah, but would you want to be the guy on the other end of the saw down in the pit?" Donny laughed.

Art laughed, too. "Guess not, but I wonder if those men had fewer injuries than today. You pushed and pulled the saw, the speed was as fast as you could go. I mean, if you take your eye off a saw today—even a band saw—no fingers!"

"Yep. Well, buddy, when do you want me back here?"

"Tuesday or Wednesday next week, but I'll text you."

"Okay. Ready to push off?"

Art drove the truck out; Donny closed the massive doors behind him. The minute the humans left the barn, Roger popped out of his den, climbed the ladder, a piece of cake for a gray fox, trotted across the hayloft to the canvas-covered cartons.

Sniffing around, he sneezed. *"Whoo."*

"It's who." The barn owl called down to him.

"Have you gotten a whiff of this stuff?" Roger asked the bird.

The barn owl glided down to a crossbeam above him. As she, too, was a predator, she thought the better of landing too close to the lightning-fast fox. Not that Roger had ever disturbed the bird, but why take the chance?

"The smell is sweet." The barn owl widened her eyes. *"But there's a tang there. I smell smoke, too, can you?"*

"Some of the old outbuildings around here and on close-by farms have this smell," said Roger.

"'Bacca sheds. Curing sheds." The owl volunteered this information. *"I've overheard people calling them that. Alfred DuCharme had an old Irish Setter—really old—and he said he remembered the last time one of those sheds was used. That was a good dog."*

"Ah, this is the stuff I see them stick in their mouths and puff, you know, when one passes in a car with the windows down. It's a human ritual I can't figure out."

"I've heard them say, 'Blowing smoke up your ass.' " the owl sagely noted.

The fox blinked, then giggled. *"But how could they do that while driving a car?"*

While Art and Donny unloaded cigarettes, on horseback, Crawford, Marty, Sam, and the young huntsman, Patrick, cast hounds behind Crawford's house. Tariq and Marty consisted of the field. A few desultory flakes twirled down. The big black-and-tan hounds picked up scent and a decent run followed.

Tariq followed Marty. She was a good rider, confident over all the various jumps Crawford had built. It was like a cross-country course, and gave Tariq occasion to be grateful to his borrowed horse.

Crawford's huntsman Patrick missed a chance to swing his pack into a southerly wind, which might have helped them after they lost the first fox. A warmer wind could send forward some scent as the temperature was dropping. But that was the day and Tariq knew the only way he'd find the kind of hunting he liked would be to occasionally go down to Deep Run or up to Piedmont, if he could cap there. Not that this was bad, just slower than he enjoyed and much of the fun was being with other people.

Nonetheless, afterward, he thanked the master, chatted with Marty for a bit, untacked and cooled down the horse borrowed from the Howards, then headed back to Custis Hall.

Sister also hunted on Tuesday. Crawford picked Tuesdays, Thursdays, and Saturdays to purposefully conflict with her schedule. Adjoining hunts, if possible, tried to select days different from their neighbors. Not Crawford.

In most respects, the Jefferson Hunt had the same kind of day that Crawford did, although the hounds found a second fox, thanks to the long experience of Shaker, as well as a bit of luck. Ultimately, any hunt is up to the fox.

In order to save gas, Sister rode in the horse trailer with Betty while Tootie rode with Shaker in the hound trailer. Sister preferred to follow with her truck or Jeep. Should a hound need to be rushed to the vet, it was easier. Otherwise, she'd have to find an unhitched vehicle or unhitch one of her trucks, which meant the horses or hounds would have to await her return. Fortunately, few accidents occurred. Given rising expenses, she played the percentages and rode in the truck on weekday hunts, although on Saturdays she would drive her personal truck or Jeep. As there were always so many people, you never knew when a last-minute errand would be in order.

Cruising along in the big dually, Sister unbuttoned her coat. They stopped at a convenience store. She and Betty liked the barbeque there so they bought up a mess to eat back at the farm. Sister opened the cigarette case, pulled out a credit card, and paid for their purchase.

"That's a good idea," Betty noted as they crossed the parking lot.

"I take this with me everywhere now," said Sister. "It's my good luck charm."

"Umm. Where do you think we lost that second fox?"

The two hopped back into the truck, which then slowly pulled away.

"I don't know where that fox went," said Sister. "I heard hounds go silent when I got up on the hill. What about you?"

"I was below you, but that's where I think we lost him. He ran up on high ground where the wind and little flurries wiped out scent."

In another twenty-five minutes, they'd reached the barns. A half hour after that, the horses were put up, clean and dry, faces buried in hay flakes.

The four of them gathered at the house for the barbeque.

"Did you look at the weather?" Shaker asked as he piled his plate high with barbeque, a touch of vinegar evident.

"Did," Sister replied, from the table. "Thursday cold, Saturday snow, but it's not supposed to get heavy until evening."

Sitting across from her, Betty smiled. "I love to hunt in the snow."

"Don't you think the hounds love it?" Tootie asked Shaker as he took a seat next to Betty.

"They do. Hounds have a lower ideal temperature than we do. We like it in the low seventies. And for horses, it's much lower."

"I love to see them play," said Sister, "throw up the snow with their noses, jump up to catch snowflakes." She could get just as excited as they could. "Hey, you all, don't forget it's St. Valentine's Day."

"I bought Bobby five sessions with a personal trainer," said Betty. "He is losing weight, but I think working with another man will push him along."

"Why?" Tootie asked Betty.

"Competitiveness. He doesn't want to lose face in front of another man." Betty prodded Shaker. "Am I right?"

Shaker smiled devilishly. "I don't know. I never have to lose weight."

The three women gave him the raspberry, then laughed.

"What'd you get Gray?" Betty asked.

"A box of Cohibas. Real Cuban Cohibas." Sister held up her hand. "Don't ask."

When everyone finished, Sister asked them to leave the dishes—she'd do them—but to hold up for one minute. She ran up the back kitchen stairs, coming down with Golly in tow, who awoke too late to be a pest at the table.

"You missed the barbeque," Rooster said, grinning with glee.

"I could care." The cat leapt onto the counter to lick out the cartons, immediately making a liar out of herself.

Sister placed a small box in front of each person. "Good luck."

Tootie tore hers open. "St. Hubert!" She held up a pretty medallion.

Betty opened hers. "Mine is red enamel. Yours is green. Hurry up, Shaker."

"Blue." He held up his medallion.

"Didn't you get one for yourself?" Betty asked.

Sister pulled a chain out from her shirt. A bright baby blue St. Hubert's medal hung on it.

The ladies kissed their master. Shaker gave her a bear hug.

"I want everyone safe and sound," said Sister. "St. Hubert's been watching over people for over one thousand years, so I think we're in good hands."

That night, under clearing skies, Art texted his boss, who texted back to call. Security was better with a landline and if one was technologically smart, which Art was, he knew the lines were clear, no taps. He called from home.

He and the boss texted in code for pickups and deliveries so Art knew the call would provide more information.

"Hey, boss."

"Art, can you go up next Tuesday?"

"Sure can."

"Donny?"

"He's a good hand."

"That's what you said about Carter. I trusted you and I'm still trusting you, but if Donny proves shaky, we got a problem."

"He's solid," said Art. "Also, he doesn't drink. I didn't know Carter fell off the wagon."

"For good."

That was the end of the conversation. When the sheriff had questioned Art, he told Ben some of what he knew about Carter. Not all, of course. He was afraid to ask the boss about the journeyman's end. Now his fears were confirmed. He sat there wondering if he could get off the merry-go-round. As long as he did his job, kept his mouth shut, asked no questions at pickups or deliveries, he thought he'd be okay. But what if something went wrong?

C H A P T E R   2 8

"I apologize for citing Tariq Al McMillan as a member of the Muslim Brotherhood," said Congressman Rickman, looking utterly distressed. "In my zeal to root out terrorists, I have done a disservice to fellow Christians. As a born-again Christian, I was not aware of the Coptic Sect. Although their religion is in many ways unlike Western Christianity, they are still Christians, and are under assault. The Coptic Christians comprise about 10 percent of Egypt's population but the official figure given is 8.6 million. I apologize for being unaware of the scale of persecution.

"As a member of the United States Congress, I will use my office to do what I can to help besieged Christians everywhere."

On network TV, Congressman Dave Rickman ate a large portion of crow but did his best to make it look like pheasant.

Sister, Gray, and Tootie watched the news report Wednesday morning.

"I'll be damned." Sister clapped her hands, which made the dogs bark.

"I'm eating," Golly complained. *"Let's be civilized."*

"I wonder who got to him?" Gray said.

"Crawford," Sister answered. "I don't know how he did it, but he did it. True to his word. At our emergency board meeting, he said he'd take care of it."

This in-studio report was followed by a news correspondent in Cairo reporting on riots on the streets of Egypt.

Tootie watched in horror. "When I talked to Tariq the last time he hunted with Jefferson, he said he was going to try and get his parents and sisters out of there. I can see why."

After Gray left for a meeting in Charlottesville, the two women finished the outside chores, then drove to Mill Ruins. Sister had asked Walter if she could feed the foxes on his property, and he'd agreed.

With the truck bed carrying twenty-five-pound bags of kibble, the first stop was in front of the old mill. Tootie hoisted the bag on her shoulder and they walked behind the mill, where a large wooden feeder box was tucked under heavy brush.

Sister fought the branches and creeper, lifting up the large door on top. "I make this hard for myself."

Tootie set the bag down, sliced off a corner with her pocket-knife, then lifted it up, pouring the kibble into the feeder box.

"They cleaned this out, didn't they?" Tootie could smell fox.

"It's been a month. If the weather is bad, with nothing left out there—which is usually the case in February, early March—I step it up to every three weeks. But it's been such a warm winter until now."

They walked back to the truck, crunching little ice crystals below in the mud. The low farm road ruts were half filled with melted snow, a skim of thick ice on top.

The second stop was way back at the edge of the property's pastures. Sister crawled over a coop and took the bag from Tootie, who then lifted herself over. Then they filled another big box in the woods.

Walking back, both women breathed a little heavier than when they started.

"I thought I was in good shape." Tootie smiled.

"Two legs. You're usually up on four when you're covering distance," Sister said. "Okay. Two more buckets at Mill Ruins, then we'd better drop some food at Tattenhall Station."

The thick mud made getting back to the big shed difficult: The bed of the truck fishtailed, but that four-wheel-drive did the trick. Finally, they made it. The door to the shed was not locked.

"No feeder." Sister got up on the back of the truck to hand down two five-gallon buckets with lids. A small hole was drilled at the edge, two inches from the bottom.

She handed these to Tootie, then jumped down to pull off a bag of food.

"I thought you put food a ways from the den. Make them travel for it," Tootie said once they were in the dimly lit shed.

"I do, but I think we'll have babies here come early April," explained Sister. "So I'm going to put one bucket by the two openings and we can walk another one to the woods' edge. When we hunted here we jumped a dog fox I didn't know. He's here with our vixen. Oh, hey, will you go get me baling twine? There's a roll on the floor on your side of the truck."

"Right. Along with the hair dryer." Tootie left quickly, returning with the twine.

Sister tied the bucket through the handle to an old nail sticking out of a support post. This way the foxes could fish out the food but not overturn the bucket.

"Ready?" Tootie then poured part of the feed bag into the five-gallon buckets.

Sister clamped the lid on top.

As they drove out after taking the other bucket to the woods, they again fishtailed left and right. A quarter of a mile from the turnoff, Art DuCharme was driving straight for them. Surprised at seeing them, he backed out—no easy task.

Sister waved as she reached the paved road. He waved back while trying to appear nonchalant.

"Wonder what Art's doing back here on Walter's land?"

After driving down the much better farm roads and filling up four huge feeders at Tattenhall Station, they returned to Roughneck Farm. She needed to make her draw list, the list of hounds to hunt, and give it to Shaker to compare. Tomorrow they'd hunt at Little Darby.

Before that, she phoned Ben Sidell. "Ben, I was at Mill Ruins filling up feeders. I ran into Art DuCharme on the road to the shed, the one that was locked up."

"I thought I told you not to go back there or to the abandoned road at the Lorillard place."

"You did, but time has passed and I need to feed the foxes. I'm sorry, I should have called you first."

"You should." He waited. "Art?"

"Right."

"Was he surprised to see you?"

"I'd say so. Probably as surprised as I was to see him."

"Well, thank you for calling me."

"Is Art a person of interest? Isn't that what you say now?"

"He is. Not for murder, but he did work with the victim, and he's had run-ins with the law before. Always for the same offense. Moonshine."

"He might have a new one."

C H A P T E R 2 9

The four-horse trailer swayed slightly as the road curved. Well accustomed to riding in the horse trailer, Rickyroo, Outlaw, Hojo, and Iota paid it no mind and continued pulling bits of hay from their feed bags. Due to the cold, the windows for each trailer berth were closed, but each horse could see outside well enough. An overhead vent provided some air circulation.

"It's those high thin clouds," Rickyroo noted.

"Supposed to snow Saturday." Outlaw always listened closely to the barn radio, as did all the horses.

"Bitsy predicts snow, too," said Hojo. He found the small owl amusing.

"Bitsy may be the nosiest animal ever," declared Outlaw. *"She's not content with reporting on the living, she has to bring reports from the dead."*

"I tell her to stop flying around the Hangman's Tree, but she perches, hears the spirits, and then scares herself," said Hojo. *"Live humans are bad enough. Why does she want to listen to dead ones?"*

"Maybe she's trying to scare you," Rickyroo teased.

"Nothing scares me," Hojo bragged.

"Me neither." Outlaw exhaled loudly. *"But I am cautious when approaching the Ha-Ha fence at Little Dalby."*

A Ha-Ha is often made of brush, often American boxwoods, and beyond it lies a ditch. If the animal did not clear it, he could push through. In general, Americans shied away from using brush as fencing, but it could work as a barrier. Ha-Ha fences were often one or two hundred years old, the hedgerow clipped, the ditches cleaned out. There was room to get your footing if you jumped the ditch, then faced the fence. If coming from the other direction, a horse could pause, then take the ditch. A few, full of themselves, took the whole obstacle. Some made it, some didn't. Being stuck down in the ditch invariably caused a scramble among riders.

"What you have to do is ignore your human," said Hojo. *"Pace yourself. Of course, if they're seesawing at your mouth and pulling your head up, there's not but so much you can do. However, the smart ones eventually learn to trust you to take the fence and to sit there quietly."*

"That's why it's called a Ha-Ha fence," Outlaw replied to Rickyroo's advice.

At this, they all laughed.

"So what's Bitsy's latest news from the beyond?" Iota asked. *"I haven't talked to her lately."*

"Okay. Now I am only repeating what she said. I'm not saying I believe it." Outlaw began with that precautionary preamble. *"Bitsy says the twelfth person hung there, Quincy Deyle—hung for rape—anyway, he told her there's a killer in the hunt field."*

Hojo was highly skeptical. *"How would he know if he's hanging on the tree? Or whatever he's doing?"*

"Takes a crook to know a crook," Outlaw said. *"He raped a lady in 1778 and then strangled her."*

"Doesn't make any sense. Why would you mate with a mare and then

kill her?" Rickyroo, although gelded, as were all the boys, couldn't understand such destructiveness.

"It's a human thing," said Iota.

The four companions babbled all the way to Little Dalby. When heading west, the crossroads at Chapel Cross was a key geographic spot in the Jefferson Hunt territory. Straight west once past Tattenhall Station, you passed Orchard Hill, then the Chapel itself. Going west, the Gulf Station was on your right, and then Old Paradise covered both sides of the tertiary road. Of course, the Jefferson Hunt could no longer hunt there.

Turning left at the crossroads, you came across some of Kasmir's land. The mountains were close here. Then you passed Beveridge Hundred, still in good shape after all these years, and finally Little Dalby. No fixture was all that distant from any other, but the road left a lot to be desired. In a car, you might go thirty-five miles an hour. Hauling horses or hounds, that speed dropped to twenty-five, maybe thirty on a straightaway.

Passing through the gates to Little Dalby, the horses lifted their heads, a current of excitement running through them, as well as Betty and Sister in the truck cab. The modest old gates, so unlike Crawford's estate, consisted of two fieldstone pillars, set wide apart. On top were brass crosses, for back in the eighteenth century, Little Dalby provided a refuge for Catholics. Even though Virginia's James Madison was the first to write about separation of church and state, religious prejudice still existed.

As she pulled in to park on the well-drained flat field, Betty said, "I wish I knew the foxes better at Little Dalby."

"No matter. They know us." Sister smiled.

"I guess they do." Betty checked out the trailers. "Don't you like seeing people already here when we pull in?"

"I do. We've got a small contingent of Custis Hall girls. The afternoon classes girls. Donny's here with one of Sybil's horses, I see. How many do you count?"

"Nineteen. Not bad for a February sixteenth—cold, too."

"Yeah, but everyone knows the season is closing in fast. We have one month left. Gotta get those hunts in."

"And a lot know the foxes are mating, which makes for great runs." Betty put on the emergency brake, even though the field was level. In a minute, the two women were out, wearing heavy bye-day tweed coats, a warm tie at their throats and each with a faded brown hunt cap—tails down, for they were staff—and brown field boots, a size too big, so they could wear extra socks.

Thin layers kept them warm more than one heavy layer. Keeping the torso warm wasn't as difficult as those toes and fingers. Eventually, cold won out.

Moving off promptly at ten, the pack headed north, pale sunlight dispelling some of winter's gloom. A northerly cast was a good choice because most of Little Dalby's land ran from the house northward.

They jumped over coops, and had crossed two tidy pastures when the hounds feathered. Moving their tails vigorously, they surrounded a long row of large rolled hay bales. Mice like to make nests in the hay bales and foxes like to eat mice. A fox had hunted there, and not too long ago.

The pack, eighteen couples, opened all at once. They trotted, continuing north. They moved in a single line over the next fenced pasture, then took the coop before the mounted folks. Finally, as they crossed over a farm road they began running. The hounds blew through three fenced-in pastures, the fox scent sticking nicely to the slightly warming frosted earth. As the sun hit those fields, the temperature rose just enough for the scent to lift off the pastures, the fragrance burst full up in those magical hound noses.

By now, everyone was glad they'd put borium on the horses'

shoes or even screwed in studs. That helped horses grip in slippery footing, which it certainly was. Mud on top of frozen ground is worse, but a slowly thawing frozen field taught you to sit deep in that saddle.

The blinding pace already claimed some victims. Two riders couldn't keep up, dropping back with Second Flight, who were running pretty hard as well. One of the Custis Hall girls, Emily Rogers, parted company with her horse at the last coop in the fence line.

The Custis Hall girls could ride, but most generally rode on flat surfaces. For a young person new to hunting, the big test was balance. Compared to what they faced now, it's easy to be balanced on the flat.

Tears flowed from Sister's eyes because of the cold and the pace. The hounds reached the end of Little Dalby, and leapt the Ha-Ha fence into Beveridge Hundred.

Trusting Rickyroo, she relaxed her hands, sank a little in the saddle and slid her leg just a tiny bit forward for insurance. Easy for the rangy Thoroughbred, the ditch was cleared, then Rickyroo hit the ground on the other side and, without taking a step, soared over the hedge.

Sister thought, *Nice bounce jump.*

Some behind her thought otherwise. Four people skidded into the ditch, misjudging the distance and the width. Two of them added insult to injury by overriding their horses. The horses, no dummies, hadn't fallen to their knees or on their sides; they turned and started down the ditch. The riders laid flat on their horses' necks because people behind were still taking the Ha-Ha fence. Once committed to a fence like that, a rider really couldn't pull up. Not going for it could prove even more dangerous.

Once everyone was over, one of the riders tried to scramble out, but the bank caved in. She had no choice but to ride in the ditch.

Loath to waste time, Second Flight master Bobby Franklin stopped his horse down on the state road and called to the four to hurry up; they could get out down by the culvert.

At last, they scrambled from the ditch with difficulty. Bobby moved on. He hated to lose the First Flight. If they ducked into a woods or headed west into really thick woods, he'd have a devil of a time finding them until Shaker blew his horn. Best to keep them in sight.

On a vigorous hunt, one by one, the horses sorted out according to breed and conditioning. The best-conditioned Thoroughbreds stayed right up front. The appendix horses—half Thoroughbreds, half quarter horses—galloped with the forward group, often right behind the Thoroughbreds. The rest of First Flight hung about thirty yards behind, but today the gap was widening. One superb half draft horse blew along with the Thoroughbreds.

They crossed Beveridge Hundred in fifteen minutes, jumping mostly log jumps, solid and well set. Then they charged into the grounds of Old Paradise.

So far this had been an eight-mile point or run.

Roger, the fox, ran flat out over the frozen ground, which sparkled white and pink as sunlight touched the frost. The rolling hills created temperature systems all their own. He ran nine miles, ten miles, and then he and the pack as one cut sharply left, heading straight for the faded grandeur of Old Paradise itself.

In the distance, the massive barn came into view. Beyond that, the house's white Corinthian columns glistened as the sun struck them.

Shaker—up with his hounds, Hojo having one of the best days of his equine life—couldn't yell encouragement anymore. The cold made blowing on the horn nasty because his lips would stick. His voice was giving out, but no matter. The pack was all on.

Closer and closer they came to the barn. Three hundred yards. Two hundred yards. One hundred yards. The fox dove under the side into his den, with hounds closing at fifty yards.

Before the hounds reached the barn, a blast hit a large tree behind Shaker as he barreled forward. Another shot rang out. The hounds stopped. Gunshots would usually stop them. Confused, they ran to Shaker.

"Good hounds. Good hounds."

"What did we do wrong?" Diddy whined.

"Good hounds, well done, come with me," Shaker said in a pleasant voice as yet another blast sprayed the branches overhead.

Shaker turned and met Sister, who stopped with six riders remaining close to her.

On the other side of the barn, Betty heard the shotgun. She knew it was coming from the hayloft, but whoever it was had opened the high hayloft door a crack, fired, then closed it. She saw no truck or vehicle nearby, but she couldn't well look. She also turned to ride on the side of the hounds.

Sybil did likewise.

Sister wasted no words. "Let's get out of here."

They trotted back a mile, then walked. From where they picked up the fox's scent to the shotgun blast had been twelve miles.

Inside the barn, the fox, Roger, heard footfalls coming down the ladder. Once he'd climbed in from his entrance outside, he stayed in his stall. Breathing hard, he desperately wanted the human to go away. A truck was parked inside the barn, and the human got in it, started it up, then turned it off. A minute later, he jumped out of the truck and left by the barn's side door.

The barn owl fluttered down to Roger's stall door.

"Jesus!" Roger caught his breath.

"Do you know there's a Jesus lizard?" The barn owl turned her head almost upside down.

"Dear God," was all Roger could muster.

The rear of First Flight and all of Second hadn't witnessed the halt of the hounds' approach, but everyone heard the shotgun blast.

Sister called to Shaker. She was worried about the hounds. "Let's get them back and check them out."

"I don't think anyone is hit." Sybil called from her side. "We'd have heard a yelp."

"That son of a bitch put someone up there." Sister swore. "Crawford had to have done it."

"Maybe," Betty called over. "But what are the chances of a run like that all the way from Little Dalby? Who would expect such a thing? It makes sense if the fixture is Tattenhall Station, but Little Dalby?"

Sister was so angry she couldn't think straight. "How do we know he hasn't paid someone to quote 'manage' the farm since the DuCharmes aren't doing it? It's his fixture now."

"We don't," Shaker replied simply.

"We have a right to follow the hunted fox into another hunt's territory," Sybil responded, close to the hounds on her side.

Shaker shrugged. "What good does that do when you're dealing with an outlaw pack?"

"I'm going to drive over to that SOB's farm and—"

As only an old friend can, Betty said, "Janie, no, you're not. Let's get to the bottom of this first. Then we can handle it. Right now, I'm glad no one is hurt."

Calming down, Sister pursed her lips. "You're right. I know you're right."

"So, we're not in trouble?" Diddy asked.

"No, we're not," Diana replied.

"But there is trouble." Giorgio had hated the sound of that shotgun.

As they rode back to the trailers, they picked up people who had fallen off, pulled up, thrown a shoe, or just couldn't keep up. The group was buzzing.

Back at the trailers, Shaker blew his horn for the riders to be silent.

Sister's voice carried. She said, "This was an unfortunate incident but, as Betty said to me riding back, we are lucky no one was hurt, horse nor hound. I would appreciate it if you'd keep this to yourselves. First, I must inform my joint-master. As you know, Old Paradise isn't our fixture anymore. So Walter and I need to discuss this incident with the DuCharmes, and then with Crawford. We need to find out who fired that shotgun. You can't fault hounds for doing their job and that was one of the best runs we've had this season. So please, keep this to yourselves."

They didn't. Human nature being what it is, a few people almost immediately phoned their best friends and swore them to secrecy. Those best friends called more best friends.

Finally, someone called Crawford.

Sister, Betty, Shaker, and Tootie had done all the chores, which took longer after such an intense hunt. Their legs proved a little more tired than they'd realized during the energetic ride. All four of them had just emerged in front of the kennels when Crawford's red Mercedes roared up Sister's driveway.

Seeing them, he slammed on his brakes, bolted out of the car, shouting at the top of his lungs before he even closed the door.

He strode toward Sister. "Goddamn you, accusing me of shooting at your worthless hounds."

She marched toward him and, without saying a word to one another, the three staff members came up right behind her.

He shook his finger in her face. "I'll sue you. I'll sue you god-damned snotty Virginian for libel."

"I haven't libeled you."

He vented more, providing lurid details from a phone conversation, in which he refused to identify the caller who swore Sister said he hired someone to keep Jefferson Hunt off Old Paradise. Isn't that always the way?

The more he recounted what he had heard, the hotter Crawford got.

When at last he had to pause to draw breath, Sister, unblinking, replied, "I said no such thing. I asked people to keep this quiet until we could investigate, and the first people I wished to call were the DuCharmes."

"But that's not what I heard," said Crawford.

"That is what I said."

"She did," Betty seconded Sister forthrightly, and so did Shaker and Tootie.

"But since you are standing here," said Sister, "I will ask you: Have you hired someone to keep us off Old Paradise?"

"Of course not," he answered, still in a huff. "No. I don't want you there, but I'm not going to shoot you."

"All right then, you do know that under the Masters of Fox-hounds Association rules, we have the right to stay on our hunted fox if that fox runs into your territory, the territory of any hunt?"

Face again red, he spit out, "I don't give a damn what the MFHA says. A bunch of snobs. Not one of them can make a dime. They all inherited it."

This was not true, but Sister knew little good would come of defending the MFHA, an organization with a big job.

"But you must understand we had to stay with our hounds," Sister persisted.

"I don't give a damn about your hounds," said Crawford. "I don't want to be accused of shooting at people. What do you think I was doing? Sitting up there in the hayloft? It's absurd!"

"Someone was in that hayloft," said Sister.

Tootie spoke up, which surprised Crawford. "Mr. Howard, is it possible someone wants you and Sister at each other's throats?"

"I— Why?"

"I don't know." Sister looked straight in Crawford's eyes. "This incident may have nothing to do with hunting. People jump to conclusions, and I confess my first thought was that you had hired a patrol. As I considered it, that seems absurd."

"Of course, it's ridiculous."

"Nonetheless, we were shot at. Three blasts from a high-powered shotgun. Sounded like a twelve gauge. Someone doesn't want us on Old Paradise."

"Well, I am going to be hunting there on Saturday. Maybe they don't want me there either."

A long pause followed. Crawford had calmed down.

Very quietly, Sister said, "I would be careful then."

CHAPTER 30

After lunch with the girls, Shaker returned to his house for a hot shower. He needed to get the kinks out.

Meanwhile, Sister, Betty, and Tootie, still in boots and britches, lingered at Sister's kitchen table, which Tootie had cleared, putting the dishes in the dishwasher. The dogs gathered below, and Golly watched from her gel pad, now a permanent fixture on the kitchen counter.

Sister was drawing on a notebook page as Betty looked on. "Good thing you didn't major in art," Betty cracked.

"Good thing you never went into politics."

Tootie smiled, wondering if she and Val would wind up like those two: teasing, prodding, bedeviling each other while offering total support. Right now Val wasn't offering much support. She texted every day ordering Tootie to return to Princeton, filling her in on all the details of everything she was missing.

"That's the best I can do," Sister said, giving up. "Tootie, you try."

Tootie sat back down, took the proffered pencil and the note-book pushed in front of her. She stared at Sister's sketch.

"You've got it," said Tootie. "It's just out of proportion."

Sister poked Betty. "See."

A minute or two later, Tootie gave the notebook back to Sister. Betty studied her simple drawing.

Pencil now in hand, Sister pointed to the drawing: a square, inside of which was a solid blue soaring bald eagle, head and neck white outlined in blue. It was a strong graphic. Underneath the eagle was a straight thick blue line to indicate water. Curved over the top of this was "American" and underneath was "Smokes" in red.

"Red, white, and blue." Betty shrugged. "Basic, but we get the message."

"Okay, can you print this up, Betty? Tootie has the proportions correct, yes?"

"Sure." Betty was intrigued. "Tell me why I'm printing this up and how many?"

"A pack of American Smokes was placed on the chest of each victim. What Tootie and I saw was a cellophane soft pack, white with this picture on front. I don't really remember if the pack itself was printed, or if this brand name was a square piece of paper slipped into the front of the cellophane covering the pack." Sister looked at Tootie, who nodded in affirmation.

"Tell me exactly what you want me to print up." Betty knew she'd have to clean up the graphic, but that would be easy with her equipment.

"Make me a sheet of squares," said Sister. "Only need, say, eight. We can cut the squares and slip them into packs of cigarettes. From far away, well, not too far, say three feet or so, the pack will look like American Smokes."

"Why in the devil do you want to do that?" asked Betty.

"We're dealing with contraband cigarettes, right?"

"It appears so." Betty again studied the drawing.

"So, I will carry a pack, and I'll see if Gray will, too, as he's always offering cigarettes to others. We just might bolt our fox out of his den."

"That is flat-out lunacy," said Betty. "For one thing, you don't know that the criminals operate out of our county."

Sister held up her hand. "I expect this covers Virginia and North Carolina. Don't know about Kentucky, but this has got to be a fairly big operation. No, we don't grow the stuff in our county, but after standing in Walter's shed I've got a hunch our county is a storage center. Look on a map. Virginia is smack in the middle of the original thirteen colonies. And just north of the Mason–Dixon line are those states with the highest cigarette taxes. Head west, you reach Illinois, another heavily taxed state."

The two other women thought a bit about this.

Tootie then said, "We are at the edge of what was once great tobacco country and we're what, two hours from North Carolina? So it's grown, cured, aged, right?" The two women nodded. "Then shredded and rolled."

"You can do it by hand or who is to say these crooks haven't got an old machine," said Sister. "So much equipment was abandoned by companies gone broke when the crisis hit. The big companies still have the very latest, but the little companies had to bail. It is possible our smugglers have equipment."

Betty was slowly getting on board. "How do the growers hide their secret stash of tobacco?"

"They don't. Who is going to go out in the field after harvest or into the shed and weigh the take against what they think it should be? Though I suppose it would be easy to shield some leaf, and it would also be easy to grow more tobacco on a place not near a road. Helicopters don't fly over to find tobacco, they fly to find marijuana. You can also grow tobacco in the center of a corn field, where no one can see it."

Betty whistled. "Pure profit for everyone on the pipeline."

"You got it. I really am willing to bet our county—in the center of Virginia, in the center of the East Coast—is the perfect way station, once the tobacco has been made into cigarettes." Sister repeated her plan to show off her American Smokes.

"I don't know," said Betty. "Are you going to tell Ben Sidell?" She raised a blond eyebrow.

"No!"

"See, you know he'll tell you not to do it because it's too dangerous. Let him do your little charade."

"Betty, if a law enforcement officer pulls out a bogus pack of American Smokes, don't you think anyone in on the game will know it's a trap?"

"Ben could give the pack to someone else."

"Won't work. And here's why this is a good plan." She omitted the danger part. "The cigarettes aren't sold here. No point. What am I doing with a pack of contraband? That's the hook."

"Oh, honey, I don't know. I don't like this."

Sister touched her dear friend's hand. "I know you don't like it, but will you do the printing for me?"

Exhaling deeply, looking down, then up, Betty finally said, "Yes, but only if I carry a pack of American Smokes, too."

"You don't smoke."

"Neither do you!"

"Yeah, but I'll say I'm carrying an extra pack for Gray."

"Do you want those cards printed up? This is an easy job. Take me maybe three hours. But I won't do it unless I'm all in."

Now it was Sister's turn to breathe deeply, stall. "Damn you, Betty."

Betty laughed. "Not the first time you've blessed me."

"All right. All right."

"Don't tell Bobby," said Betty. "He's out of the shop this afternoon trying to drum up business. I'll bring the graphics back around six." She quickly made a copy of the drawings.

"You know, if I really had a sick sense of humor I'd slip a pack of our American Smokes into the front seat of Crawford's fancy car or better yet, his hunt jacket."

Betty laughed. "Pretty perverse."

"I shouldn't waste time thinking about how to get even with him but occasionally, I do." Sister stood up and stretched. "Let's do it. Come on, Tootie." The three women left. Upon hearing everything, Golly left her gel pad to look at the two drawings.

For good measure, she sniffed them, too. *"Be much better if this were a cat."*

Down on the floor, Raleigh—irritated that he wasn't going with Sister—snapped, *"No one is going to smoke a cigarette or buy anything with a picture of a mangy cat on it."*

She spit at him, then turned her back.

Rooster, too, listened to everything. *"I know you love Sister but, Raleigh, this is a stupid plan."*

Golly turned back around. Although she hated to agree with Rooster, she said, *"Nothing will come of it."*

CHAPTER 31

The Norfolk and Southern route ran through Tattenhall Station, a wooden Victorian train station much like others built during the heyday of rail travel. Now only freight trains rumbled through, their schedules irregular, unlike the old passenger trains.

Over time, this station and many others like it fell into disuse, then disrepair. When Kasmir Barbhaiya bought the property a little over a year ago, he stabilized the structure, repaired the plumbing, cleaned it, and repainted it. He couldn't bear to see the destruction of such tiny bright pieces in the mosaic of a grand past. This Saturday, the large parking lot, with its potholes all filled, gave promise to a huge hunt field.

Kasmir's vast holdings were well foxed with reds and grays.

Coyotes stuck closer to the Blue Ridge Mountains and, as this was a year when game was plentiful, they posed little problem at Tattenhall Station. For now.

It was always in Sister's mind, and Shaker's, that this omnivorous adaptable species was as lazy as a human. If coyotes could eat without working for it, they would. Any farmer with fowl not secured at night found themselves the next morning without their geese, ducks, and chickens. Then, too, coyotes were happy to pick up puppies, kittens, and small house dogs. Best of all for the rangy canines was the humans' garbage, easily torn up. No working at all for that. Unwittingly, people brought the coyote closer.

However, even like a fundamentally lazy human such as Carter Weems had been, coyotes will work when pressed.

Hunting at Orchard Hill three weeks ago, Sister had seen coyote tracks. She had known they belonged to a coyote because, although the size of a domestic dog, they are in a straight line, the hind feet often stepping into the prints left by the forefeet. She wasn't too worried about it because it was their breeding season, too. Males travel long distances to find a mate. All the female has to do in most mammal species is throw on a little lipstick and wait.

Directly across from Tattenhall Station was the red brick utilitarian volunteer fire department building on the east side of the tracks.

Sister lifted up on Matador as Shaker mounted Kilowatt, Kasmir's gift to the club last year on February 19. This was February 18, and unknown to Kasmir, the nonhunting members of the club—usually married to hunting members—had decorated the inside of the station with a banner thanking him and declaring it St. Kasmir's Day. The hunt breakfast would be the usual fare, but today High Vajay and his wife, Mandy, had also brought special Indian dishes beloved by Kasmir.

The focus of all this gratitude was utterly unaware of it since the hunting ladies of the club, directed to divert his attention before taking off, easily did so. In his mid-forties and widowed, Kasmir was ever mindful of the ladies.

Shaker looked straight up at the lowering gray clouds. "The Weather Channel was right."

"I give it an hour," said Sister. "What about you?"

"Think you're right." The huntsman agreed with his master that the snows were due soon.

Betty and Sybil were already mounted and waiting to move off. Betty had Tootie with her. Sister wanted Tootie to ride with each whipper-in a number of times and once or twice up with Shaker, so she would know how the huntsman operates. Tootie had to work up to Shaker though.

"Well, let's do it," Sister said to Shaker and then in a louder voice for the field, "Hounds, please."

They walked behind the station, a huge expanse of pasture before them, wire fence interspersed with coops. Kasmir would eventually fence the property, which would cost a fortune but look terrific. Right now his energies were focused on bringing the pastures back and fixing up the modest Virginia farmhouse he lived in. Someday he might build a larger home, but that would be something he would do with a wife, if someday he found another woman to love, who would love him for more than his money.

Sister, as always, counted heads. Thirty-two in First Flight. Bobby shepherded fifty. Many people had come out because they hoped it would be a good day, and others because the word had passed about the celebration for Kasmir.

The group walked along, hounds fanning out in front, searching for scent. On the nearby road heading to Old Paradise, Sister spotted Crawford, his hound van, Sam driving the horse van, and three stock vans driving by—also, Tariq in his Saab, looking longingly at the huge field.

"Doesn't miss a chance, does he?" Sister heard Edward Bancroft say to his wife and Gray as they rode up behind her.

"He had to see us, too," Sister remarked knowing Jefferson Hunt's large field would inflame Crawford.

The banter ended. Strictly speaking, it was out of line, as

hounds were drawing in at the end. They all saw Tootie and Betty, horses' heads pointing south, hats off.

Softly calling to his hounds, Shaker turned them south. Asa, out today, surged forward with Diana. Right behind them were two young entry, Parker and Pickens. The youngsters stopped, turned slightly right toward the west, noses down, and opened.

The older hounds rushed toward them, noses down. They opened, too. The fox zigzagged a bit, then straightened out. He was a large red fellow with a magnificent brush.

This section of Tattenhall Station—all pasture—afforded everyone a fabulous view of a fox running well ahead of hounds, all of the dogs singing and running as one.

The snowflakes began to fall. The fox disappeared in a slight swale, then reappeared farther down, heading back toward the tracks. Gaining a little more time on the pack, he really opened up. Diddy, Diana, all the young entry and second-year entry moved as fast as they could. The older hounds comprised the middle of the pack. This early in the hunt, no one lagged behind. On those long days toward the end, a few hounds would be perhaps ten or twenty yards behind the pack, a sign that they should be retired at the end of the year.

No one popped off. The tight footing wasn't slick yet. The mostly flat pasture had a soft roll here and there, such as the little swale the fox had used.

The big red fellow crossed the north–south road. Sister cleared a stiff coop in the fence. She had three strides before she was out on the road, then over that. Three more strides and over the stone fence at Beveridge Hundred. Out of sight now, the fox dodged into the Christmas tree rows at Beveridge Hundred, a little sideline for the farm. The bushy Douglas firs, already over Sister's head, blocked any sight of the clever critter. She could see some of the hounds in the row in which she ran, but the hounds were all forward, in many rows.

Silence.

She came to a halt. Shaker and the pack stood at a culvert under the farm road, a forest on the other side. Hounds cast, furious to relocate the scent, which had been hot, hot, hot. Nothing.

"I know it's here," Pickens cried in frustration. *"He has to be here."*

Shaker moved them along into the woods. Nothing. He came back out, walked down the farm road toward the house, which was a mile distant. Nothing. Then he returned to the spot where the hounds lost the scent. Zilch. After moving in all four directions, he sat for a moment, collected his thoughts, then collected the hounds.

How a fox can vanish has mystified people since Aesop's time. Shaker sure didn't have an answer.

Shaker walked down to the state road, turned left, dropped over the slight bank onto flat ground. Walking along the fence line, he kept the pack off the road and the field was now behind in a single line. A coop appeared in a thick forest on Tattenhall Station land. Cleanly set, one had only to face it squarely and leap over into a nice path in the woods. Rarely used, the black coop was only two and a half feet high. But a horse had to jump from open land—a wide view—into a dark woods and a narrow lane.

Sister, legs of iron, gave Matador a firm squeeze. Over they went. The horse appreciated a clear signal and was a bold fellow anyway, a source of argument back in the barn: Who was the bravest? Matador knew that he was. The Bancrofts got over the coop nicely, as did Kasmir, High Vajay, Mandy, and Xavier, who had lost a lot of weight, which his horse greatly appreciated. For whatever reason, Ronnie Haslip crashed the jump. Ronnie was a good rider, too. Even moving off, Sister heard the crack behind.

When a horse refuses or you part company, you must return to the rear so as not to impede anyone else's progress. Ronnie walked his horse back and mounted up. But when horses see another horse refuse a jump they are certain a horrid goblin lives under the coop. Today's riders that were behind Ronnie had a devil of a time getting over that small obstacle. It quickly became clear who had a solid horse and who was a solid rider. The worst was when one horse rode right up to the jump, then slammed on the brakes. His rider took the jump. He didn't.

Sister couldn't wait for those who had fallen. To do so meant losing the hounds. Maybe the field master can find hounds and maybe she can't, but if she winds up blowing the covert because she's in the wrong place, there goes the hunt, or at least the hunt on that fox. The people in the rear of the field, now upset, strained to hear if the hounds had picked up the scent of a fox.

The person assigned to ride tail today was Ben Sidell, a fairly new rider but on a bombproof horse, Nonni. Ben had had his hands full at the coop. Fortunately, everyone was fine, as were their horses, but Ben couldn't get into the woods until everyone was safely over.

When one lady's horse refused three times, Ben said nicely, "Best you go back to Bobby Franklin." Down the road at a gate, Bobby was in the pasture bordering the woods.

Without a word, the lady did as she was told. All very proper, but disappointing to the rider.

Snow fell heavier now, caps turned white, shoulders also. However, it didn't feel as cold as a freezing rain or sleet, and the beauty of it, as well as the sound of snowflakes hitting tree limbs and pine needles, delighted most everyone.

Hounds moved along, a bit of scent here, a bit there, but not enough to open. They stuck to it. These are the situations that demonstrate the ability of a pack. Any group of hounds looks great when scent is burning. And there's nothing a pack or the huntsman can do on those dead days, when nothing sticks. It's the in-between times like today that are the test, and Jefferson Hounds were all business.

No one even grumbled.

Parker lifted his head once to see what everyone else was doing, then quickly put his nose to ground. The line, so light and teasing, would break. They'd have to widen their cast, pick up the faint reward, and push on.

The walk turned into a trot, but still no music. The woods opened up onto a rough pasture, broom straw sticking up through the cut hay stubble. It would take a good long time for Kasmir to focus his renovation labors back here—best to concentrate on the really good pastures near the roads. Also, the soil varied at Tatten-hall Station. As Kasmir rode on his gorgeous Thoroughbred over the field being dusted with snow, he made a note to take soil samples back here.

Large fallen trees bore witness to high winds. Their split-open trunks showed they were old, and had weakened.

Hounds leapt over a sycamore down by a narrow stream. They crossed the stream, as did Shaker, then Sister. They met another woods, mostly hardwoods and a few pines. Hounds kept on, but still not speaking. The snow fell steadily.

The low pressure should help scent, but an old line is an old line. Shaker and the hounds hoped it would warm up. They emerged on a large eastern field, a giant walnut in the middle, so thick three men could maybe get their hands around the trunk. Its bare winter branches were black with vultures. They looked down at the horses, then toward the humans and horses moving toward them. None of them moved.

Sister had seen vultures in a denuded tree many times, although not in the snow. Sooner or later, they'd lift off, returning to better protection. She hoped they didn't lift off as the horses rode by, for surely it would spook a few.

The birds stayed eerily still, continuing to watch.

The hounds lost the scent in the middle of the field. They cast like spokes in a wheel from the center, which was Shaker. But to no end.

Shaker figured they might as well hunt back. They'd been out an hour and a half. With a little luck there was still hope for another run. Shaker returned to the woods at a distance from the vultures, and drew the dogs along the edge of the woods. He patiently walked along, Betty and Tootie now in the middle of that field, battling winter winds.

Sybil was in the woods. She let out a holler. "Tallyho!"

Hounds moved toward her voice, as did Shaker, finding a path in. He caught a glimpse of his whipper-in, hat off, snow already on her hair, for it was coming down fast now. Sybil's hat and the horse's nose were pointing due north.

Quickly, Shaker got on the deer path, moving in that direction. Sister found the wider path, tractor-wide.

Within minutes, good old Asa opened, and off they ran, due north, straight into the snow and now light wind. Sister couldn't see and really, Matador couldn't see all that well either.

The hounds burst out of the woods and into another large pasture, but the fox was nowhere in sight. They blew through that, cleared a coop, as did Shaker, then Sister. Betty and Tootie jumped an old tiger trap farther up the fence line, but all still ran true north. Fifteen minutes later, the hounds crossed the east–west road and flew into Orchard Hill.

An unexpected siren jolted Sister, who held up the field at the roadside jump, which was three stout logs lashed together.

At first she thought it was the fire department, but then a

squad car—sheriff's department, sirens blasting, lights flashing, which Matador did not appreciate—screamed right by her. An ambulance raced behind.

She waited. Waited a bit more, for the snow seemed to soak up sound. Then she jumped the logs, crossed the road carefully, and jumped into Orchard Hill over a break in the three-board fence. Orchard Hill needed some help, but in these hard times so did a lot of other farms. As she moved along, she gave thanks that when she talked to the owners, they'd said they would not give way to Crawford.

Straining to hear the hounds, she finally picked up the sound. Ride to cry, which she did. Galloping through the orchard and the wide roads around the different types of apples, she made up the ground. This is when you want to be on a Thoroughbred. She scarcely felt the ground beneath his hooves, nor could she hear anyone behind her.

The hounds cut north. She caught a glimpse of Sybil, low on her horse, galloping straightaway.

Three tiers of square hay bales lashed together, now snow-covered, filled in for a jump. It was a nice jump, really. Matador had a split second of hesitation as he looked at all that white. He didn't remember white, and horses remember everything. One good smack on his hindquarters with her crop and he sailed over, grateful that none of his stablemates had seen that split second. Matador was only a year into foxhunting so he still had a bit of learning to do. Still, his talent was above reproach, and he showed it as he flattened out.

Sister couldn't remember the last time she rode so fast. Snow hit her more on the right side now, but she had to squint to see. She could still make out Sybil's back as they blasted over an open field, then had to draw up and shift down into a trot. She'd run up right on Chapel Cross itself.

Hounds surrounded the foundation of the stone structure, the cross somewhat visible in the driving snow. A religious fox had dug a cozy den at the foundation. However, he wasn't there.

Wise in the ways of hounds, the fox being chased had jumped into the unoccupied den, which had a tunnel opening farther down along that same foundation. The sly fox then hurried out and over to the graveyard surrounded by trees. If you positioned your den just right vis-à-vis the headstones, graveyard dens were cool in the summers and often warm in the winters. The hounds had no idea their quarry was only fifty yards behind them.

One by one, the field gathered behind Sister. Most had made it over the jumps. Those with faster horses kept up. Others trickled in until finally Bobby and Second Flight arrived.

Shaker dismounted, blew "Gone to Ground." Praising his hounds, he turned his face away from the snow. The church's sexton chose not to come out and celebrate with them, but Mr. Vega did like hunting.

"Shaker, let's go in," said Sister. "This thing is turning into a real blaster."

"Righto, Boss."

"Why don't we walk back and through the gates?" she said. "No point in jumping if we don't have to and that was a hard run. We've been out—"

He looked at his watch as she looked at her grandfather's pocket watch, saying first, "Three hours and twenty-one minutes."

She giggled. "I was going to say the exact same thing."

How she loved a snowy hunt. Hounds, tails up, pranced, some even twirling around, as they made their way back to Tattenhall Station.

People in both fields laughed, talked excitedly, and shared their flasks. Nothing like a sip of spirits to warm the body and loosen the tongue.

Moving at a brisk walk, they arrived at Tattenhall Station twenty minutes later, and everyone hurried to take care of their horses.

That done, they couldn't get into Tattenhall Station fast enough. Helped by Vajay until everyone was inside, Mandy held up Kasmir with one thing after another. Then they led him in. As he walked through the station doors, a cheer went up.

Out of her coat and into a tweed, proper for a breakfast, Sister held up a glass to toast. "To Kasmir Barbhaiya on his saint day, with thanks from Jefferson Hunt. What would we do without him?"

At that, three cheers lifted the rafters and all the women rushed to kiss him. Kasmir blushed.

He simply said, "It is an honor and a joy to be part of Jefferson Hunt and hunting over lands that Mr. Jefferson himself once knew." He paused. "And, of course, the kisses from the beautiful Jefferson Hunt women make it all worthwhile, but I have not yet been kissed by our master."

Grinning, Sister came over, kissed him, and gave him a big hug. She knew how lucky she was to have someone like this in the club and in her life. He was one of those men who made life deeper, more colorful. She'd long ago learned if there's someone who robs your life of color, get rid of them. Here she was, surrounded by those who were giving instead of taking.

"I do mean it, Kasmir," she said. "My guardian angel smiled on me the day you first rode with us."

He whispered in her ear, "I came back to life on that day, Sister. I thank you."

What he didn't say was that, later that day of his first hunt with Sister, he had distinctly heard his late wife's voice saying, as though she were in the passenger seat of his car, "Husband, I'm dead, you live and love and laugh."

If there were ghosts at Hangman's Tree, there were also ghosts at Tattenhall Station. Spirits who remembered stepping off a train to greet a husband, wife, children, parents, or dear best friends. But love lingered, too, and this breakfast glowed with that, and the strong friendships in the group.

At the rear of First Flight, Ben had heard the sirens, but didn't know one was from his department. Realizing that, Sister made her way over to him. "Ben, one squad car roared by."

"Thank you." He moved away, fished out his phone to call headquarters.

"Lillian, I'm at Tattenhall Station. I was told that a squad car came out here. Why?" He guessed Art got caught with his still as he waited for Lillian to read the exact call-in.

He heard the report, thanked her, and hurried through the crowd.

He found Sister. "Apologize to Sybil for me. I won't be back at the barn to help with Nonni."

"Of course. Is there anything I can do?"

He looked into her eyes. "Crawford Howard was shot at Old Paradise."

CHAPTER 32

Art looked stricken. "I walked outside, slipped, and the gun went off. It was an accident: Crawford is about to write a big check to my father. I'm not going to queer that deal."

Still in hunt kit, Ben sat opposite the distraught young man down at the police headquarters, quiet on this snowy Saturday.

"You have a permit for the twenty-two. Checks out."

"Sheriff, if I was going to kill someone, would I do it with bird-shot?"

"No. But can you tell me where you were on Thursday, when Jane Arnold and her hounds were shot at not far from your barn?"

"Well, I don't know the time of that but I was in the garage most all the day."

Ben didn't know about the shotgun incident until Crawford had called the sheriff to loudly declare the libelous charges levied against him ridiculous. It took Ben ten minutes to find out what was ridiculous because Crawford's telephone rant continued that long.

Later that evening, Ben called Sister, who'd made light of the incident. She had enough trouble losing Old Paradise and she wasn't going to do anything to cause difficulty for the DuCharmes. Whoever fired the shots wasn't trying to harm her, Shaker, or the hounds. She assumed those shots were a warning to stay off of Old Paradise.

"Art, do you own a shotgun?" Ben asked.

"I own two. A twelve-gauge over and under, and a twenty-eight-gauge single barrel. The twelve-gauge is so loud, such a kick, I'm going to sell it. I prefer the twenty-eight when I'm bird hunting, which I rarely have time to do."

"Did you know about what happened Thursday at Old Paradise?"

"No. Why didn't someone tell me or Dad?"

Ben tilted his head slightly. "That incident was reported to me by Crawford, who swore he didn't do it. And Sister, who was following hounds, did not report it—even though hounds, Shaker, and the master were fired upon."

"Someone aimed for them? A shotgun has a big spread. You'd think they'd be hit. Or was it a rifle?"

"Shotgun, and it was fired over their heads from the hayloft of the barn, so they think. But they didn't see the person. I find it very odd that two firing incidents have occurred on Old Paradise."

"Hitting Crawford was an accident. I should have unloaded the shells. I know better, but I was only walking to the truck, which was parked outside the barn."

"Your father and mother live on one side of your family's property and your uncle on the other. You live closer to your uncle than your father. Does this create tension?"

"No. Uncle Alfred and I get along, but I'm careful. I don't want to hurt Dad, but neither Margaret nor I want any part of their fight. Since Margaret's at the clinic or the hospital so much, I usually check the farm at night. I check the barns, the outbuildings.

There's nothing to steal, but sometimes people will sleep in them. With these hard times I've found a few folks. I do turn them out. How do I know they won't light up and fall asleep? Our outbuildings are built with huge timbers. I don't want a fire, especially in the barn, which I'm hoping we can rehab with that big check."

"Did anyone other than Crawford see you trip and fall with the twenty-two?"

"Snow was coming down. Still is. Tariq Al McMillan was behind him. He called the ambulance to report Crawford had been hit, and I guess they called your department."

"Yes, they did. Art, obviously I'm not going to arrest you. Crawford made a statement that it was an accident and he was embarrassed that an ambulance came, but he does have shot near his eyes."

"I'm really sorry about that. Tomorrow I'll go to his house and try to make amends somehow. I don't know what else to do. It was a stupid mistake."

"That it was. Right now, we're being extra careful. We want to solve Carter Weems's murder. No law enforcement agency wants an unsolved murder."

"Yes, sir."

Released, Art drove back to Old Paradise going twenty-five miles an hour, as the roads had deteriorated. It really was an accident, shooting Crawford. Firing over the heads of the Jefferson Hunt hounds was not.

He knew that Crawford would be hunting at Old Paradise Saturday, but he didn't expect Sister. The more he'd thought about the tobacco being in that barn, the more he knew he had to move it. The chances were slim that anyone would go inside the barn, but he didn't want to risk it. His father would blame it on his uncle. A lot of questions and snooping would result. By himself, he had loaded up his truck, parked in the closed-up barn, and was ready to go back down the ladder when he heard the hounds. Later, after the shooting, he returned and drove the truck to his house, parking it outside. Right now that seemed safer than anywhere else, and he would be ready to drive north come Tuesday.

He had to find a better storage place. He had a furniture delivery Friday on his way back from New Jersey. It gave him a cover. As for storage, he'd think of something.

After hot showers, Sister, Gray, and Tootie sat in the den. Sister had bought a DVD of *The African Queen*, which Tootie had never seen. Sister liked to unwind after a hunt and was looking forward to watching the movie, which she hadn't seen for forty or so years.

She'd found out that Crawford was okay. His wife, Marty, told Sam, who told Gray. Sam drove out, drove the horses back, leaving his car there. He wouldn't be getting it for a few days. He was lucky to get the horses back. Marty had driven the hound truck. Tariq drove with her so his Saab was at Old Paradise as well.

Sam drove the young teacher back to his lodgings at school after they both put the horses up. Marty lent him her four-wheel-drive Lexus.

On the coffee table in front of Sister rested six packs of American Smokes. From a distance, they looked fine. Close examination would reveal the card slipped inside the cellophane. Betty had given them the cards after the hunt breakfast. Sister and Tootie slipped the graphics in at the kitchen table.

Two pair of socks on, his heavy robe wrapped around him, Gray slumped in the sofa. "I don't know why I'm so tired," he said.

"Long hunt, hard riding, and the cold can beat you up." Sister sat next to him while Golly curled around next to the cigarettes. "I'm tired, too."

Tootie sat in the club chair. "I couldn't see my hand in front of my face at the end."

On the coffee table by the doctored cigarette packs, Golly looked over at the two dogs. *"Why don't you start smoking?"*

"For what reason?" Rooster asked.

Raleigh sat up, now peering over at the cat. *"Why should we smoke?"*

"It will improve your mood." The cat smiled.

"You're the one who needs help," Rooster replied.

"Just a suggestion." Golly half closed her eyes but what she was thinking was if they smoked maybe they'd die soon.

CHAPTER 33

Snow fell throughout Sunday. A storm of such intensity hadn't been forecast. Roads became impassable. Even the interstates had sections closed, especially crossing the Blue Ridge Mountains or in the Alleghenies.

Sister was glad to have Tootie's help, and they trudged their way to the barn, as Shaker did the same to the kennels. Sister couldn't plow out the farm roads because the snow just kept falling. When it slowed down, she'd take a crack at it.

The hounds tucked up in the kennels. A few stayed in their outdoor condos, stuffed with straw. At a human's appearance, a head would peek out from the heavy canvas, which covered the hound-sized opening, only to duck back in.

Wearing their heavy blankets, the horses were turned out to play by Sister and Tootie. It's never good for a horse to stand hours in a stall, and "stall rest" is one of the dreaded phrases from a veterinarian's lips. Even the best of horses, laid up for a time, could become sour or destructive. An early warning signal was banging a feed bucket against the wall.

Fortunately, the horses walked through the snow, kicking up snow for the fun of it.

"Tootie, wouldn't you like to be a horse just for a day?" Sister asked as they slipped the halters and flipped the lead ropes over their shoulders. Like the horses, they kicked up snow as they walked back to the barn.

"A Thoroughbred, deep heart girth, wide nostrils, long and powerful hindquarters, and a well-developed stifle. I'd love it," the young woman answered as they pushed through the two feet of snow, with more coming down.

The *rat-tat-tat* on the Blue Spruces by the barn bore evidence to the storm.

"Studying conformation, are you?" asked Sister. "You know, my mother had the best eye for a horse of anyone I ever knew. Well, let me amend that—Mother, Kenny Wheeler, the late Jean Beegle, and the very alive Joan Hamilton. It's like they have X-ray vision. Well, I digress. Sorry."

Tootie smiled. "I like listening to you."

"You're kind. God, I don't want to turn into one of those people who live in the past and the past is always better than the present. In some ways it was, any past, any century, but in other ways not. I believe the present is pretty good. Remember that when you're in the dentist's chair."

They both laughed.

"Your mother"—Tootie slid open the barn door, which they'd had to shovel snow from—"her turnout was really perfect."

Sister had a few photographs of her mother in lovely frames throughout the house. With one exception, Mother at the beach, they all showed the gracious lady on horseback.

"Proper attire for every occasion," said Sister, following Tootie into the barn. "I liked hunting kit, obviously, but she even loved the rest of it, tea dresses, afternoon gloves versus evening gloves. The right shoes. When to wear high heels and when not. Colors. Tootie, when I was young, you couldn't wear white before Memorial Day. It just wasn't done."

"A lot to remember, but your mother must have remembered everything."

"That she did." Sister walked along the center aisle, placing the halters and attached lead shanks on the brass hook on the side of each door. "Can't let Lafayette grab his halter. For whatever reason, that horse lives to destroy leather. He's happy with his gel pad though, now that I had another one sent. I'll never be able to take the one in the kitchen from Golly. She'd tear down the house." Sister paused, then laughed. "How could I miss what's under my nose? Golly and Lafayette are good friends. They egg each other on to demolish whatever they can."

Also hanging up halters and shanks, Tootie asked, "Did your mother love animals?"

"Good Lord, mother picked up every stray, every unwanted animal she ever saw or even heard about. She'd get in the station wagon, had wooden sides, and off we'd go. My poor father put up with it. Well, he loved her. We all did. Especially the rescued animals." Sister laughed.

Just as Bitsy was looking down, Tootie looked up. She said, "My mother isn't hard-hearted, exactly, but she never wants anything to be trouble."

"A lot of people are like that. Inanimate objects have more value than living things."

"Odd, isn't it?"

"I know what I was going to say before I went off on a trip

down Memory Lane. Mother used to say, 'Movement is the best of conformation.' Remember that."

"I will."

As they threw down three flakes of hay for later, when they'd bring the horses back into the barn, they heard the outside tack-room door open and close. The door into the center aisle opened.

Gray shoved his gloved hands into his pockets. "You've got puppies."

Sister was confused. "I haven't bred anyone."

"A stray crawled into the hound trailer, the side door was open, and she had four puppies in that deep straw. I put out food and water for her."

"Great day." Sister stood, then moved toward the ladder up to the hayloft. "And I was just talking about my mother, Sister Teresa to all abandoned animals."

"Do you have an empty stall?" asked Gray. "I think we should move her into the barn and put down an old blanket." He looked up as Sister threw down a plastic garbage bag from a storage area in the loft. It was filled with blankets in need of repair.

"Bombs away." She then said, "Tootie, pick out the best blanket from the bag and get that back stall ready. I'll go help bring mom and the puppies in."

Walking through the snow with Gray, heads down, Sister asked, "Is she mean?"

Gray shielded his eyes. "I don't think so, but we haven't handled her puppies yet."

The aluminum trailer afforded protection from the storm. The straw helped with the cold, but the barn would be better.

Sister knelt to pet the dog's head, a mix, but some boxer was in there. "What a good girl you are. Four beautiful puppies."

The exhausted dog wagged her tail.

"Why don't you carry the puppies and I'll carry her?" said Gray. "She's tired and I don't know if she'll follow us, although she'll probably follow her babies."

"Yeah, but we don't want to expose them to the storm. Let me run into the kennel. I've got some old towels there. We can wrap the puppies and I'll carry them inside my coat." Sister left and was back in ten minutes because the slow going just ate up time.

Gray gently lifted the mother up and she offered no resistance as Sister carried the puppies in a towel.

Together they made their way back to the barn, carefully depositing their burdens in the now fixed-up stall. Tootie put a water bucket in there with a plate of kibble. She added more wood shavings to the stall floor so they were deep. Two blankets had been arranged in the corner. Gray laid the mother down as Sister placed the puppies at her side.

Tootie knelt down to stroke her head. "She needs a name."

"We'll think of one." Gray smiled. "She should be fine in here. How smart of her to find the hound trailer."

"I bet she's been at the edge of this farm for a while, but clever enough for us not to find her," Sister remarked.

Back in the kitchen, they watched the Weather Channel, which promised the storm would abate in early evening.

Gray called his brother. "I'll pick you up tomorrow and we'll fetch your car," said Gray. "The Land Cruiser can go through anything, even this snow."

"Sounds good to me," said Sam. "Tariq's car is there, too. I know my old Outlander can make it, but I don't think his car has four-wheel drive. Might. There was so much going on I didn't pay attention."

"I can imagine," Gray replied. "As I recall he drives an old Saab. Front-wheel drive. He might make it out if he stays in our tracks. Well, the first thing is, this storm has to stop. The big roads will get plowed out first, so we might have a hell of a time getting back to Old Paradise."

"Isn't going to be that easy getting here to the house either."

"No problem, Brother. You're going to drive the old tractor down the drive and cut big deep tracks for me. I told you we should buy a snow plow."

"I don't have enough to pay for my half. Besides, Gray, how often do we get a snow like this?"

"Yeah, yeah. First thing tomorrow morning, your ass better be in that tractor seat." Gray laughed, then hung up.

The quiet day restored their energy. Being cut off lets the mind go free and the body repair. Even the nighttime chores were fun, as the snows turned deep blue with the fading light.

All was well, even for a stray dog and her four newborn puppies.

The humans sat in the den after supper, Tootie on her laptop, Sister doing needlepoint, and Gray rereading Schumpeter. Gray closed the book for a moment, reached over on the coffee table, and slipped a cigarette out of the pack.

He read the fine print on the cigarette. "Camel."

"I looked everywhere for soft packs and those were the only ones I could find."

Tootie looked up from her research on equine veterinary history. "We had to buy a carton because Sister knew we'd destroy some packs."

"Why is that?" Gray lit the unfiltered Camel, surprised at how it tasted. It had been decades since he'd smoked a Camel.

Wasn't bad.

"We had to carefully unglue each pack, then turn it inside out so it would be white."

"Janie!" He laughed. "Wouldn't it have been easier to fold white paper?" He picked up the pack. "How many packs did you ruin before you got it right?"

"Eight," Sister replied.

"We wanted to have more to give out, but it was too hard," Tootie said. "But the American Smokes graphic looks really good."

He looked up at the pack again. "Does." Took a few more puffs. "Damn, these burn fast."

"Less tobacco than the old days," said Sister. "All the popular and discount brands are cheating on content."

Snubbing out the cigarette, Gray blew smoke from his nostrils. "Pisses me off."

"Pisses me off when you smoke in the house," Golly complained from the desk.

"What are you reading on your computer? You've been as quiet as a mouse," Sister asked Tootie.

"There are no mice in this house," Golly grandly announced. *"I patrol the place. I am a first-class mouser."*

"Smoking opium," Raleigh, a snoot full of tobacco smoke, said.

"I'm reading history," said Tootie. "The first vet school in England was established in 1791. We didn't have one in our country until 1879 and we didn't have a four-year program until 1903. Iowa State both times."

"So who treated horses?" Gray was puzzled.

"Blacksmiths," Tootie answered.

"That explains it." Gray drummed his fingers on the arm of the sofa.

Sister looked up from her needlepoint. "Explains what, sugar?"

"Blacksmiths still think they can treat horses. And they never seem to get along with vets."

"Some of that, to be sure." Sister returned to her task. "My favorite is the new horse owner who had just read an explanation of some medical condition or hoof problem. They then tell the vet or the blacksmith what to do, based on their research." She looked at Tootie. "The Internet really creates havoc. Everyone is an instant expert."

"That's a fact." Tootie smiled.

"Then again, think how much you learned about tobacco and taxes from the Internet," Gray added sensibly to the conversation.

Sister dropped her hands in her lap. "Up in smoke."

"Smoke gets in your eyes," Gray fired back.

"Smoke and mirrors," Tootie chimed in.

"Holy smoke," Raleigh said, but they didn't get it.

"We'd better get back out into the world tomorrow." Sister laughed. "We're getting loopy."

CHAPTER 34

Gray drove slowly through the snow, heading out toward Old Paradise with his brother, Tootie, and Tariq in the car. "Plowing is done by independent contractors for the most part."

The Land Cruiser could go through most anything, so he gladly played taxi.

"Remember thirty years ago, something like that, when we had that odd snowstorm in October?" Sam said from the backseat. "So many branches fell down because leaves hadn't fallen yet."

"What about the Easter blizzard in, um, 1969?" Gray recalled.

"I wasn't born yet." Tootie teased them.

"We know," both brothers said in unison.

Tariq, also in the backseat, remarked, "Neither was I."

"When were you born?" Sam looked at him.

"1986."

"Well, buddy, it goes fast," said Sam.

Gray turned on his windshield wipers as he neared a large tractor plowing snow, the driver snug in a heated cab.

"Wonder what he makes an hour?" Sam mused.

"More than you do," Gray replied.

"Everyone makes more than I do."

"You're breaking my heart," Gray said, then added, "Did Crawford make it home before the storm really hit?"

"Just made it and, you know, a couple of those pellets were close to his eyes," said Tariq. "He's actually okay about it. I mean, he's not mad at Art because he says Art's too stupid to get mad at. Actually he said, 'Not the sharpest tool in the shed.' "

They crept along, finally able to go thirty-five miles an hour on the freshly cleared part.

Tootie stared out the window, the land resplendent in fresh snow. "It's good to get out of the house."

"We were about to drive my beloved crazy," said Gray.

"Don't forget we have a five-gallon bucket of kibble with corn oil in it," Tootie said.

"Why is that?" Tariq inquired.

"Sister says there's a fox in the barn at Old Paradise. Hounds were heading straight for it. She doesn't think Crawford knows enough to tend to his foxes so she'll do it until someone, not her, can teach him."

"Don't hold your breath," Sam said. "Tariq, bet you wish you were back with Jefferson Hunt."

"I do, but he took care of the Rickman mess. I'm grateful and he lends me horses."

"You're doing him a favor by riding them in the field," said Sam. "I can't ride them all, and Marty, while not a bad rider, can't really handle a green horse."

Gray glanced at Tariq in the rearview mirror. "I never asked you where you learned to ride."

"My father got me lessons as a child in Egypt. Riding, wherever you find yourself, opens many doors. I learned a lot in England, too. In the old days, Nasser and a lot of Army officers rode. Our Olympic teams were pretty much made up of officers or former officers."

"Used to be that way here, too," said Gray. "They came from the cavalry and competed in uniform. Looked wonderful. I don't remember it, but I saw pictures of them." Gray slowed again as they turned on the road to Tattenhall Station and beyond.

"This hasn't been plowed," said Sam. "Bet they don't get to it until Thursday." He peered out the window.

"One set of tracks so someone got out." Gray made sure to get his vehicle in those tracks.

It took them a half hour to reach the entrance to Old Paradise whereas it usually took fifteen minutes.

Turning, Gray noticed that the tracks they followed came from Old Paradise. He passed Alfred's tidy cottage, then Margaret's, and finally Art's, from which the tracks had come.

"Well, Art was the one who got out," Sam simply noted.

"I'm sure he had a delivery given these long dark nights." Gray laughed.

"A delivery?" Tariq asked.

"Oh, Art makes moonshine," said Sam. "Well, he used to. Maybe he had other important business." Sam paused. "I wouldn't be surprised if he was over at Crawford's. He does have to see him face-to-face."

"I was loading up horses. Never saw it, just heard it," Sam mentioned.

"Me, too," Tariq said. "I turned and saw Sam running to Crawford. It was snowing hard. So I ran. Art was down on his hands and knees with Crawford."

"It's always something," Gray said, pulling his vehicle near the snowbound two cars. "Let's see what we can do here."

They stopped, piled out, and retrieved two snow shovels from the back of the Land Cruiser where a five-gallon bucket with some baling twine wrapped around the handle also sat.

Tariq dug out his car and Sam dug out his.

"Want me to take a turn?" Tootie asked.

Sam grunted. "No, honey. If I can't dig out my car, I need help."

"All right then." She knocked on the window of Sam's car, where Gray had started the motor, letting it idle.

He rolled the window down. "Yes?"

"I'm going to take the feeder bucket inside."

"Fine. Let me know if you smell fox." Gray rolled the window back up.

Tariq had started his car, too, hoping the heat from the exhaust would melt a bit of snow. His years in England taught him a little bit about functioning in snow and cold, but he would never become accustomed to it, beautiful as it was.

He got out, picked up the shovel, and started shoveling out his front wheels.

Tootie slogged to the barn, tried to kick away snow from one door so she could slip in. Without a shovel, this was unpromising. She knelt down in the snow to use her hands. Finally she'd cleared just enough from the front of one of the big doors to crack it open and slip inside.

Looking up, she beheld the rustic beauty of this structure, built to last centuries. February sunlight filtered through the stall windows. They had mesh over them so if they did break they wouldn't shatter all over the place. The beams were squared tree trunks. She noted everything: the stalls, the old wrought-iron fittings, the hard-packed dirt floor.

Dripping with cobwebs, the inside seemed surreal and majestic. She wondered about the horses who had lived in those stalls.

And, yes, she did smell fox. Carefully walking down the center aisle, she peeked into each stall, for the Dutch doors were opened, fastened to the side.

She found the stall with a large hole in it, a pile of earth around it. The bottom door opened with a creak. She walked softly inside.

Roger heard her and smelled her but the fox didn't peek. He stayed still to listen.

She looked around for a spot to tie the bucket. No nails protruded low and the hooks for the long-disappeared water buckets hung too high. The thick-planed oak boards for the stall had no spaces between. Defeated on that count, she set the bucket down in the middle of the space. She unwound the baling twine and walked out, closing the door. She knew foxes well enough to know a healthy fox could easily jump to the top of a Dutch door, the bottom part.

Fascinated, she soaked up everything. She touched the saddle racks by each stall door, all made from planed and sanded wood to hang down flat when not in use.

She opened the tackroom door. Again, cobwebs festooned the twenty-by-twenty room. It was planed heavy oak, little lines of caulking between the boards to make it airtight. Bridle half moons lined one wall, permanent saddle racks lined another in two vertical rows. Everything else was handmade of wrought iron, even the lanterns hanging on the walls. Covered with dust outside, their candles were still inside.

Tootie knew this was the saddle horse barn. She wondered how many workhorse barns there had been at Old Paradise—mule barns, carriage barns—all fallen down now, probably. Or if they were still here, she didn't know where, as she had only hunted Old Paradise a few times while at Custis Hall.

She stood in the tack room marveling at the handiwork, imagining the grooms bustling in and out, knowing that many had been slaves. One couldn't really appreciate the hands that made this country hum until you saw their fine work.

She could almost hear the talk about poultices, the right bit for a young horse, the pride in breeding fine horses and driving horses, too.

Curiosity got the better of her. Laying the baling twine down, she climbed into the huge hayloft, saw the remains of barn swallow nests tucked into eaves and places where joists were. The birds would be back in the summer. Swallows were reliable that way. Looking all the way up, she saw the barn owl's nest in the cupola. The barn owl looked down at her.

Gave her a chill.

She took a deep breath. Another one. Tobacco.

She followed her upturned nose until she found the place where the hay remnants were completely flattened. The odor was stronger here.

"You in here?" Tariq called out.

"I am." She walked to the side of the hayloft.

"We're ready to go," Tariq said. "Think both Sam and I can make it." He held up his hand to her.

"I'll back down."

After climbing down, she bent over once in the center aisle to pick up the baling twine she'd left there. Silly, but she didn't want to leave any debris. A pack of the bogus American Smokes fell out of her breast pocket. She bent over to pick them up, a cigarette falling on the floor. She also scooped that up, slipping it back into the soft pack.

"Tootie Harris, when did you start smoking?" asked Tariq.

"I don't, really."

"You just carry around cigarettes for your friends?" He laughed at her. "I've never seen that brand."

"Contraband." She smiled broadly. "Really, I don't smoke. It's a long story."

"If you do smoke, let me give you a Cleopatra." Tariq reached into his inside coat pocket and pulled out a pack. "I never smoke on the grounds at Custis Hall."

"I really don't smoke. I'm just carrying this around for Sister. Actually, she doesn't know I filched a pack." Tootie lifted her shoulders in an innocent gesture, then smiled.

The young woman was so beautiful, Tariq, transfixed for a moment, had to snap back to reality. "Let's go."

With Gray leading the way, both men managed to drive their cars off the property.

In the passenger seat of Gray's Land Rover, Tootie enthused about the barn on her way back. "Know what was really weird?"

"What?"

"It smelled like tobacco in the hayloft."

Gray pulled over at Tattenhall Station, waved on Sam and Tariq, then called Ben Sidell.

The sheriff arrived an hour later, thanks to the roads. Gray had turned around and they had driven back to Old Paradise.

In the barn, Roger heard the door open and ducked back into his den. The corn oil on the kibble was delicious.

Tootie, Gray, and Ben hurriedly climbed the ladder.

Hands on hips, Ben said, "Sure smells like tobacco."

"Here, smell this." Tootie pulled out the pack, fetching one cigarette.

"It is or was tobacco," Gray firmly noted.

Ben took the pack from Tootie's hand. "What in the hell are you doing with this?"

Tootie explained why she had the pack.

Ben took her by the arm, looked into her eyes, and said, "You get rid of these. Better yet, give them to me." He turned to Gray. "It's one accident after another. Gray, you're in charge of that crazy woman. Burn the packs. I will call her myself. I will cuss her out, too!"

CHAPTER 35

Water gushed from drain spouts, ran across low spots in roads, filled streams to the top of their banks and threatened to overflow. Tuesday's cold temperatures were followed by mid-fifties on Wednesday, and even the low sixties on Thursday.

Unpredictable as central Virginia weather can be, this provoked comment from everyone. The elderly swore they'd never seen anything like this temperature bounce. Weathermen produced graphs, other dates in history, and all concluded this had to be in the top five temperature fluctuations. Sister canceled Tuesday's and Thursday's hunts, hoping still for Saturday. The weather report for the weekend predicted mid-forties, some clouds, no precipitation. She hoped it would be so.

Her mud boots were green wellies, but appeared brown right up to the tops. The house décor now included muddy paw prints. Even though Raleigh and Rooster had their sisal rug to wipe their paws on, there was just too much mud out there. When Golly made a foray outside, she allowed herself the pleasure of walking all over the cars, then shot back inside where she exhaustingly groomed her paws.

What's the point of trying to keep the house clean? Sister decided she'd wait until the mud dried before mopping floors and wiping down all the surfaces. No matter how hard they tried, the humans, too, tracked in bits of mud, even after taking off their boots.

Betty and Sister stood next to each other in Sister's big bathroom with the double sinks, washing their faces. Somehow, mud covered their faces, too.

Betty wiped off the brown. "That hot water feels good."

"Did you ever use one of those face steamers?"

"No, did you?"

"Yeah. It did get the dirt out. But it's like everything else, Betty, you have to make a regimen of it. Finally, I gave up."

Cleaned up, they repaired to the den, where Sister checked her emails and Betty sat down with a stack of old studbooks for hounds. The two had promised each other to go back with Asa's bloodlines to find the perfect nick to one of the girls' bloodlines. If only it were that simple.

"After you check your emails, put in the MFHA disc on bloodlines, will you?" Betty asked.

"Hmm." Sister read avidly. "Well, Betty, score one for the narrow-minded."

"What?"

"Charlotte Norton has sent Tariq's resignation letter to the board. He states this will be his last semester. He doesn't wish to cause problems for Custis Hall and he feels he must go back to his family during these tumultuous times. There's more, but that's the essence."

"Rickman did recant." Betty opened another small red studbook. "Don't you wonder what Crawford threatened him with?"

"Money. Campaign funds from Crawford and his friends. You no sooner get in the House of Representatives than you have to run again, so Rickman is already fund-raising. Maybe there's more to it than that, but I expect that's the meat of it."

"If I had that much money, I wouldn't waste it on politicians." She scribbled some names and dates—foxhunting club names, too—in her hound notebook. "Janie, you haven't told me the whole story about Ben."

"Uh, I guess I deserved it, but he told me in vivid terms to never do anything like making those cigarette packs without talking to him. He said I was exposing myself and others to serious danger."

"Any more?"

"No. He also said acts like that could compromise an investigation." She slipped the MFHA disc into her computer. "He's right. I didn't think our sheriff's department was working seriously on this contraband matter but I guess they are. It's not my business. Obviously, they have more on their plate than that Carter Weems murder, which is old, I mean in police terms—at least I guess it is."

Betty got up, notebook in hand, and pulled up a chair next to her friend to study bloodlines. It was easier on the screen than pulling out a book for each year, although Betty did like to check the books.

"Name the puppies' mother yet?" she asked.

"Tootie calls her Zoe, for life. She's a sweet thing, those floppy ears and that boxer face."

The two scrolled through different bloodlines for Sister's prized Bywaters blood. A good match wasn't so easy to find these days, as that type of American hound began to fall out of favor in the middle 1960s, though in recent years it was somewhat coming back.

"You just know that Zoe and those puppies will wind up in your house," Betty remarked calmly.

"I was hoping they'd wind up in yours."

They read some more as Betty wrote in her notebook. "Do you really think you're in danger?"

"No," Sister, fearless to a fault, replied.

This time it was a fault.

CHAPTER 36

The hounds, restless from being in the kennels all week, stood on their hind legs in the large draw pen in the kennels. Everyone wanted to go, so Sister and Shaker took most of the pack—with the exception of Asa, who needed rest, and Cora. Cora and Dragon did not get along; fangs would be bared and insults traded. This would go on even during hunting, if one tried to outrun the other. So master and huntsman decided to take the slightly younger hound.

In the girls' large run, along with three youngsters not quite a year old, Cora pleaded her case. *"You can't go without me. Dragon is an idiot. He overruns the line. He has temper tantrums. Take me! Take me!"*

Hearing Cora cry, the three young girls cried along with her. They didn't know why they were howling since they hadn't yet hunted and would not be doing so until next season, but if this lead hound was making a fuss, they would, too.

A large field of hunters patiently waited by the kennels. Everyone, like the hounds, was stir-crazy. Walter was at a medical convention, so he wasn't there, which was too bad. It's always good to have your joint-master with you when footing is questionable. Actually, it's good to have your joint-master out anytime.

Tootie would ride with Sybil today and Betty would, as always, take the right side, on Magellan. Sybil was working with a young Thoroughbred, Buster. She figured a sloppy day like today was good for the five-year-old.

With Sister on his back, Lafayette was calm, while waiting for Howie to open the gate. Felicity rode in the field with the Custis Hall girls. Donny Sweigart was out. In fact, everyone who could throw a leg over a horse seemed to be there.

As the people waited, Bobby overheard a lady telling another that Art DuCharme had been pulled over yesterday, his truck searched. That caused a ripple of comment and the lady in question didn't like Art, since he had not succumbed to her charms. The fact that Art would one day inherit Old Paradise along with his cousin was not lost on a certain type of woman.

"Found nothing," she said. "Full of furniture and a large box of furniture polish."

"I'm sure that furniture would look wonderful in your house, dear," Renata Meroveus cooed.

Others smiled, but behind their gloved hands.

"Hounds, please," Sister called and off they walked.

The only possible first cast would be on higher ground and the foxes would fly low as soon as they could. For all the melting, some snow remained in low spots, though yesterday's high winds swept over meadows, speeding up the drying process.

Sister could hear sucking sounds as Lafayette walked along the mucky farm road heading toward Hangman's Ridge, but it could have been a lot worse.

Shaker cast in the apple orchard. Hounds ran to Inky's den.

"I'm not coming out," Inky called up from her living room.

Dragon stuck his head into the main den entrance. *"Spoil sport."*

"Come along then," Shaker commanded and the hounds walked back out to the road and popped over the jump into the large open field between Roughneck Farm and After All.

The hounds tried, were so focused. They headed to the foundation of the first cabin, the stone still relatively intact. A big walnut tree grew out of the middle. The fox called Target had been there; his scent was strong enough to open.

Speaking, but not in unison, the hounds trotted from that foundation to the middle of the field.

They split, one half going straight to After All and one half going toward Hangman's Ridge. Both sides were now screaming.

Shaker followed the half heading toward the ridge, figuring the ground rose higher, hence better footing.

After All had good footing in the woods, but Broad Creek would be an obstacle on a day like today.

Betty easily took the hogsback into After All, although she could feel Magellan's hind hooves sink deeper than usual in the mud. Hearing the huntsman's horn in the other direction, she had to try to turn the pack back to him and the other half of the pack—no easy task on open ground. In woods, it's even more difficult. She urged Magellan on, trying to get ahead of the pack, which she did. Then silence.

Betty wisely waited. No point in rushing right back. Better to remain still and listen. Someone would yelp, or she'd hear something underfoot. The footing in the woods was pretty good. Slushy snow stuck to the paths.

She heard a yip, then a yap. Then silence again. She headed Magellan toward the last yap, picking her way through the woods. She came upon the hounds casting about and, as she did so,

Trooper, farther into the woods than the others, let out a clear signal. All the dogs ran to him and off they went, all speaking.

Damn, damn, double damn, Betty thought as she fought her way through the overhang, dead branches on the ground. She swerved Magellan around fallen trees. Finally, she made it out to a narrow deer path heading north and south. Hounds wailed, and she could hear the other half of the pack, full cry.

She pulled ahead of the hounds, whom she could see as they ran through the woods. Now that she was on a path, she figured she'd stay parallel to them. If they turned inward, she'd go back in, but her best shot would be if they'd come out and cross the path. If not, she'd do what she could to get up on their shoulder. There was no way she was going to get ahead of them if she had to plunge into the woods again.

Sure enough, they turned, Trooper in the lead, right toward her. She had just enough space to crack her whip and she did. It sounded like rifle fire. All heads came up. Her shouting could be ignored and sometimes was. This, maybe not.

"Leave it!" Betty bellowed.

A few hesitated. "I said, 'Leave it.' Come to me."

"We'd better do it." Tootsie warned. *"She sounds really mad."*

One by one, they came to the path, as they weren't but ten yards off of it when Betty cracked the whip.

Looking down, Betty noticed large human footprints on the path. The footprints led directly into the woods where the hounds had been. Curious, she walked in and saw footprints again, now a line, and a brush along the snow. There were no fox tracks. A drag. Someone had dragged a foxtail through here.

"What in the hell is this?"

The hounds looked up at her on Magellan and Taz chipped, *"Fox scent."*

"Hounds, this isn't good. In fact, this is terrible."

How terrible Betty didn't know but she picked up a trot, keeping the hounds with her by using encouraging words. She headed for the horn, the sound of which grew farther and farther away.

Sister followed the other half of the pack, staying about twenty yards behind them as they zigged and zagged over the meadow, then ran under the fence back onto the farm road just below Hangman's Ridge.

The jump, already sloppy, would become even sloppier as each horse in the field took it.

Sister gave thanks that she was second over; Shaker had been first. Tootie and Sybil had to be somewhere in the orchard.

The hounds lost the scent on the road. Some hurried into the orchard, others kept trying to the right of the road.

Sister moved up and out of the way of the jump. As she did, Dragon opened, nose down. Moving deliberately, he ducked into the tangle at the bottom of the ridge. Deer paths, passable but full of switchbacks and some rough spots, allowed Sister to get closer to the hounds. Obviously, the farm would have been ideal, but this fox had other ideas, moving farther east at the bottom of the ridge.

She could hear more hounds open now, as those in the orchard came to Dragon. She walked along the bottom, as she knew a path near a large rock overhang. She'd have to pick her way up, but it could be done. Behind her, she could hear people hung up at the jump.

Turning around, she saw the forward riders trotting to catch up with her. Knowing her mind, Lafayette stepped onto the paths and began the upward climb.

The rock outcropping reminded her of Devil's Den at Gettysburg. It felt colder suddenly; snow filled many crevices. The path curved toward the giant rock, then climbed above it. She came out on the ridge above a pile of huge rocks. Large old conifers and some deciduous trees grew here. Their branches, having been pulled down by snow, still hung low. Some of the pines still had tufts of snow on the needles.

Lafayette snorted. Sister heard horses below her beginning the climb. She heard a crack, a slash of fire from high up in one of the pines, then felt a hard hit over her heart. She slipped off Lafayette, hitting her head on the ground.

The horse didn't move, but put his face down to the unconscious woman.

Target doubled back, looking up at the horse. The fox swiftly moved beside the woman who fed him. He touched her cheek. The hounds had turned, so he sped off without saying anything to Lafayette.

The dogs reached Sister just as the first rider climbing the path did.

"Hold hard," Edward Bancroft called.

He maneuvered his horse to the right of Lafayette. There wasn't much room.

Dragon already had his nose to Sister's and the pack surrounded her.

"She's alive," the head hound called.

Shaker was blowing the hounds back to him, but they didn't obey.

Betty had no idea what had happened and was trying hard to get to the horn.

The shooter, down from his perch, was sliding down the steep side of the ridge, progress hidden from view. But the hounds heard him. Dragon wheeled away from Sister in pursuit. The pack followed.

Dragon let out a deep call, which the hounds with Betty heard. They, too, took off.

Shaker struggled to get up with his pack, as did Tootie and Sybil.

Betty pushed Magellan on. A fast horse, she made up the ground. She saw the pack ahead of her, closing fast on a man with a rifle strapped across his back. He cut back into the woods, climbed up a tree just above the hounds, unslung his rifle, and focused through his scope. Betty was dead center. Dragon and the hounds leapt up, one grabbing the toe of his boot as he fired. The shot hit the top of her hard hat, creasing it.

The force knocked Betty off Magellan. Unhurt, she picked herself up out of the wet field, then laid back, flat, her helmet upside down in the field. Magellan took off toward the barn.

Hearing the hounds, Betty, face muddied, looked up. She saw the hounds around the bottom of a tree and a man in it.

She crawled, then rolled. He didn't fire.

With no time to think whether she was crazy or scared, she stood up, sprinting toward the woods. She'd be a tougher target out of the clear.

Reaching the edge, she got behind a tree. Peering out, she saw the hounds yanking at Tariq's feet. He kept kicking at them, but he couldn't get his rifle properly aimed downward.

She saw Sybil and Tootie emerge above him on the old trail.

"Get out!" Betty shouted.

Tariq didn't see but he heard the two women above him. He could fire up and he did. Then he reached up, pulling himself up a bit higher, in the tree, firing in Betty's direction. She heard the bullet whiz past yards away, then thunk into a tree.

Sybil ordered Tootie, "Get back up on the ridge. Take my horse with you."

With that, she dismounted, slipped her .22 pistol with ratshot out of the holster and crept downward, one tree at a time.

Tootie did as she was told. Fit to be tied, Shaker was calling and calling his hounds. Tootie hollered to him for all she was worth.

He made his way to her as she headed to the ridge. She told him what she had seen. He dismounted, taking his ratshot, handing Hobo's reins to Tootie.

"Wait here." The muscular huntsman ran down the deer path.

The hounds, treeing their human quarry, set up a booming racket.

Much as Tariq wanted to shoot them, he knew people were coming for him. Cursing, because he might have made it, he reached into his pocket for more shells.

Sybil and Shaker, working together now that Shaker had reached her, fanned out, moving toward Tariq.

The hounds heard them coming, but the Egyptian did not.

A flurry of ratshot hit the tree. He ducked, turning away from the shooter. He realized he had a chance to get away if he could kill or wound the hunt staff, especially Shaker and Sybil, who were closing in. Betty was below him. He didn't know who was above him, but he figured it had to be staff.

Betty left her tree and ran to another.

She picked up a small rock jutting out of the soft earth, threw it for all she was worth. It clattered, hitting a tree near the one the hounds surrounded.

It was enough to draw Tariq's attention. Shaker, who had been stealthily making his way down, fired, as did Sybil, from the opposite direction.

Tariq tried to fire at them, but lost his balance and fell from the tree, the rifle discharging into the air. That fast, Dragon ripped out his throat.

CHAPTER 37

"I've always wanted a purple boob," Sister told Betty, Tootie, and Gray as she sat in the den, her feet up.

"Thank God you bought that cigarette case," said Gray. "I'm glad I didn't say anything about the cost." He smiled. "It's priceless."

He picked up the case from the coffee table. A bullet wedged in the middle of it, the tip flattening against the back side.

Gray and Tootie had brought back Sister from the emergency room. After cleaning up, as she'd been muddy from head to toe, Betty had met them at the house. She'd brought her cap for them to see the crease on the top made by Tariq's bullet.

Sister sighed. "We can give thanks Dragon killed him before he shot anyone else. If Tariq could have gotten his rifle up he would have fired."

"Odd," Betty mused. "He fell out of the tree but he never loosed his grasp on the rifle."

Tootie said, "He was such a good teacher. I liked him so much. What happens to people?"

The three older people didn't immediately respond.

Even Golly, quick with a criticism, said little. Events had shocked her, too.

At last, Gray offered a partial explanation. "I guess anyone can justify what they do if they believe they are doing it for a great cause. For Tariq, raising lots of cash to help protect the Coptic people, millions of them, was worth a few American lives. That's all I can think of, but I know we all underrated Ben Sidell." Gray moved his thoughts to something he could understand.

Gray had spoken with the sheriff once they got Sister to the emergency room, where she regained consciousness. "Ben knew contraband was moving out of our county. At first he assumed it was illegal liquor, but then realized it had to be tobacco. The laws have changed to allow smaller batches of liquor to be sold. That isn't to say there still isn't money in moonshine, but the 'shine is off, forgive the pun."

"How'd he know that?" Tootie asked.

"Pretty much the same way Sister figured it out: Albemarle County and central Virginia are the perfect distribution centers for the northeast, and even into Chicago."

Sister leaned on Gray's shoulder for a moment. "But Tariq. Never in a million years would I have thought he was behind something like this."

"The real leadership of his smuggling operation is in Cairo. He was important, had a great cover, spoke perfect English."

A knock on the back door sent the dogs barking. Tootie hurried to see who was there, and shortly afterward she and Ben Sidell returned.

"Did you learn anything new just lately?" the genial sheriff asked Sister.

"Yes, you're a good sheriff."

"Butter me up. I ought to slap you with every citation I can find. Sister, you damn near got yourself killed, nearly blew our operation. And furthermore, I had to spend a damned whole hour with Animal Control convincing them the hound was protecting his owner. I spun a lovely tale for Dragon. Madam, you are a lot of work."

"I am. I'm sorry. How can I make it up to you?"

"A stiff Scotch would help. I'm finally off duty."

Gray walked to the bar to pour Ben a serious amount of single-malt Scotch. "Anyone else ready for a libation?"

"I think I might have a whiskey sour." Betty stood up, served Ben his drink, then returned for one of her own. For himself, Gray made his usual Blanton's and bitters.

"Thank you." Ben gratefully took a sip. "High-test."

"Hard day." Gray smiled as he sat down, his own drink in hand.

Betty turned to Ben. "Is the embassy informed?"

"Yes. It is our great good fortune that a former secretary of state lives in Albemarle County. He told me to simply hand them the report of events. Nothing more."

"Which means they know about the contraband?" asked Sister. She may have ached, but her mind was sharp as ever.

"Sure." Ben put his glass down. "We've been working on this for over a year. This is an annual multi-hundred-million-dollar business. The only monies that come to our citizens are those growers and workers in on the deal, the chain of true tobacco people or as they say: 'bacca. Then there's the chain of truckers and those who distribute in the big cities. The hubs of distribution collect the cash. In other words, everyone who buys American Smokes in Boston, those store owners pay directly to the distributor and with cash. There are no records that we can find of the transactions. We've uncovered only one player in this entire network. And he's dead."

"Good Lord," said Betty. "Tariq never spent much money." She thought out loud. "Old car. Decent clothing, but nothing to suggest such income."

"He didn't have that much. Oh sure, he had more than Custis Hall paid him, but he wasn't motivated by profit. Tariq was a true idealist. He believed he was protecting, saving even, Coptic Christians." Ben folded his hands together. "Maybe he did. Who knows."

"But how? The military will control Egypt one way or another and those men are mostly Muslim. They harass the Christians and the Muslim Brotherhood will go back on every promise they make about protecting all Egyptians. They believe in Sharia, which sure isn't good for Christians. The Brotherhood and the Army are enemies but both are anti-Christian. The embassy has to be alert to all this."

"The secretary of state was not exactly forthcoming about why this needs to remain silent, but after working on this case, talking to him, reading everything I can get my hands on, and watching Arab TV, in translation, I have a pretty good idea." Ben unfolded his hands, placing them on his knees. "We believe dictatorships are bad and that every country should be a democracy, preferably in our image. England has been working on democracy since 1215; little by little, France flip flops since the French Revolution. We believe she'll remain mostly democratic. Look at the European nations, and the Scandinavian ones; close as they are to us, not all of them are successful at it."

"Neither are we." Gray laughed. "But what you're saying is this is an impossible dream for a Mideast country."

"He feared the Muslim Brotherhood are elected in force and that they will go back on their word of working with others. It's a case of the lesser of two evils. The fear of Tariq was that the Muslims will wipe out the Christians or drive them out of Egypt. Religious extremists are rarely motivated by profit. They are much harder criminals to catch."

"Better the Devil you know than the Devil you don't," Sister remarked.

"Yes." Ben drank his drink down to half. "Graft, payoff, are a way of life in most of the world. You can't do business in South America without it and not over there either. I didn't know that the military in Egypt can run businesses, but they can. Anyway, Tariq felt his people would be much safer with a military neutral about Coptic Christians. Maybe he was right. All the money made from contraband is funneled into the pockets of the colonels and generals."

The four sat there for a time; even the animals were quiet.

"Ideology kills, doesn't it?" Tootie asked the dagger-to-the-heart question. "Doesn't matter what it is."

"It damn near killed Janie," Gray said in a strong voice. "You could have been killed as well as Sybil and Shaker."

"I heard you all kept coming for him," said Sister, "and you Betty, no ratshot even." She smiled at her best friend.

"I can't believe I left my gun on the saddle, but I needed to get out of that open field."

"I was wrong, Ben, I truly was and I apologize," said Sister. "I expect the sight of that American Smokes pack is what set him off. And I also expect that those men killed with packs placed on their chests were killed because they wouldn't sell the contraband."

"That's what we think. Tariq was in New York when Adolfo was killed. We think other operatives were in Boston and Chicago to kill those noncooperative shop owners. It was a strong warning to others." Ben enjoyed the crackle and the odor of the fire.

"Carter Weems?" Sister asked.

"I expect he was hauling the stuff out of here and became a liability in some way."

"And Art?" Sister asked again.

"Art is up to no good, but we can't catch him at it. But I will give Tariq credit, he held it together, kept the trains running, so to speak, and only lost it at the end."

"Tell you one thing," said Betty. "Tariq was smart. He laid a clever drag and waited for the right day. Tracks don't hold in footing like this. If he'd accomplished his goals, who would have found the drag line?" She raised her eyebrows. "I say the hounds are the real heroes."

"Always are." Sister held up Gray's glass, then took a swig. "How can you drink this stuff?"

Though sore as hell where the cigarette case had pressed against her heart, Sister was returning to true form. "Ben, you've been wonderful. I know you live alone. Let me give you a puppy. It's the purest love in the world."

CHAPTER 38

E arly March came and, cold though it might be, it lifted spirits because spring couldn't be far. Hunting season for Jefferson ended mid-March.

Despite the bruising, Sister rode, drove her truck, and fell in love with Zoe and her puppies.

Tuesday's hunt on March 6 was at a new fixture, Close Shave. It couldn't have been better. They didn't really know the territory yet, didn't know their foxes, but as the foxes ran so did they.

After everyone was put up, Zoe given warm food, Sister shepherded Betty and Tootie outside to her truck.

"We're going to scare people," she said.

"I do that anyway," Betty joked. "Especially without my makeup."

Tootie sat in the rear of the truck. Betty hopped into the front seat, picking up the dryer. "Will you throw this thing away? You are not going to get it fixed."

"Put it in your lap," ordered Sister.

Sister drove near Roger's Corner, where the small crossroads is. She parked where she'd seen the police cruiser weeks before.

"All right. Now I want you, Betty, to sit in the passenger seat and look serious. Tootie, I want you to stand behind me and hold this." Sister handed Tootie the box used for the Johnson tracking collars. She kept the door of the driver's side open, opened the window, stepped outside, and rested the black hair dryer on the windowsill.

Crouching behind the door but clearly visible, Sister pointed the hair dryer at the road. "Tootie, lift the tracking aerial over my head."

"Are we going to get in trouble for this?" Tootie asked.

"I will take full responsibility. Here comes one. Look serious!"

A car heading for them over the speed limit braked dramatically, then glided by.

"Gotcha!" Sister said.

Those three women at their phony speed trap stayed out there in the cold for an hour, scaring the pants off people who thought they'd get a ticket. In a flash, Tootie had an idea of what Sister was like when she was her age.

Back in the truck, heading home, through her tears of laughter, Betty said, "You are crazy."

Sister replied, "It's good to be alive."

To the Reader:

Tobacco is interwoven with the history of the New World. I found it fascinating. Should you wish to pursue the subject, you might begin with:

http://archive.tobacco.org/History/Tobacco History.html

For an overview of government response to tobacco, try:

http://www.fda.gov/tobaccoproducts/guidancecompliance regulatoryinformation/default.htm

You will find much more if you search using your computer.

As this is a work of fiction an extensive bibliography is out of place, but works on tobacco and tobacco families are not difficult to find.

If you took chemistry in high school, you will be able to battle through technical publications and monographs. If you pursued chemistry in college you might find the analysis of varying chemical compositions of the different tobacco types exciting. Even with my limited background in chemistry, I was amazed at how tobacco can be manipulated, for lack of a better word.

At bottom, tobacco helped build the United States. It is worth studying.

All best,
Rita Mae

ACKNOWLEDGMENTS

One of my hardest riding hunt club members, Mrs. William Johnson (Maria), has set up a Facebook page so that you may ride along with Sister Jane.

http://www.facebook.com/sisterjanearnold

We'll see you in the hunt field.

RITA MAE BROWN is the bestselling author of a series of foxhunting novels—*Fox Tracks, Hounded to Death, The Tell-Tale Horse, The Hounds and the Fury, The Hunt Ball, Full Cry, Hotspur,* and *Outfoxed*—the *New York Times* bestselling Sneaky Pie Brown mysteries, and *Rubyfruit Jungle, In Her Day,* and *Six of One,* among many other novels. An Emmy-nominated screenwriter and a poet, she lives in Afton, Virginia, where she is master of foxhounds of Oak Ridge Hunt Club and one of the directors of Virginia Hunt Week. She founded the first all-women's polo club, Blue Ridge Polo, in 1988. She was also Visiting Faculty at the University of Nebraska in Lincoln. Visit her website at www.ritamaebrown.com.